For your glory, Lord!

ACKNOWLEDGMENTS

My deepest thanks go Krista Stroever and
Joan Marlow Golan for their wisdom and
willingness to take on this project. Also to
Ellen Tarver, whose insights and comments
made the story readable. Finally, thanks to
my family, who traveled through Taiwan with me,
and prayed for me as I wrote this book. You all are
great blessings in my life.

WISER THAN SERPENTS

SUSAN MAY WARREN

Steeple
Hill®

Published by Steeple Hill Books™

STEEPLE HILL BOOKS

Steeple
Hill®

ISBN-13: 978-0-373-78620-6
ISBN-10:   0-373-78620-4

WISER THAN SERPENTS

Copyright © 2008 by Susan May Warren

www.SteepleHill.com

Printed in U.S.A.

AUTHOR'S NOTE

I had just tossed the magazine in my growing TBR pile, not sure when I would read it, if ever. My husband happened to pick it up, captured by the title on the cover: The Global Slave Trade. "Hey," he said, "did you read this?"

I sat down with the article and everything inside me tightened as I read about the epidemic of slave trade around the world today. From women and girls held in captivity to children and men in labor bondage, it's a horrific situation. 600,000–800,000 people are trafficked internationally each year. Approximately 80% of them are women and children. And it happens in the United States, right under our noses.

One of the organizations trying to do something about it is the International Justice Mission. Think: a team of real-life Jack Bauers rescuing victims caught in the web of slavery. Lawyers, criminal investigators, social workers and volunteers from all walks of life who live Micah 6:8 daily: To seek justice for the oppressed. And they don't just rescue victims (sometimes at the cost of their own lives!) but they also provide care and counseling, pursue legal justice and fight to prevent it from happening again.

The writer inside me was captured by this idea; the woman inside me ached for the girls forced into sexual slavery, and the Christian inside me said, "Do something!" Suddenly my adventures in Taiwan flooded back to me. We'd gone there for a month of recovery following a traumatic experience in Russia, and after reading the statistics on how so many people are transported through Asia, I knew Taiwan would make the perfect setting for this novel.

David, my American hero, was just the guy to fight this battle. Moreover, with so many of these victims being Russian, I just had to get Yanna involved, also.

Human trafficking is real. It's an abomination. And must be stopped.

You can help:

Sign up to be a regular prayer partner with IJM, and receive weekly e-mails highlighting prayer requests.

Keep your eyes open to the world around you, and care enough to pay attention to possible illegal abuses of power, even slavery, right in your own backyard.

Finally, give financially to help IJM fight slavery. Over the past ten years, their lawyers, investigators and social workers around the world have rescued thousands of victims of sex trafficking and other forms of abuse and oppression.

I also want to help, and I'll be donating 15% of the royalties from this book to support this cause. Thank you for helping me help them. For more information, visit www.ijm.org<http://www.ijm.org>.

Thank you for reading *Wiser Than Serpents*. I pray it makes you wise, and aware of the serpents in our world.

In His grace,

Susan May Warren

Prologue

Out of all FSB agent Yanna Andrevka's bright ideas, masquerading as a mail-order bride ranked among the most stupid. This thought took root as she blinked against the sudden flood of sunlight and stared at her *groom*-to-be, Kwan, as he'd so kindly introduced himself—five foot nine of cut, Asian muscle, a scar running from his chin to his ear, an eyebrow pierced with a curved barbell, and eyes that looked like they could spear through her and take out her heart.

Here comes the bride. Only this bride felt disheveled and grimy, her long hair hanging in strings over her face, her body stiff after being locked in a pitch-black storage room alone for what seemed like an eternity. That things were about to get worse seemed apparent as her captors/hosts/groomsmen dragged her blindfolded from the belly of wherever they'd stashed her, led her to Kwan's office, sat her down in a chair and handcuffed her arms behind her. She'd had the presence of mind to fist her hands as they secured them, allowing for jangle room on her wrists. She twisted her hands, keeping the circulation pumping, fearing it might take her longer than she hoped to get out of them.

Yanna silenced the moans of fear that rose from the depths. Of course she'd recognized Kwan, even before his kind introduction. He'd been at the top of her Most Likely to Kidnap and Traffic Women search list. Thankfully, she'd also shared her suspicions with her FSB cohorts, which would be only slight consolation when they found her body floating with the fish.

What had she been thinking?

Kwan stood over her, hands loose, her blindfold dangling from one fist, his stance unassuming. The confidence in his body language turned her blood cold in her veins.

She raised her chin and managed to find her voice. *"Wŏ zài nei li shì?"* Not that she expected an answer to her question—where am I?—but it bought her time as her brain spun and tried to fix on her surroundings. She smelled the brine of seawater, and small square windows evidenced a ship's office. Streams of fading sunlight splotched the thinly carpeted floor and turned a smooth black desk to onyx. Her nausea clinched it— last time she'd been at sea, she'd lost half her stomach overboard and gained a new respect for the *rebotnik* who fished the Amur river near her home in Russia.

When Kwan didn't respond, Yanna asked again, "Where am I?"

It occurred to her that she might be saying something that would earn her another slap, like, *Touch me again and die, you pig.* She hadn't used her Mandarin for years, and she might be letting loose any one of the threats she conjured up for this man who'd kidnapped, and possibly killed, her sister Elena.

Kwan stepped back from her and leaned against the desk. He picked up a *pero,* a ten-inch knife, probably intending to terrify her, and chose a star fruit from the bowl on his desk. She ignored the press of hunger in her stomach. Her last meal had been about three decades ago, courtesy of the hotel at Incheon Airport, Seoul, Korea.

Kwan cut the fruit slowly, his gaze steady. *"Qingwèn, ni shì bu shì Meiguó rén."*

Was she an American? She hid a flare of indignation and gave him instead a quivering smile. "Do I look like an American?" she asked softly. She hid the flinch as he gave her a head-to-toe perusal, starting at her calf-high supple leather spiked-heel boots, past the black leather skirt, up to the sheer silk blouse and camisole. American? Hardly. Americans dressed in baggy jeans and sturdy hiking boots. Maybe not all Americans, but the ones she knew prided practicality over form. Missionary Gracie Benson nearly had to be coerced into wearing the pretty dress FSB agent friend Vicktor Shubnikov purchased for her trying to save her life. And Sarai Curtiss, Roman Novik's girlfriend and humanitarian doctor, ran around the

Khabarovsk University Hospital in a pair of yoga pants and running shoes.

Then again, a sturdy pair of Reeboks just might come in handy in about ten seconds when Yanna kicked that juicy smirk off Kwan's face and demanded Elena's whereabouts.

After she got out of the handcuffs, of course.

Kwan wore a smile, but it didn't touch his eyes as he used the knife to bring a piece of star fruit to his mouth. The ring he wore on his middle finger sparkled in the fading sunlight, and she attributed the nasty bruise on her cheek to the snake's head with the ruby stones. Finishing his silent assessment, he raised a thin black eyebrow. "You speak English."

She nodded, purposely keeping her eyes down, catching a view of the two thugs who stood slightly behind her. She'd named them Fu and Wang, they looked like extras from a Jackie Chan movie. "I thought I was meeting my future husband. My *American* future husband," she mumbled, hiding completely the simmer of terror that lurked just below the skin. Was this how Elena had felt? Had the two goons behind her also drugged the twenty-three-year-old Russian with some sort of drug, perhaps in her plate of dim sum while she waited for her flight to America in the Korean airport? Had they escorted/dragged her through Incheon airport and onto the plane, sat flanking her like Dobermans, and whisked her through customs and passport control in Taiwan like she might be a head of state?

Had they shoved her into a waiting sedan, then clamped a cloth over her nose and mouth, laughing while she kicked and fought and succumbed to yet another drug?

Most importantly, when she'd awoken, had Elena's stomach turned to knots and threatened to climb up her throat when she realized that no one knew where she was, and that she'd been swallowed whole into a world of human trafficking, bondage and slavery?

Only these thoughts kept Yanna from kicking Kwan in the throat, making a fast break for the door, hurtling herself overboard into the cold China Sea and freestyling it toward shore. These, and the belief that following her hunches might lead her to her little sister. *Elena, why didn't you listen to me?*

Kwan laughed at her. He nodded to Fu and Wang to leave as he finished off the star fruit. Then he stood. As he left, Fu handed Kwan her passport, the one listing her as Olga Rustikoff. Through the briefly opened door, Yanna glimpsed bruised skies, blue sea, and heard the sound of a speedboat. How far were they from mainland China?

Kwan paged through the passport. Yanna heard the ship's motors fire up, felt the boat list as it moved. For the briefest of seconds, she wished she'd listened to Roman and Vicktor, trusted their sources, their concern. And she wished David Curtiss, best friend and American soldier, had answered her e-mails. Yes, he'd told her he'd be undercover, deep under, in fact, but that hadn't stopped him from writing before. From checking into her life. From caring. The fact he'd been ignoring her for nearly three months hurt more than anyone could ever know. He may think of her as a kid sister, but his friendship filled her world with a light and hope she couldn't put into words.

She'd never told him that, of course. At this rate, never would. Her body would simply wash ashore on some foreign soil and he'd never know that after fifteen years, she still dreamed he'd fly halfway across the world to take her in his arms and tell her he couldn't live without her.

It was the drugs in her system talking. Because she—an FSB agent, and David, an American Delta Force major had as much chance of hooking up as she had of escaping this ship and not being devoured by sharks.

Apparently, her backup team, the ones with a supernatural connection—Roman and Vicktor, Gracie and Sarai—needed to up their piety because God certainly hadn't heard their prayers for her safety. Either that, or Yanna was simply correct in her belief that prayers to an unseen—and uncaring— God accomplished nothing. After ten years fighting crime in Russia, she could have told them that.

Kwan picked up his metal garbage can, set it at his feet. Then, taking his lighter, he ignited the passport and dropped it into the can. The acrid smell of plastic filled the room. Yanna stared wide-eyed at the black smoke.

"Why—?"

But she knew why, even as the word left her mouth. Kwan reached behind him and held up a tube of lipstick. Saying nothing, he uncapped it and twisted the base. Yanna held her breath as a three-inch curved blade extended.

Kwan nodded. "Want to explain to me how a schoolteacher smuggled this onto an airplane? Or better, what is this?" He pulled her cell phone from his pocket, one of her best designs, the one with global GPS active 24/7. When she'd given one to Roman, it had helped save his life, and she'd counted on the little transmitter planted inside to save hers. "This doesn't look like a Nokia from the central market."

She kept her expression cool, but inside dread pooled like blood.

Why, oh, why, had she talked herself into believing she could do this alone? Every muscle in her body tightened when Kwan dropped the phone into a drawer and pushed himself off the desk. He approached her slowly, dug his fingers into her hair, then yanked her head back. Her scalp screamed, but every nerve centered on the sudden cold prick of her not-so-cute-anymore knife scraping the well of her neck.

She swallowed. "I…my…cousin works airport security. He—"

"Agent Andrevka, I'm not that stupid."

She refused to flinch, to give any indication that his words sliced through her, leaving her cold.

Yes, this was definitely the dimmest of her bright ideas.

"I'm not sure, exactly, what to do with you." He ran his hand down her hair, smoothing it. "You're very beautiful—"

A knock came at the door. With a sigh, Kwan let her go and stepped back from her. She felt his gaze on her like daggers, or maybe it was simply her pounding heart, cutting her chest to shreds. *Get a hold of yourself, Yanna.* She hadn't worked in the field since her training days, but she'd been taught how to think ahead, look for opportunities.

To have backup. Oy. She hoped her other transmitter was still operating.

"Enter," Kwan said, hiding the knife behind his back as he crossed his hands.

The door opened, and Yanna heard footfalls even as she kept her eyes ahead of her. Fu spoke quickly, softly. "He's here."

Kwan's breathing, and the silence that followed felt like a noose, choking off her air. *Think, Yanna!* Now might be her one and only chance for escape…but what about Elena?

"Escort him in—"

"But the wom—"

Kwan raised a hand, cutting Fu off. Every muscle in Yanna's body coiled as she watched Kwan sit down at his desk. He closed the lipstick case, capped it. Folded his hands. His silver eyebrow spike gleamed against the sunlight.

Yanna twisted her hands in her cuffs and, for a moment, considered a prayer, just in case she might be wrong about God caring.

She heard voices at the door, and Fu entered the room followed by a tall, broad-shouldered man. She scrutinized him through the curtain of her long hair, wondering how many steps it might take to break free and launch herself out the door. The visitor didn't look her way as he entered, but she glimpsed ponytail-long dark hair, a close, trimmed beard and an arrogance in his step. She looked away. Dressed in a pair of designer jeans, a gray silk shirt and a pair of black hiking boots, he looked American. Of course. The center of the human-trafficking trade. Yanna worked her hand-cuffs as she listened to their conversation with her rusty Mandarin.

According to her translation, Mr. American slave trader wasn't exactly fluent, either. But he made his point. His shipment waited in Taiwan and he wanted to set up an exchange.

She wondered if she, or Elena, might be among the cargo.

Yanna studied him, took in his wide shoulders, the way he held himself and a memory stirred inside her. Fu saw her perusal and slapped her.

Pain exploded in her face and tears rushed to her eyes. As she cried out, the visitor turned. She saw his body jerk, and she looked away, hating the foolish bravado that lied to her and told her she was field material. Too much time spent with her hero pals Vicktor and Roman.

She was a computer tech, with a knack for gadgets. What had made her think she wouldn't face the same fate as Elena? Or worse, the same fate as Katya?

Nothing but desperation.

"What is she doing here?" the voice said, and Yanna looked up. Blue eyes, *familiar* blue eyes looked down at her, and for the briefest of seconds, they filled with horror.

She'd seen that horror before. Just outside Red Square in Moscow fifteen years back, right after a man had grabbed her and wrestled her into the shadows.

Right after David Curtiss had jumped him and pulled him off her.

And two seconds before she'd lost her heart forever to a six-foot-two, blond-haired, blue-eyed American boy with a soft spot for the oppressed.

No, it couldn't be. But under all that dark hair, the flashy California attire and the painful Mandarin she plainly recognized the guy on the other end of her e-mail dreams, Preach, aka David Curtiss. She stared up at him, and shock turned her pale. This was his big undercover assignment? The truth flashed across his face.

He recognized her, too.

"You like her?" Kwan asked, finding his feet.

Yanna looked away, not wanting to see David's expression when he answered.

"I do," he said, and something inside her turned

warm at his words. Even though she knew it was an act, tears of relief filled her eyes. Yes, let Kwan give her to David. Together they'd find Elena and—

"She's not for sale."

Yanna closed her eyes.

Kwan came around the desk, leaned against it.

"Why not?" David said, his voice low. "I want her."

And then, Yanna realized exactly how Elena might have felt. Cheap. A commodity. A sickness welled inside that had nothing to do with the sea.

"She's not who you think. She's a Russian agent." Kwan nodded to Fu, who clamped her around the back of the neck and forced her face up. She kept it averted from David's, fearing the look of derision in his eyes. Whatever undercover plot he had strung together, her appearance might just be unraveling it, and fast.

"An agent?" David repeated. "Then why do you want her?"

Kwan was silent. He drummed his fingers on his arms, staring at her. She winced as Fu's grip dug into her neck.

"I don't," Kwan finally said. "We're done with her." He reached across his desk, behind him.

"Then let me—"

"No."

Yanna recognized the lipstick tube and her blood drained from her body as Kwan opened it and twisted out the blade. He glanced at Fu, who let her go and it was all she could do not to collapse. But she wouldn't do that. Not in front of David.

Never in front of David.

Out of her periphery, she saw Fu pull out a small silver Makarov pistol that looked painfully like the one she had back home. He leveled it at David.

Yanna's eyes widened as Kwan stepped up to her and smiled at David. The man she loved.

"I'm going to kill her," Kwan said softly. "And then maybe we'll do business."

Chapter One

One week earlier

Yanna Andrevka hadn't spent the past ten years of her life putting her kid sister through college to watch her throw it away on some pudgy, bald American named Bob.

Then again, she wouldn't be doing cartwheels if Elena were marrying a hip, urban Russian named Sergey or Ivan, either. The very fact that her bright, beautiful sister put any man before finishing her law degree had Yanna turning the beet she was chopping into a blood-colored mash.

"About finished with the salad, Yanna?" Katya asked as she drained off the water from the mashed potatoes into the sink. Steam rose, cooking the already stifling galley kitchen. The tourists who thought that Siberia in summer still meant glaciers and bitter winds should spend a day in her apartment in August. The Gobi Desert was probably cooler; certainly it was less humid. Yanna scraped the beets into a bowl along with onions, pickles, diced cooked potatoes and cooked carrots. She picked up a wooden spoon and began to stir.

"Where's Elena? She's supposed to be back by now." The fact that her sister had lifted nary a finger for the goodbye send-off she'd planned gave Yanna sufficient ammunition to let her anger simmer. It felt better than facing the fact that in twenty-four hours, she'd be alone in their two-room flat, no one to greet her when she stayed too late at volleyball practice, or harass her about having no social life.

She had a social life. Namely, Elena. Especially now that Yanna's other friends—Vicktor and Roman—had ladies who took up their free time. Ever since Elena had moved back to Khabarovsk two years ago, after getting her undergrad degree in Saint Petersburg, Yanna's life had taken on new vibrancy. Maybe it was watching Elena come into her own and blossom into a beauty like their mother. Or maybe it was living vicariously through her soap-opera romances, or listening to her dreams of life after school. Until two years ago, Yanna had seen her kid sister as a nuisance, a leech, just another price Yanna had to pay for her mother's foolishness.

Now, she wasn't sure just how she'd survive without Elena snuggling up to her when she arrived home from a date, or a class, regaling her with her latest drama.

Bob had better be worth it. Or Yanna would cross the ocean in a single bound and spike his head across his two-story beach house. The pictures did look nice, however.

"She's picking up her wedding dress," Katya said. "I told her they have dresses in Seattle, but she says she wants a Russian dress. You can take the girl out of Russia, but you can't take Russia out of the girl." Katya looked up from the potatoes she was mashing. Skinny as a sixties-era model and wearing a pair of jeans and a sheer white blouse, Katya looked like she hadn't the strength to mash a pea. With long, bottle-bleached hair and brown eyes, the twenty-two-year-old English teacher had a ticket to Seattle with Elena. She'd continue on to Jersey to meet her prospective groom. She poured more milk into the potatoes. "I'm getting my dress from a store in New York. I already told Mario that."

Yanna swallowed a remark and turned back to her salad. She added oil, salt, pepper, and tried not to let her cynicism leak out. She should be happy for the two girls. They'd won the lottery, according to too many Russian women. American husbands. Life in the promised land. True, most women in Russia today struggled to find jobs and, when they did, pulled in less than eighty percent of the salary men did. Yanna had to be twice as good at her profession to get half the respect a man did. Still, after seeing what loving the wrong man—too many times—and living with a permanently shattered heart had done to their mother, well, Yanna wasn't about to mess with the good thing she had going. Decent friends, a solid job, an apartment to come home to…she had more than most women could hope for.

Besides, she had already found her true love. And, even if he never knew it, their e-mail relationship was enough for her. Actually, it was probably safer, even more rewarding her way. If he never knew how she felt, he could never reject her, could he?

Yanna poured the salad into a glass bowl then, lifting it above her head, squeezed past skinny Katya and out into the family room. She'd set up her dining-room table, pulling it out from the wall and placing it in front of the sofa. Three chairs were set opposite the sofa, and with an end table added from her bedroom, she'd made seating for at least eight. The rearrangement left little room to maneuver, what with her shelving unit running across one end of the room and her television on the other. Khrushchev forgot to leave room for breathing when he designed the tiny single-family flats.

The doorbell buzzed. Yanna grabbed her key from the latch by the door and peered out the peephole. Elena smiled broadly. Her teeth looked huge in the domed view.

Yanna pulled open the inner door, then unlocked the outer door. Her fellow FSB pal Vicktor had installed the vaultlike steel barrier during the reign of a serial killer a few years back. It squealed on its hinges as it opened.

Elena squeezed past Yanna into the narrow entry hall. She toed off her sandals, setting a bag down beside her. "Guess what I got?"

"Your wedding dress?" Yanna closed the door.

Elena's face fell. "Katya, you rat!"

"Oh, please," Yanna said as she brushed past her sister. "I spy on people for a living. If you think I didn't know what you were up to, you haven't lived with me since you were a kid."

"Oh, I have no doubt you have my computer and my cell phone bugged, as well as listening devices planted throughout the flat and in my schoolbag." Elena placed a kiss on her sister and scooted into the kitchen as Yanna finished setting the table.

Sometimes, she seemed so much like Yanna, it was difficult to believe not only their fifteen-year age difference, but that they had different fathers. Long, mink-brown hair, flashing dark eyes, a reserved smile—these things Yanna recognized of herself. But Elena's willingness to embrace new ideas—like Internet dating—or even her belief that she could make marriage work with a man she'd never met, these were from her father, their mother's youngest and most outspoken boyfriend. Her mother had been wildly happy with Genye, the dreamer. Until he'd been arrested for drunk driving and beaten to death in his holding cell.

After that, something had died inside their mother, as well. About then, Yanna had graduated from college, stepped in and taken over the raising of Elena.

Perhaps this was why Yanna couldn't forgive Elena for abandoning her for a man. This, too, felt like a legacy from their mother.

In a few days, the only thing she'd have left of Elena would be her hand-me-down jeans and one of the matching silver lockets they'd exchanged last year for Christmas.

Katya emerged with the potatoes as the doorbell rang again. Yanna opened it to three of Elena's group-mates from school. They charged into the flat, dumping their sandals and book bags, and turned up Valery Meladze on the stereo. Yanna felt young again as the music found her heartbeat. The bell rang a second time, and Vicktor, Roman and Sarai stood just outside the metal door. Yanna's contingency.

Sarai gave her a quick hug. "How are you holding up?" She had to nearly shout.

Yanna shrugged. Although she and Sarai had only met for a summer years ago, and hadn't seen each other until this past winter when Roman rescued Sarai from becoming a political prisoner, Yanna felt as if she had known the blond American doctor all her life. Or maybe she simply reminded Yanna of Sarai's brother, David. Probably another good reason Yanna enjoyed having Sarai around.

Roman handed her a bouquet of flowers. "For the bridesmaid." He gave her a kiss on the cheek and Yanna was touched by his kindness. The Cobra captain with the tawny-brown hair and hazel-green eyes seemed so much happier with Sarai around, and the wounds he'd received in gulag had healed nicely, especially under Sarai's care.

Walking in right behind them, Vicktor caught her before Yanna could follow Roman and Sarai into the flat. Vicktor had an intensity about him, from his dark hair to his toned frame that scared away most women. But Yanna and, most of all, Gracie, his fiancée, knew that underneath that take-no-prisoners exterior resided a man who would give his life for his friends.

"Gracie said she'd meet Elena in Seattle. She's there working with a new project, so she said she could sneak away. I sent her the flight information."

Yanna nodded, hating the sudden prick of tears his words caused. His blue eyes softened, and he reached out and gave her a one-armed squeeze.

"Thanks, Vita," she said. She'd planned on asking her friend Mae—a national guard pilot who'd recently moved to Seattle—or even David to keep tabs on Elena, and the fact that Vicktor had suggested his fiancée, well, all at once Yanna felt that maybe Elena would be okay, after all.

Yanna followed him into the family room, where everyone crammed around the table. Some merciful soul had opened the windows to her flat, and when Katya switched off the music, street traffic three stories below drifted up, adding an early evening ambience. The smell of hydrangeas and dahlias lifted from the bouquet on the table, now covered with bowls of salads, cutlets, mashed potatoes, and glasses of prune *sok*.

Elena emerged from the kitchen, carrying her masterpiece, a tall Napoleon cake of thin layers and abundant cream. Yanna couldn't help but notice how she glowed, just like a bride should. She'd pulled her dark brown hair back, and it cascaded in curls along the neckline of her sleeveless tank. With a hint of tan on her arms and nose, she looked about sixteen. Yanna could hardly believe this was what Elena really wanted. But then again, if Yanna were to look deeply, perhaps her dreams weren't so very different. Not really.

Someone to love her? To count on? No, that wasn't so foreign a desire.

Yanna picked up her glass of *sok,* raised it to the group. "To Katya and Elena. *Cheslivaya Vechnaya!*"

"Happily ever after," they all chorused as they touched their glasses for a toast.

He'd never eaten deep fried frog on a stick, but David Curtiss was a patriot, and he'd do just about anything for his country.

"Shei-shei," he said as he took the delicacy from the vendor, fished out a New Taiwan dollar and dropped it into the vendor's hand.

He wondered what might leave a worse taste in his mouth, fried frog, or meeting a man who had beheaded the two undercover agents who had tried this trick before David. But if all went as planned, his culinary sacrifice would lead him to the identity of Kwan-Li, leader of the Twin Serpents, the largest organized crime syndicate in eastern Asia.

The smells of night market were enough to turn even his iron gut to mush—body odor, eggs boiled in soy sauce, fresh fish and the redolence of oil from the nearby shipyard. Even worse, the fare offered in the busy open market sounded like something from a house of horrors menu: Grilled chicken feet, boiled snails, breaded salamander, poached pigeon eggs, and the specialty of the day—carp-head soup.

"What did you get me into, Chet?" he whispered, wondering if Chet Stryker, his cohort for his unfortunate op, was grinning at the other end of his transmitter. "Squid or even snails, okay, but a frog?" Chet had set up this meet—and the frog signal. "Next time, you're going to be drinking asparagus juice, buddy." He hoped Chet's silence meant he still had his eyes on him. David hadn't seen his partner in the forty-five minutes he'd been walking around the market—a sign of Chet's skill, no doubt.

David looked at the brown and crispy frog and wondered if he was supposed to add condiments—he'd noticed a sort of ketchup and horseradish at the bar.

A few more seconds and he'd have to take a bite. It wasn't enough to just stand here and try to blend in with the crowd, not an easy task given that every man who brushed by him stood around chin height. Even with David's long dyed-black hair, silk Asian shirt and designer jeans, he knew he looked like a walking American billboard. Thankfully, foreigners flocked to the novelty of night market in this part of Kaohsiung in Taiwan.

He saw a couple of Americans stroll by, listened to their comments about the food, the smells. A short blonde, slightly pudgy, wearing a blue Taiwanese shirt and shorts set probably purchased in a local beach shop sucked on the straw of a jujube shake. Next to her, her husband was finishing off a grilled squid. Aid workers, probably. The island had a plethora of Americans working in relief and humanitarian aid agencies. Especially after the last earthquake.

If only that shaker had dismantled Kwan's organization. But unlike the hospitals and island utilities, organized crime kept their systems up and running without a hiccup, transporting heroin out of mainland China, and arms and munitions in, where they ended up in rogue countries like Afghanistan, or even Iran, and in the hands of rebel groups like Abu Sayyaf in the Philippines, and countless crime syndicates from Thailand to Malaysia.

But the disruption of services in Taiwan had given David what he needed to slip under Kwan's radar and place himself on his doorstep. If he played this right, Kwan would agree to his offer of pistols, automatic rifles, rocket launchers, mortars, and the promise of a light howitzer, in exchange for 150 kilos of heroin. The exchange of weapons for drugs would accomplish two goals—intercept another shipment of heroin and trace the trail of arms.

Most of all, David hoped to put a face to the boss of one of the largest drug and arms trafficking rings in Southeast Asia.

Then maybe he could cut his hair, take a bath and get out of his sweaty duds and into his uniform, where he felt most comfortable.

And he'd finally write back to Yanna, who by now probably wanted to strangle him. He'd never gone this long without corresponding and every day that passed without hearing from her felt a little like a part of him had died.

Sorry, Yanna.

Perhaps, however, this time-out from their daily e-mails and instant messages had told him one thing—how much she meant to him.

He checked his watch. Kwan's man was late. Which meant he'd have to take a bite of froggie.

He lifted the amphibian to his mouth.

"Lipley?"

He heard his alias on the lips of a small, bowed man. "I'm Ripley," he said.

The Asian man—David placed him at fifty—nodded once and moved past him. David ditched the frog and followed, dodging shoppers, keeping the man in his sights. "Contact," he said softly into his transmitter. But probably Chet had already seen that.

They left the press and smells of the market and crossed the street into the shipyards. The container yard of Kaohsiung Harbor—the third largest in the world—had been an easy place to mask their shipment of Remington M-24 Sniper rifles, Colt M-16s and Commandos, and way too many H & K MP5s. The CIA had also thrown in Smith & Wesson .45

caliber pistols. David had watched from the roof of a warehouse earlier today as Chet checked the supply with the head of CIA in Taiwan after sweeping the area beforehand. He'd heard Bruce okay the transaction, and even reiterate the agency's agreement—and policy—to disavow should things go south. Figured.

Then David had cleared Chet to lock the container tight and leave, alone.

He hadn't heard from his partner until they met over an hour ago outside the market. Until Chet had told him about the frog.

The moan of ships moving out into the South China Sea, the smell of seaweed and oil, and the sound of seagulls calling brought David back to his last trip to Russia, only eight months ago. After helping his best friend Roman escape from a Siberian gulag, and making sure his stubborn-as-a-Russian sister, Sarai, was safe, David had accompanied Yanna to a volleyball match in Vladivostok. And afterward, they'd walked down to the wharf to watch the lights of the ships glimmer against the black sea and listen to the water lap against the massive steel hulls. Her long mink-brown hair blowing in the cold wind, and that mysterious smile on her face had nearly made him take her in his arms.

Nearly.

But he'd been dodging that impulse, with success, for almost a decade. Well, all but once. Still, starting a relationship—the kind he wanted to finish—with Yanna could only lead to heartache. And not just because they lived on different sides of the ocean. But because they lived on different sides of eternity. For now. He'd never stop hoping that might change.

"Wait here." The little man stopped him with an outstretched hand, and David stood still, his heart thumping as he watched the man disappear behind a three-story stack of metal containers. From behind him, he heard footsteps. He turned and tried not to flinch as two of Kwan's muscle materialized. They both looked like they'd done time in a Chinese prison—their noses set poorly, bodies wedged into ill-fitting suit pants and silk shirts. Homemade tattoos lined their forearms. He recognized silver Russian-made Makarov pistols in their grips and he kept his hands out from his pockets. "Where's Kwan? I agreed to meet with Kwan."

"He wants a sample of the merchandise before he's willing to meet with you," said the taller, nastier-looking of the two.

David shrugged. The guns were real enough. They had to be, to make it overseas and into the right hands. Yet inside each gun, the CIA had installed a surveillance chip to leave a trail that David and the other members of this op could track.

Hopefully, in the end, they'd bring down Kwan's organization. Before they sacrificed precious lives. "Fine, I'll want a sample of his merchandise."

One of them smiled, and it sent a warning into David's gut. Something didn't feel right. He'd been undercover in enough hot spots over the world, first as a Green Beret, and then as a Delta Force operative, to recognize something sour in the air.

But he said nothing as he turned and wound his way to the container he'd set up for just this scenario. He hoped Chet had heard the exchange and had him in his sights.

Not that Chet would step in should the op turn ugly. This was important enough to both of them, to the war on terror, to the thousands of soldiers in Iraq and Afghanistan being mowed down with their own American-made weapons to sacrifice David's life, should it become necessary.

David stopped before a locked container and entered the code to the mechanical lock. The door came open with a teeth-grating whine.

"Inside."

With the moon rising over the water, streams of hazy light raked the container yard. But it couldn't penetrate the palpable blackness of the container. However, David had personally secreted the one crated box of weapons in the container and now walked over to it without hesitation. He reached out to crack it open when a light flickered across the crate.

"Stop."

The voice came from the darkness, and David couldn't make out the face of the speaker. When the light panned the floor, he plainly recognized the man writhing in the pool of luminescence, bleeding from the head, his hands tied behind him.

Chet.

David stared at him and everything inside him turned to liquid. "What's going on?"

"We have a problem."

David narrowed his eyes, trying to get a fix on the speaker.

"We caught your partner here working with the CIA."

Chet glanced up at him, his face granite. David leveled the appropriate glare at Chet. *Lord...*

"We'd like to think that he was double-crossing you, Ripley."

Was that a question? David walked over to Chet, grabbed him by the hair. "Is that true, O'Hare?"

Chet looked at him, and slowly nodded.

Pain cut through him, and David thought he might gasp. Instead he backhanded Chet. His partner fell back and the sound of Chet's ragged breathing filled the container, burned right into David's soul.

"I think we'd like a demonstration now."

David looked up, into the shadows. He made out a taller man, deep-set eyes, a thick build. "I was supposed to meet Kwan."

"First a demonstration. Then Kwan will see you."

Which meant that David couldn't end this here, couldn't somehow shoot their way out in a blaze of gunfire and fists.

"What demonstration?" he growled.

The man nodded past him, toward one of his men. David heard the crate being wrenched open and bile burned in his mouth. He met Chet's gaze with a coolness meant to mask his feelings. Chet glanced away from him, closed his eyes.

No, God. It wasn't supposed to be this way. Especially since Chet was more than a partner. In a way, he was family.

How would David ever tell Chet's cousin Gracie— who just happened to also be his pal Viktor's fiancée?

He heard one of the men behind him uncrating the Smith & Wesson double-action .45 semiautomatic from the straw and oil that kept it dry and secure. He then heard the ratchet of the eight-round magazine as it slid into the chamber. He tightened his jaw, fixing a hate-filled look he didn't feel on his "betrayer."

The cold, round end of a pistol pressed against David's brain stem as another man stepped forward and handed him the pistol.

David nodded. "Step back. It'll be loud, so be prepared for trouble." He took the gun by the shiny silver handle, felt the weight, the cool grip.

Chet's captor stepped away from Chet, leaving the man alone and helpless on the floor. David heard the men behind him also move back, perhaps not wanting to risk soiling their clothes.

What about their souls? *Please forgive me, Lord.*

He aimed the pistol at Chet and prayed.

Chapter Two

Yanna couldn't decide which place felt more dismal—her basement office at FSB HQ, with the harsh fluorescent lights, the musty smell of mold and cement, cables snaking the floor like land mines, the sharp neon eyes of endless computer screens; or her third-story, two-room flat, with the dark brown carpet, the occasional hot water, the temperamental electricity. She'd dreaded Elena's departure for months, and when it happened, she found herself running from the echo that greeted her at the end of the day.

She flicked on the light to her office. The fluorescence played coy for a moment, then flooded the room with wan light. Tossing her workout bag onto her faux-leather sofa, she moved to her desk, wiggled the mouse to bring her computer to life, then logged in.

A schematic of her newest project flashed on her screen. She'd designed a microsize GPS radio transmitter to fit into a chip no larger than a one-carat diamond.

Her latest tweak included a "panic" button that reported a precise latitude/longitude/time. She hoped that one of her surveillance applications would earn her an office with a view of Red Square in Moscow.

It also gave her something to do during the long weekends that Roman spent with Sarai, or when Vicktor holed up in his flat IMing Gracie, back in Seattle.

No, she wasn't lonely. Really. She had all the humming CPUs to keep her company. Yanna clicked open her e-mail program, checked through a list of recent messages. One from Artyom, a techno engineer inside the FSB who helped her refine her applications. One from Gracie, confirming Elena's flight information. Two from her volleyball coach, detailing upcoming meets and practices. Noticeably absent were any e-mails from David.

As usual, she clicked her Internet icon, logged on to the net and entered a private chat room. More often than not over the years, she'd found David logged on and waiting for company. Good thing he didn't know how often she'd rejected face-to-face company, curled up on the sofa with her laptop and spent the night tapping to him. Sometimes it just seemed safer, especially with David five thousand miles across the ocean, to unlock her secrets to a computer screen than to those who saw her every day.

"Where are you, David?" Things would have been just fine if she hadn't seen David less than a year ago. He'd swooped in with his confidence and bravado and unshakable loyalty to help spring their pal Roman from a Russian gulag during the coup in Irkutsk. But David might as well have escaped with her heart, also, because seeing him after all those years had reminded her that although she might not *need* a man she *wanted* one.

The wrong one. Because, according to her last assessment, David Curtiss wasn't only an American, but one in the business of fighting terrorists. And the recent headlines from Moscow said that their governments didn't exactly see eye to eye on whom, exactly, the terrorists were. More than that, David was religious. Vicktor and Roman called him Preach, and rightly so, because she couldn't have a conversation with him without it turning spiritual. Not that he attacked; on the contrary, he answered questions. And took God seriously.

But she'd seen too much of life to really buy into the idea that God cared, *really* cared about the details, or even the big picture. One quick glance at the headlines across the world told her that God had checked out long ago.

No, she'd let David and Roman and, lately, Vicktor do the praying—the spiritual surveillance— while she designed the physical equipment.

Are you there? She typed the words in the chat room, but his name wasn't lighted on her list of contacts and she didn't hold out hope for a response. I miss you, she almost typed.

Instead, she minimized the window and wrote a

note to Artyom, detailing a new idea. Then she sent a letter to Elena, wondering if she'd checked out of her hotel at Incheon airport yet. Two days without a word from her sister had started to annoy Yanna. Especially since she'd found her brown spike-heel boots missing and had an idea of where they'd run off to.

"Dztrasvootya." A knock followed the greeting and Yanna looked up to see Vicktor at the door, one hand on the jamb. "What are you doing here this late?"

"I should ask you the same question." Yanna leaned back in her chair. "Working a case?"

Vicktor gave a half nod. "Chief Arkady sent it over. His department found a body behind the Amur hotel. A woman, someone from Thailand or some other Asian country, it looks like. We're running her ID now. Meanwhile, we have the man listed as her husband in custody. Looks like he ran up a gambling debt, and took his frustration out on the first available target."

As an agent in the international crimes department of the new face of the KGB, the FSB, Vicktor spent too much time in the Russian casinos and strip clubs, tracking down foreigners trying to run from justice.

Yanna winced. "And people wonder why I don't want to get married."

Vicktor shook his head. "I'm not sure these two are married—he's Russian and the girl looked awfully young. Besides, not every man in the world is like your many dads, Yanna. There might be a few good ones left."

"Maybe," Yanna said. "So, what brings you down to my lair?" Yanna oversaw the Internet and IT department, something that had earned the respect of her fellow FSB agents. But what Vicktor didn't know was that she'd put in a request to transfer—to Moscow. The idea had been simmering for months, and when Elena had announced her potential engagement, Yanna took it as a sign.

Besides, with Vicktor engaged, and Roman and Sarai spending every free moment together, she needed to get on with her life. Alone. And far away from any reminder of the man she could never have. Because, really, why torture herself?

"Gracie called." Vicktor didn't smile, and the omission made Yanna uneasy.

"How's Elena? Did Gracie get her settled in? I really appreci—"

"Elena never got off the plane, Yanna."

Yanna's breath hitched. "What?"

"Gracie searched the terminal, then contacted the airline. Elena wasn't on the flight."

"But that's the right flight. I wrote down the numbers myself." She leaned forward, pulled up her e-mail to Gracie. Then she opened another Internet window and typed in the address for Korean Air. The numbers matched.

"She wasn't on board. Just to be sure, I checked all the incoming Korean flights over the past two days. And then I checked the flights to San Francisco, Los Angeles, Chicago and New York."

Yanna's chest tightened. "None of them?"

Vicktor shook his head. He sighed, looking past her, worry in his eyes.

Yanna let the information sink in, settle like acid into her bones. "I don't understand. I saw her get on that plane, Vicktor. I walked her right through passport control, right into the gate area, watched her climb the stairs into the plane. Saw it take off. I'm telling you, she was on that plane."

Yanna typed in her access to international passport-control information. "Did she clear passport control in Korea? She wasn't supposed to exit the international side of Incheon airport—her hotel was right in the airport, and she didn't have to go through passport control to stay there." She scanned the screen, scrolled down and answered her own question. "No."

The spiral of panic hit, affected her voice, lit her nerves on fire. "What about Katya? Was she on the flight to America?"

"No."

Yanna pressed her fingers to her temples, her voice low. "Where are they, Vita?"

Vicktor shook his head, a grim look on his face. Then he stood. "There's something else, Yanna. The M.E. called. The Korean embassy faxed over a picture from their morgue. Utuzh needs you to come down to his office and identify a body."

Yanna's breath left her, and something inside snapped. She heard a moan deep down inside, but she wouldn't, couldn't let it surface. *"Ladna,"* she said, agreeing to his request in a voice she didn't recognize. She stood and followed Vicktor from the office.

"I just want to know one thing, Bruce. How did Kwan find out about Chet?" David kept his voice low, but his tone meant business as did the barrel of his Glock 47. He'd been asking himself that for three days as he lay low, not returning to his house, or the humanitarian aid company he used as a cover business. Three days of waiting before he could sneak into the Kaohsiung hospital and see for himself that Chet was going to live.

Three days to sort through his brain the scenario at the docks, and come up with an answer. Three days before he could track down Bruce, bribe a waiter and yank his CIA contact away from dinner with a group of loud Americans and meet him in the bathroom. Where, just because he was angry and on edge and not entirely sure who to trust, he met Bruce with right hook and a knee to his spine.

He drove the muzzle into Bruce's jaw, the other hand he used to tighten his submission hold on Bruce's hand. He leaned close and leveraged the thinner man onto the grimy bathroom floor. Yeah, like that smell, pal? "How did he find out?"

"Back off, David."

"Listen, I'm living off the grid. I look and stink like something that crawled out from under a dock and it'll take very little for me to simply disappear.

I've already shot one friend, so it just may become a hot streak if you don't start talking."

"You were there. We were alone. What do you think happened?" Bruce tried to wiggle out of David's grip, and earned a moan.

"I think that you—or someone inside your department—is on Kwan's payroll."

"Why would I—"

"And I'm going to find out who."

The silence behind that statement told David that Bruce heard him, and well. He swallowed. "I know."

David said nothing.

"Yes, okay, we have a mole. But it's not me."

David didn't move.

"C'mon, Curtiss. You know me well enough to know that I'm a patriot. We've worked together for years. I wouldn't turn over a friend." He lowered his voice. "And I wouldn't shoot a friend."

David flinched, but he let Bruce go. Bruce instantly found his feet. Stepping away from him, David watched the man's hands in case he delivered a payback swing, but Bruce preferred the far end of the room.

He smoothed his dress shirt, his office haircut, and his hands shook slightly. "Believe me, I'm as sick about Chet as you are."

"You didn't shoot him."

"You had no choice, David. Chet told me what happened. He told me they jumped him, and that it was either him or both of you. You did the right thing."

David wished he could agree. Wished he didn't hear Chet's agony every time he closed his eyes.

If it weren't for the high drama the sounds of the shooting wrought, and the need for immediate egress, Chet would be lying in the Kaohsiung morgue and not in ICU. David had gotten clear and called Taiwanese police in time to save his life. Meanwhile, Kwan's men vanished and David went dark. Three days later, David wasn't sure if he might find a bomb in his scooter's carburetor, be dropped with a clean shot to his head from some sweet-potato kiosk, or if a Thai call girl might show up on his doorstep as a gift from his new business partners.

The entire thing made him sick and the smell of raw fish and tofu emanating from the café kitchen only made his stomach roll. He wished that someone would remind him, again, why he was trying to take out Kwan? Because lately he had a hard time figuring out which side he was really on.

"I've run the scenario through my head a thousand times. The leak had to come from someone inside."

"We'll figure it out, David. Only a handful of people knew about this op. Me, my director, the American attaché to Taiwan. And even they didn't know names. We've swept our phones for taps, scanned all communication going in and out of the embassy. I don't know, but I promise, I'll find out."

David closed his eyes, ran his hands down his face. He sighed. "Now what?"

Bruce stepped to the door, opened it and glanced

outside. When David shanghaied him, Bruce had been dining with two Taiwanese ladies and a small contingency from the American Institute, aka the American embassy in Taiwan. "I'll talk to Lee. See if he knows anything."

Lee Quinn, the khaki-wearing, apple-cheeked man from Iowa who ran the American Institute? The boys on Bruce's staff called him Q, mocking his ability to even boot up his computer without crashing a system or two. Yeah, he was sure to have insider information.

Bruce closed the door. "Now we wait. Kwan's men saw that you meant business, and got a taste of the merchandise. So, you let them bring that message back to Kwan and let him get hungry."

"Kwan could be on to me. My cover could be blown."

"Maybe. Or maybe you're one step closer to putting a face to the name and bringing down his operation."

"So another criminal can slide in and fill his spot?"

"Kwan has fingers all the way from Canada to Thailand, and well into America. We bring him in, we cut him a deal and nail his counterpart, the other Serpent. Then we start to dismantle the Twin Serpents from the top down. And it's not just arms. It's drugs, and human trafficking. It's twelve-year-old girls from Burma who get to go home. It's making life safe for the people you care about." Bruce reached out to David and squeezed his shoulder. "It's doing the right thing and looking at yourself in the mirror every morning and living with the person you see." Bruce raised an eyebrow, patted him once and left.

David let him go, not sure what to believe. Not sure that he could live with the man he saw in the mirror. And not sure who, exactly, might be on that list of people for whom he fought to make the world a safer place.

No, wait, he knew exactly who topped that list of those he fought for.

Wait for Kwan. David had been a soldier for so long, it felt unpatriotic to even question Bruce's words. But suddenly he longed to jump ship and vanish. Head north by northwest to Russia. He felt so close…on the right side of the world, at least.

He waited five minutes then stepped out of the bathroom and cut left, past the kitchen and out the back entrance. Quick-stepping through the alley, he came out onto the sidewalk. Twilight bent shadows around the three-story apartment buildings that lined both sides of the street. The main floor housed business, restaurants, grocery stores, kiosks of clothing and household goods. On the second and third floors lived the families who ran the stores. Toward the edge of the sidewalk, leaving a narrow path between building and machine, a thousand scooters lined up like dominos. He smelled grilled something—chicken or pork—stuck his hands in his pockets and walked down the street.

After checking for traffic, he crossed the street and entered an alley to the next street, ducked into an

Internet café and crossed to the back booth. He sat down, aching for something, *someone,* to connect to. He'd been sleeping in flophouses for three days, eating strange food from street kiosks and he'd begun to despise his own smell. All he wanted was a friendly face. Words to remind him that if he might be shot and left for dead in a shipping container, someone somewhere would miss him.

At least he hoped so.

He opened a page on the Internet and accessed his chat room. Something sweet and wonderful washed through him when he saw Yanna's icon lit. He knew he shouldn't—he'd been deep for so long that to screw up now would be colossally stupid—but, well…

He opened the chat screen and discovered she'd been looking for him.

Are you there? she'd written.

Yes, he typed back. I'm here. I'm sorry I've been out of pocket for so long. How are you?

He waited, watching his cursor blink. Blink. Blink. Blink…now in time with his heartbeat. Disappointment filled his chest. Probably it was wrong, even dangerous for him to long for something so much. But he couldn't help it. Writing to Yanna had become more to him…well, he couldn't rightly put it into words.

All he knew was that sitting here staring at his cursor was the only thing that made any sense to him at the moment.

C'mon, Yanna, I'm here. I'm right here.

* * *

Anyone who knew his son would know that he'd raised an idiot. All those boarding schools in England, and later Japan and America. The years of private tutoring, of taking the boy under his wing, and how did his son repay him?

By nearly blowing his cover.

By letting David Curtiss, operative and potential troublemaker, get too close.

Kwan stared out of his office window, to the snarl of scooters and traffic below, watching the trucks spit exhaust. The view in Moscow had been grander—overlooking the old district, with its bold architecture and cobblestone streets. He'd loved to stroll Arbot Street and dine with the ambassador at Spaso House. His time in Mongolia and China had been equally rewarding, and he'd learned things he couldn't put a price on. But it had been Hong Kong that had changed his life. Where he'd learned exactly who his parents were, and why he'd been born. Where for the first time, he understood the nature and sacrifices of love. And where the future had been conceived.

He'd only accepted the post in Taiwan for his son's sake. And now, he'd have to clean up the boy's mess.

And what was worse, Curtiss was good, too good. Kwan had been looking for him for days, and the man had shown up right under his nose, during a meal of boiled tilapia. Kwan had lost his appetite right then.

The pencil Kwan held snapped between his grip

and graphite spilled on his silk shirt. He stifled a curse and threw the shards down onto his desk.

They'd have to let him get closer.

Only then would he, and his legacy, be safe.

Chapter Three

"This is crazy, Yanna, and I'm not letting you do this." Roman leaned past her, grabbed the jacket she'd added to her duffel bag and threw it across the room. If the frustration in his voice left any room for doubt, the abuse of her leather jacket clearly displayed exactly how he felt about her little undercover op. The jacket fell across the desk where her computer worked away, steadily retrieving all of Elena's e-mail and Internet correspondence over the past three months. Anything that had to do with Zhenshini & Lubov, the mail-order service Elena had used to find "Bob."

"Hey, what if it's cold where I'm going?" Yanna retrieved the jacket.

"Which is exactly my point," Roman snapped, now taking her jeans out of the bag. "You don't have the faintest idea where Elena is."

Yanna picked up her jeans and held them with her jacket to her chest, hating the accuracy of his words.

Elena's "Bob" didn't exist. Or rather he did exist—a lot of him, in the form of a long list of aliases, including Katya's New Jersey boyfriend. Hence, why when Yanna had done her initial background Bob check, he'd turned up wealthy and healthy and a good churchgoing man. He probably fit the criteria for every prospective bride registered on Zhenshini & Lubov.

She had never felt so thankful for Vicktor's fascination with America—and the fact that he'd done an internship in Seattle a few years prior with the police force—as when he'd picked up the phone and pulled in favors across the ocean. The Seattle detectives had tracked down "Bob's" address and found a vacant lot. So much for the swanky beach house.

Which only turned the ball of pain inside Yanna to living fire. The address listed for the bridal service in Moscow also turned out to be phony—the only link to actual, live people she could squeeze information from being the Web master who hosted the site from a tiny two-room office in Saint Petersburg. And after Roman's fellow Mafia-fighting FSB/Cobra pals in St. Pete had wrung the Web master dry of information, she'd learned roughly…nil, nada, *nichevo*.

Which led her back to Elena's university friends and a thin brunette named Olga, fellow subscriber to Zhenshini & Lubov, recently—and conveniently—engaged. With Yanna's credentials and a little brutal reality, Olga had handed over her airline ticket to America.

"I'm an idiot," Roman said, making a grab for her duffel bag to—what, toss it off her third-story balcony? She hip-checked him, a skill learned from their days playing street hockey. He banged into her closet, his hazel-green eyes sparking. "I should have known you were up to something when you issued yourself a new passport. You used Olga's name, didn't you? You're hoping that whatever happened to Elena will happen to you."

"Is this why you woke up all my neighbors in the middle of the night trying to break down my door?" Darkness pressed like coal smoke against her windows.

"I would have taken it off at the hinges with a blowtorch if you didn't open it. And if you don't listen to reason, I'll call in reinforcements. I'll tell Sarai to bring enough sedatives to knock out a tiger. By the way—" he scooped up the passport lying on the bed "—you do realize that you're at least ten years older than the age listed for Olga, right?"

"I'll pass for her. Just you wait until you see what I'm wearing."

"You had to say that, didn't you?" He tossed the passport onto the bed. "I hate everything about this."

"I have no choice, Roman. My sister has vanished." Yanna rolled her jacket into a ball and shoved it again into the bag. "Apparently you've forgotten that when you went running off to a province under martial law to rescue Sarai—against orders, I might add—I was the one to drive you to the airport." She grabbed her makeup bag and tucked it in next to her jeans.

Roman just stood there, hands on his hips, glaring at her. He looked a bit ragged, even dangerous, in his black jeans and matching T-shirt, his tawny-brown hair tousled beyond repair. If he got serious, he could keep her from leaving. One of those wide, muscled arms across her door, and well, she just hadn't kept up the hand-to-hand combat skills she'd learned in the military. Besides, Roman not only worked out every day, he had a passion about him that never said quit. It used to scare her. Today it only made her angry. "I'm going, Roma. End of conversation."

"Then I'll go with you—"

"You don't have a ticket, and the flight is full—"

"I'll drag someone off, or bribe them or maybe I'll just tell the pilot that a crazy woman is on the flight who needs *constant medical attention.*"

Yanna grabbed her lipstick from her purse, refusing to be baited. "I'll be fine. I have a weapon—see?" She uncapped the tube and turned the base. A knife protruded.

"That is not a weapon. That's a toy." He tried to snatch it from her, but she pulled away.

"I probably won't even use it."

"It probably wouldn't help if you did. Especially if someone tries to grab you." Roman raised his hands in the air in a gesture of frustration, turned and stared out the window. He was visibly shaking and, for a second, the concern in his posture muted her.

Maybe this wasn't such a good idea after all.

Maybe, in fact, she should wait for Roman or Vicktor to go with her. Or even David, to whom she'd written after returning from the morgue.

Seeing pictures of Katya's battered body had made her nearly retch, but the relief that poured through her kept her from going right over the edge and into the comfort of a pint of vodka.

But she wasn't her mother. Not yet. Hopefully not ever. And the hope that Elena might still be alive galvanized Yanna. Kept her upright and thinking. Believing that she could find her.

Yanna had written to David, three times, in fact, over the last few days since her sister disappeared. And not a word. She tried not to be angry. Really. He was probably deep undercover. But the truth felt hard and glaring—the first time she'd ever needed the famous Preach and perhaps his prayers and, well, he wasn't there.

However, Roman filled David's shoes well; she could practically hear David. "Yanna, you're not a field agent—never have been. You're a computer whiz. Let Vicktor and I find her."

"I need to find her now, Roma." Yanna sank down on the bed, feeling suddenly, overwhelmingly, exhausted. "Every second matters. If she's still alive, the window for opportunity to locate her closes with every day. I think she's been trafficked, and worse, by the Twin Serpents. Apparently, people in your department, I might add, have been watching this group for years. It's been almost one week since she got on that plane. I need to leave on tomorrow's flight."

Roman turned back, and she saw the tension in his bloodshot eyes. "I hate this. Everything inside me is screaming that I should drag you down to HQ and lock you in a holding cell until we find her."

"You wouldn't do that," she said, her voice shaky.

He sighed, his shoulders falling. "I might. I should." He ran his fingers into his eyes, rubbing them. "No. I wouldn't."

She rose and came over to him, putting her hands on his broad shoulders. Once upon a time, she'd had a crush on the dashing Mr. Charm. But then again, so did half of Moscow, and three-fourths of Khabarovsk. Every single woman her age she knew had entertained fantasies about Roman Novik. But he'd only ever had eyes for the girl who got away. The girl for whom he'd surrendered everything. The girl who had helped him find himself—David's kid sister, Sarai.

"Roman, listen. I'll take my cell phone. You know it has global GPS. And I'm wearing my new earrings...see?" She touched her ears, the tiny faux diamonds that Artyom had made. "They not only have GPS, but one-way transmission abilities and a panic button. You can find me anywhere on the planet."

"But I can't get to you if I'm in Russia."

"Then follow me. I'm leaving on this morning's flight to Korea. And I'm going to find Elena and bring her home."

Roman took her into his arms and held her, and

she felt his heart thumping. "I'll be praying for you, Yanna. Be careful. Please."

Yanna nodded. "I'll be fine, Roma. I promise."

David sat in one of the deep plush seats of Kwan's thirty-six-foot high-performance speedboat, Gladiator, the wind parting his hair, his face against the salty seawater, his hands gripping the gunwales. Kwan had expensive toys, and David knew that by motoring him out to his yacht, Kwan hoped to impress him, Ripley the gunrunner. Yet David's mind couldn't stay fixed on the hundred-twenty-foot yacht looming on the horizon. Worry edged his thoughts, his focus. Yanna had never answered his instant message, and he hadn't been able to return to the Internet café. But something in his gut didn't feel right.

Lord, wherever she is, please watch over her. David lifted his gaze to the sky, the twilight sending fire across the dark water. Glancing back at his chauffeur, he also raised a prayer for himself.

A week since he'd shot Chet, David was finally going to meet Kwan. David wore a digital recorder sewn into the lapel of his leather jacket, and with twenty-four hours of recording time, he hoped to nail Kwan through his own words. Somehow he had to stay in character, reinforce the fact that Chet had been a rat, and that he lived to make as much cash as fast as possible and any way he could—no questions asked.

There were times, like now, when he wished his life, his job, might be simpler. Like his sister, Sarai's. Save lives—that felt like a pretty decent job description. The things he did and the choices he made felt so far from the side of good, at times he wondered if he cost lives rather than saved them.

By the time he calculated the cost, he usually found himself already neck-deep in trouble. Like the night he'd met Yanna Andrevka.

"Pomegetye!" David should have known, from her terrified scream for help that found its way to his soul, that he'd never quite get over meeting her.

Sometimes he went back to that night. Heard his and Roman's footsteps as they walked toward Red Square. Felt the screams ignite his adrenaline as he dove into the shadows and found a lithe girl wrestling with a man twice her size. He tasted the fury as he tackled the man, who kicked him, wrenched free and took off running. David's legs had reacted on pure instinct. He'd nearly had his hands on the attacker twice before the guy ditched him in the alleys off Prospect Pushkina.

He'd returned to find his hockey pal Roman being decked by a second attacker, and he'd leaped on that man. Roman had got a lick in just as Yanna turned to David, digging her fingers into his arms.

"Please, let him go," she'd said. Although her voice shook, he saw in her demeanor a strength and a concern that reached past her own terror to stop a brawl. It turned out that the second man he'd tackled had been her date, and a hockey pal of Roman's. And, after raking her date—Vicktor—over good, he and Vicktor had parted allies and, soon after, became friends.

David pinpointed that moment in Red Square as the precise second Yanna had knocked the wind out of him. He'd never really recovered. It wasn't just those beautiful brown eyes, or her feisty, independent spirit or even her femininity that made him a little breathless.

It was the fact that she trusted him. At least over e-mail. Face-to-face, it wasn't quite that easy. The last time he'd seen her he couldn't escape the sense that Yanna was hiding something. Holding back.

Which meant that maybe she didn't really trust him, despite her words.

The boat bounced over choppy waves, jarring his teeth, turning David's attention back to his mission. After waiting far too long for Yanna to check in to their chat room, he'd finally returned to his flat—a two-room dive above the Anchor, a grocery store/ CIA front. From the shop below, the putrid scent of tea eggs—eggs boiled in soy sauce and tea for a zillion decades—destroyed his appetite. Especially when Kwan's contact tracked him down and invited him for a rendezvous on his yacht.

The chauffeur cut the speed and David felt the boat settle into the water, slowing as it motored toward the silver-and-black yacht. *Keep your eye on the ball, Preach.* David found his expressionless look that gave him one of his few advantages. Besides, after shooting Chet, nothing that Kwan threw at him would faze him.

They glided up smoothly next to the aft deck, and the boats nudged each other as the ocean rolled them. Tying the boats together, the chauffeur nodded to David. The man had already patted him down and searched for weapons, coming up empty. David wasn't that stupid.

David climbed across the seats, glancing at the sleek dual console with its gauges and padded steering wheel. In another life…

But he didn't have another life. This was his life. Mingling with murderers…only being honest via e-mail with a person he could neither touch nor see.

Head in the game, David. He couldn't keep living in the what-ifs. Not if he wanted to stay alive and unearth Kwan.

Not if he wanted to be the soldier he'd dedicated his life to being.

He followed the chauffeur up the stairs and stopped obediently, waiting, finding his sea legs as the man disappeared into a compartment.

David recognized the two thugs who appeared along the rail. They'd had a bonding experience in a dark container on the wharf in Kaohsiung. He gave them a dark nod, noting again the shiny Makarov pistols they carried. Sometimes he wondered at the love/hate relationship China had with Russia. They sure shared their toys well.

He walked between them along the starboard deck until they reached a door. Again he waited as Kwan's muscle introduced him. As if Kwan might be royalty.

King Kwan. David barely hid a smirk, evidence again that his head still wasn't quite on the game.

From this vantage point, Taiwan appeared as a smudge on the horizon. David wondered how far Kwan parked from mainland China, and if this location might be under the protection of certain Red Guard patrols. How deep did Kwan's Chinese influence run?

His escort reappeared and gestured him into the office. A young man sat behind his desk, his eyes cool and dark. He wore a silk shirt, a flash of silver at his neck, and another in a bar that ran through a pierce in his left eyebrow. David hid his surprise, and a spurt of anger. Clearly, he'd been duped again. This man was young—in his late twenties. The Twin Serpents reign of terror had begun in the eighties. This Kwan hadn't been shaving long enough to helm an organization like the Twin Serpents.

David approached him with a swagger that he hoped projected confidence. Across from "Kwan," he saw a thin brunette who'd clearly had an ugly twenty-four hours sitting slumped in a chair, her head down, her hair tangled and hanging over her face, her hands cuffed behind her. She wore the attire of a working girl—stiletto boots, a short skirt, see-through blouse—and David refused to let his thoughts untangle the scenario. Taking down Kwan would also dismantle his human-trafficking business—the third largest moneymaker for organized crime around the globe. An added benefit would be if they caught his suppliers, from Russia, across Asia, and even into America. Human trafficking had no geographic bias.

He ignored the woman and the pulse of pity inside, and faced the Kwan imposter.

"I was told I was meeting Kwan."

The man said nothing. Raised the pierced eyebrow. Then smiled. "I am Kwan."

David didn't react, didn't betray his frustration. Instead, he folded his hands over his chest. "Why did you make me wait? I have other buyers, if you're not interested." David watched the so-called Kwan, weighing his reaction.

Kwan said nothing, let his eyes run over him. Then he lifted one shoulder. "I have other sources, also."

David maintained his silence.

Kwan smiled, slowly. "But none at your price."

David nodded. "Then let's do this. I say where, you say when."

"No. We'll go right now, today."

David narrowed his eyes, shook his head. "How do I know you're Kwan and not someone—"

Behind him, he heard a slap. The woman cried out and David turned, fighting his reflexes. He didn't care who the woman was, he wouldn't stand here—

Ice flushed through him even as she looked away. His breath actually left his body, and for a long, painful second, he couldn't move.

Yanna.

Yanna?

He felt sick, staring at the welt across her face.

Sickened and just short of launching himself at the man who'd hit her. "What is she doing here?" He'd had to wrestle every emotion back to its starting pad to manage the cool, somewhat annoyed tone, and not sound as if the world had just slid out from under him. What *was* she doing here?

Her gaze snapped up to his, and for one raw, awful moment, he knew. She recognized him. Even under his long dyed-black hair, his Mafia garb. She now knew exactly what he'd been doing the past three months. An odd hint of shame rose, right alongside the nearly rabid panic that surged through his veins. Yanna…

"You like her?" Kwan asked, standing.

Yanna looked away, and something inside David broke. "I do," he said, painfully aware at how real those words felt. Real and terrifying.

Especially when tears glazed her eyes. *Oh, Yanna.* His horror nearly choked him.

"She's not for sale."

Yanna closed her eyes. David felt as if he'd been belly punched.

Kwan came around the desk and leaned against it.

"Why not?" He kept his voice detached, and should have won an Oscar for his prize-winning, nearly wolfish tone. "I want her."

But oh, how it hurt to see Yanna close her eyes in a slow flinch.

"She's not who you think. She's a Russian agent." Kwan nodded to his man, who grabbed Yanna around the back of the neck and forced her gaze up. David's breathing quickened and he fought it. *Look at me, Yanna.* But she didn't. She kept her beautiful eyes averted, as if ashamed.

What was she doing here?

"An agent?" David somehow said. "Then why do you want her?"

Kwan was silent. He drummed his fingers on his arms as he stared at her. David caught her wince of pain. He glared at the man holding her neck. *Keep it up, pal, and you'll find out just how that feels.* David flexed his fingers at his sides.

"I don't," Kwan finally said. He looked at David, a smirk on his stupid, pierced face. "We're done with her."

David felt a whoosh of relief so strong it nearly took him down at the knees. "Then let me—"

"No." Kwan reach behind him and pulled out a tube. Of lipstick?

David glanced at Yanna, saw her nearly go white as Kwan uncapped it and twisted the base.

A tiny knife appeared.

Oh, this was bad, very bad mojo. Kwan glanced at his man, as if giving a signal, and he released Yanna. She shook out of his grasp, swallowed, lifted her chin.

Now there was the Yanna he'd met ten years ago. The one with composure and courage. The one who had stolen his breath clean out of his chest.

Oh God, help! Not only was he sorely outnumbered, and undergunned, but if he did what his gut screamed for him to do, he'd erase months, even years, of hard work. Chet's suffering would be in vain.

And Kwan would go deeper underground.

What was Yanna doing here?

That things were going to get worse seemed apparent when Yanna's attacker pulled out his pistol.

Then Kwan stepped up to Yanna. Grabbed her hair, tilting back her head.

"I'm going to kill her," Kwan said softly. "And then maybe we'll do business."

Chapter Four

Think, Yanna, think! Yanna stared up at David, at the horror on his face as he watched Kwan clutch her stupid little knife and her brain went blank. Aside from being exactly the last scenario she would have conjured up for meeting David again, she knew beyond a shadow of a doubt that right now his brain was checking out every possible egress route, every possible angle where he wouldn't have to blow his cover to save her life.

And probably coming up empty.

Contrary to current appearances, Yanna made her living using her brain and solving problems. And from her viewpoint, David had two options.

Watch her be killed or be killed himself.

And neither of those seemed acceptable. At least, not to her.

Yanna caught David's eye and then, with everything inside her, slammed her stiletto into Kwan's ankle.

She connected in a bone-jarring crunch. Behind her, a gun fired, missing David's head, or where his head had been, because the moment she acted, he turned and slammed his fist into the face of Fu, or maybe Wang. The Chinese thug went down, bleeding from the mouth.

Yanna followed with an inside kick to Kwan's knee. Her cute knife went spinning across the floor. Kwan collapsed, but not before he grabbed her arm, pulling her with him.

She landed on top of him, pinning him with her chair.

She looked up just in time to see David scoop up her knife and turn it on Wang. In a second, he'd appropriated Wang's gun.

For one endless moment, all Yanna heard was panting.

"Let her go," David said, pointing the gun at Kwan. "I won't ask twice."

Outside, shouts, feet thundering across the deck.

"You'll be dead long before they get here," David added.

Kwan released his hold on her hair. "You're the dead man," he said. David pulled Yanna to her feet, helped her wiggle from the chair. Before he could force the handcuff key from Kwan, the door burst open.

"Run!" David pushed Yanna ahead of him, toward another door. Yanna stumbled through it to a narrow hallway.

Shots fired behind her, then David burst through the door and slammed it behind him. "Run!"

Yanna fought for balance, her hands cuffed behind her. She reached the stairs and tripped up them.

Twilight, the sun setting on the far horizon and turning the ocean to fire, beckoned from the bow of the yacht.

David had her by the arm, running, pulling her, now flinging her right over the edge into the frothy depths.

Cold! The ocean gulped her whole, sucking her under, stinging as she went down. She kicked and kicked, surfaced with a greedy gulp of air.

And David was right there, arm around her waist, pulling her against him. "Kick!"

Yeah, okay. She coughed, but kicked hard, letting David drag her against the hull of the yacht. Above, voices yelled, clearly searching for them.

"Shh." David's cheek rested against hers, his voice calm, as if they might be out for a leisurely swim. "Stay calm."

Calm? Yanna shivered, and she fought to keep her breath steady. But inside, her pulse raced at full tilt in her throat, and David's heart hammered against her as he pulled her tight to his chest. Clearly, neither of them were in any state of calm. She kicked, willing herself to trust him, to trust his arm around her waist as he trod water, pulling them into hiding. The voices came toward them.

"Deep breath," he said a second before he pulled them under. She closed her eyes. Don't panic. But David had a death grip on her and the breath in her lungs leaked out too quickly, began to burn. She fought the urge to struggle, but couldn't stop herself as fear spewed into her arms, her legs.

She opened her eyes and saw the yacht hazy above them, David swimming hard toward another boat. Oh, please, oh, *please.* With everything inside her, she kicked, too. Just as she knew she would have to breathe, even if it were water, they broke the surface.

Shouting came from the front of the yacht. David pulled out her knife—where'd he get that?—and lunged at the rope tying the boat to the platform of the yacht. The boat began to float away and David grabbed it with one hand, keeping a hold of her with the other.

"I gotta get aboard. Then I'll pull you up."

Shots zinged the water next to her. He was leaving her here? "Wait!"

"I'm not going to leave you, Yanna. Just tread water."

His voice, so calm, so David, went straight to her thundering heart. For a second he turned her, holding her arms, and looked her in the eyes.

He seemed to promise without words that he wouldn't leave her.

"Don't die," she rasped.

"Right." With a nod, he let her go and she sank into the water. In a second he'd pulled himself over, into the belly of the boat. More shooting, and she hugged the boat, like he had, kicking to keep her chin above the surface. *Hurry, David!* But he didn't lean over for her; in fact, she heard the engines fight for life and the boat begin to move. "David!"

And then, just as the boat began to pull away, the

last protection between her and a very angry Kwan, David grabbed her arms.

He dragged her over the edge, unceremoniously dropping her in a seat as he dove for the controls and hit it.

The boat surged to life and Yanna landed facefirst in the back of the seat, ground into submission by the gravity of however much horsepower Kwan's machismo demanded.

"Stay down!" David shouted as a shot whistled over his shoulder and chipped out a portion of the windshield. He ran the boat in tight zags, making it jump and churn, and Yanna fell into the seat and huddled, praying she wouldn't be sick.

"They can't catch us, not in the yacht."

Yanna stared up at David, breathing for the first time. He braced one knee on the seat, both hands on the wheel, glancing back over his shoulder now and again. The wind parted his long dark hair, which sailed out behind him, and, in his flamboyant silk shirt and wet jeans—which had torn somehow in their great escape—he looked uncannily like some modern-day pirate.

All he needed was a tattoo.

And, look at that. As his shirt flapped open in the breeze, what did she see but the etchings of a design. An eagle.

David Curtiss had turned into a high seas buccaneer.

She looked up at him, and for a split second couldn't help but smile.

Apparently, however, he had the demeanor of a pirate, too, because he frowned back. "We're not outta trouble yet, Yanna." Then his eyes softened, and something so much like relief filled them that she felt herself completely wordless.

He was right. At least *one* of them was in serious trouble, indeed.

David could hardly keep up with what had just happened. Without hesitation, almost instinctively, he had reacted to Yanna's bravado and suddenly here they were, he and Yanna, parting the ocean in Kwan's cigarette boat. And, to his even greater shock, the woman he so wanted to love huddled at his feet, staring up at him as if he might be some sort of South Seas swashbuckler.

His head had most definitely checked out of the game. He exhaled, stifling a word his persona might use. Instead he slammed his hand down on the steering wheel.

At his feet, Yanna made a wry face. "That bad, huh?"

He looked at her, then sat on the driver's seat and pulled her up. The wind buffeted her eyes and she looked down, blinking. Then she turned sideways, searching the ocean behind her. "I can't even see them."

"Trust me, they're behind us. Maybe even tracking us with some onboard GPS. We gotta ditch this boat as soon as we can find another ride."

Yanna hunched her shoulders and brought her legs

through her handcuffed arms one at a time, until her hands were in front. David glanced down at the jewelry. "I'll get you out of those as soon as I can."

"I know you have your hands full," she said, without looking at him. "I'm sorry I got you into this."

"I think it might be the other way around," he said, frowning. "What were you doing there?"

Yanna glanced at him, a pained look crossing her face. Then she shook her head and looked back toward their pursuers.

Okay, don't *tell me why I just blew a multimillion-dollar operation.* David concentrated on driving. Just. Drive. Get to shore and then maybe he'd confront the feelings roiling through him, the ones he couldn't get a fix on. Relief? Fear? Anger?

Why was it, every time he got near her, *really* near her, he couldn't seem to get a hold of his emotions?

Staring at the shivering mermaid next to him, he could see her as she'd been, a beautiful coed with a brain that could run circles around his, tying his heart into a messy knot of confusion as they sat in the kitchen of his Moscow flat, trying to unlock advanced calculus.

"It's not so hard, David." Her laughter always made him feel the wind under him.

"It would be a thousand times easier if it weren't in Russian." It was these times, with the night pressing against the windows, the cool spring air carrying in the scent of the late night, of rain, and the occasional bark of a dog, that he wondered how he would have made it through those years at Moscow University without her.

"If you want to graduate, you have to nail this final," she had said, pushing the book toward him. "I'll translate if you can't get it."

He'd looked up at her. It hadn't been the words that confused him. It was how he was supposed to pack up his bags and climb on an airplane and live the next decade without Yanna in his life.

His face must have shown it, because her smile dimmed. "Are you still hoping to go to grad school?" Those brown eyes had roved over him, her long elegant hand tapping her pencil on the linoleum tabletop.

At that moment, he hadn't known what he wanted. Well, besides Yanna. Because it wasn't just her exotic beauty—those dark, mysterious eyes, the silky dark hair, the strong frame honed by championship volleyball. But the way she had kept up with him, outthought him, even challenged him.

They said that opposites attracted, but sometimes Yanna felt like the other side of himself, even in the way she could read his thoughts. "I don't know. How about you?"

She had leaned back, rolled her pencil between her fingers. "I'm…being recruited for the military, or something like it."

It had been the way she said it that made his eyebrow quirk up, made his plans unravel. "What kind of military?"

She made a face. "I can't tell you."

Oh, that kind. He didn't say anything, but panic had reached up and wrapped around his throat. Yes, America and Russia seemed to be getting along pretty well, but if she joined the KGB, or something like it, and he planned on filling out the forms from the recruiting office, well… Somehow he had resisted the urge to pull her to him, perhaps run for Siberia.

"Hey," she had said, smiling. "It's adventure, travel, education. Power."

Her words hadn't sounded so different from his own to his father, when he'd told him he might join the military. But as he had seen her tap her pencil on her leg, he had heard the words behind her statement. Power…as in, not weak, not helpless. "This is about your mother, isn't it?"

She had shrugged, not looking at him.

"Yanna, just because your mother made stupid mistakes with men, buried her pain in a bottle, doesn't mean that you can't get married, find a nice guy…" He had just about gagged on his words. Because even as he spoke, he had felt the words cut into his heart.

She had looked up at him, her mouth in a tight line. "No, David, I'm never getting married. Ever."

And since that moment, he'd felt so deeply ashamed of his relief.

Now, they bounced over the waves, and David steered them in and around the fishing boats that trolled the sea. "If they have us on radar, maybe we can confuse them."

Yanna still refused to speak. He noticed the wind had caused her eyes to water. If he didn't know better, he'd guess that she was crying. But Yanna didn't cry. Not his Yanna.

He finally maneuvered behind a large freighter, hiding the boat between the massive ship and the shoreline. He cut the motor down to idle.

In the far distance, the shoreline had become a dark shadow under an indigo sky. The moon traced a line across the now-settling waters, and the breeze turned calm, despite the increasing nip in the air.

With God on their side, they just might make it back to shore in one piece, sneak back to the safe house and sort out how to get Yanna home safely.

And him back in the game.

Yeah, that would take a miracle. David ran his mind over the fireworks that had played out on the yacht. Why would Kwan kill Yanna in front of David? Was it just to show how tough he was? Or could it be that Kwan had already figured him out? Had the mole blown David's cover, too?

David looked out over the boat, toward the open sea and Kwan's yacht, somewhere in the darkness hunting them down.

"These things usually come with a dinghy." He climbed past her, toward the back and opened the hatch over the smooth stern. Then he reached inside, pulling out a bundled mass of rubber. He tossed it toward the water, hanging on to the rope. The dinghy unfolded as it flew and hit the water half-inflated. He went back and extracted a small motor. "That Kwan knows his water safety."

Even in the darkness, he could see that Yanna didn't smile at his attempts at humor.

"C'mon," he said, reaching for her. Yanna offered her hands and he pulled her to him, helped her up to the side. "Climb in. I'm going to push you off, and turn the boat around."

She scooted forward, then jumped off the hull toward the dinghy. She landed with a thud in the center of the dinghy and rolled to her back. David handed her down the motor, then shoved her away from the boat.

Turning the speedboat around, he cut a length of rope and secured the wheel. "Hopefully they'll follow it out to sea," he yelled to Yanna, a second before he gunned it. He jumped over the edge as the boat hurtled toward open water.

The wake rocked the dinghy and he waited a moment before hauling himself aboard. When he did, he lay beside Yanna, breathing hard, staring into the now-dark sky. His wet clothes pressed him into the dinghy, sucking out his energy. He refused to let fatigue have its way. Not until he'd at least gotten Yanna to safety.

Beside him, he felt Yanna shaking.

"You cold?"

She said nothing and he turned on his elbow, staring down at her. In the rising moonlight, she looked painfully frail, not at all like the capable agent she'd become, and everything like a scared, broken woman. And yes, she was shivering.

"Yanna, what are you doing here?" He didn't wait for her answer, but scooted his arm under her and pulled her tight to his chest. She let him and curled in close, bringing her arms up between them. He cocooned her with his leg, putting his chin on the top of her head. "Shh. It's going to be okay."

And then she started to cry. Deep, racking sobs that so shook him he didn't know what to do. The Yanna he knew didn't even cry at sappy movies—*Love Story, Brian's Song,* even *The Way We Were.* She hadn't even emitted so much as a whimper when she'd been attacked on the streets of Moscow so many years ago.

And she'd never, ever let him hold her like he was doing now, like he'd longed to for way, way too long.

What had she been doing with Kwan? For the first time David let what-ifs fill his mind. What if she was on a special op for the FSB? If so, where was her backup? Where was Vicktor, or Roman, who dealt specifically with Mafia? What if Kwan had planned on selling her to the slave market?

What if David hadn't come along?

The thought tightened his chest, made him suck in a long, deep breath. *Oh, thank You, Lord, for letting me be here.*

He closed his eyes. Breathed in deep the scent of the ocean in her hair, felt her cling to him, heard her shaky sobs start to calm, tasted her skin salty against his and, in that moment under the stars, with the sea lapping against the dinghy, he didn't care why she was here.

Just that she was.

Chapter Five

She must be dreaming. Must be, because only in her dreams would Yanna wake up with David's arms around her, holding her as if he'd never let her go. His heavy breaths made his chest rise and fall, and seawater scented his now-drying silky shirt. His skin was warm and dry and his arms secure around her. Yes, she could probably stay right here, forever, in this perfect world.

Except, this wasn't the real world. In the real world, Yanna Andrevka didn't collapse sobbing into anyone's arms. And she didn't let her fear turn her into a cowering ninny who let fate push her from one disaster to the next.

She opened her eyes, leaned back and was surprised to see that David was awake. He met her gaze, concern in his dark eyes. His long hair had dried, and now hung wavy and dark around his face. "Feeling better?"

"I feel like I could sleep for a year, thanks to the adrenaline drop."

He smiled and ran his hand down her hair, pushing it behind her ear. "If it helps, you didn't sleep long. And, most of all, you didn't drool."

She narrowed one eye. "How do you know? I'm sopping wet. I might have drooled all over you."

"I would have noticed." Of course, if he had, he still wouldn't have said anything, because if she knew anything about David, honor came miles before his own comfort. That's probably what had drawn her to him first—well, right after all that powerful *I will save you energy* he brought into their relationship. It had taken her years—long after he'd returned to America—to admit that his protective spirit had touched her in ways she could never express. David wasn't just a hero at heart; he was also military—top-secret-go-up-against-the-extra-special-bad-guys-in-the-world kind of military.

Which was precisely why he'd been on that boat, acting like a gunrunner.

Oh, David. Why was it that as soon as she thought she'd gotten him far enough away to breathe again, he rushed back into her life with a velocity that made her reel? Apparently, right into his arms.

He hadn't released her, which felt more intimate than the moment demanded. Still, she didn't exactly put up a fight. In fact, as she watched the moonlight caress his face, she knew it was now or never.

If she wanted to kiss David, show him exactly

how she felt about him, well, she'd probably never get closer.

But she couldn't. She'd tried that once, and it was quite possible she still harbored old wounds, if not scarring.

"Thank you, by the way, for what you did back there, on Kwan's boat," she said softly. "I know that I destroyed whatever undercover mission you were on." She smoothed his hair against his shirt. "I'm not sure I like the fact your hair is nearly as long as mine. And since when did you get a tattoo?"

He didn't smile. "It's henna. And please tell me that Kwan didn't, um—" he closed his eyes, as if even asking it caused agony "—rape you."

Her stomach did a little painful twist. "No. He hit me a couple of times, but no, no one hurt me like that."

A muscle pulled in his jaw as he digested that information. His arms tightened a little more around her. "I about lost it when I saw you sitting there. I've never felt such an urge to hurt someone as I did Kwan." He ran his hand down her cheek. "I'm sorry he hit you. No man should ever hit a woman."

Of course he would think that. If only that standard might be adopted worldwide.

"David, I have to ask…why were you there? What did I walk into?"

His mouth turned into a wry smile. "Can't tell you. Not if I want you to stay alive."

"Covert American op to stop drug smuggling?"

"Something like that."

She dug her fingers into the lapels of his shirt. "I just can't believe I destroyed it. All your hard work—"

"What exactly were *you* doing there?"

Yanna closed her eyes, a spike of pain making her tremble. Idiotic tears wet her eyes. David deserved to know, but she knew the moment she revealed her stupidity, he'd react like Roman. Maybe even worse.

She couldn't tell him, not yet. She needed this moment with him to be…good. Especially because it might be the last one.

Perhaps he took her silence for fear. Or a post-traumatic response. She had no idea what David might be thinking, but surprisingly, he didn't push her.

"I'm just glad I was around to…intervene."

And then, the way he looked at her made everything inside her go a little weak. As if he might be contemplating exactly her thoughts.

Which, at the moment, entailed her lifting her face to his and letting him see how glad she truly was to see him.

No, this was not a good idea. Because, had she so easily forgotten what happened to Elena when she trusted her heart instead of her head? And if that weren't clear enough, Yanna just had to take a look at her brokenhearted mother.

Most importantly, she simply had to remember the last and only time she'd kissed David and tell herself that one delicious moment in David's arms, letting her emotions off their leash, would destroy ten years of friendship, so carefully carved out and honed. She needed David as her friend. Her best friend, sometimes.

Yet longing stirred within her, the one she'd buried over and over. David. Her David. The man who took her breath away.

The man who had saved her life. She smiled up at him, the kind of smile that told him exactly what was on her mind.

He didn't flinch. But he swallowed. And wet his lips, an invitation....

But even as she opened her mouth, even as she considered touching her lips to his, the dinghy rocked. Seriously rocked, as if it had had enough of both of them and wanted to dump them in the drink.

Yanna jerked out of David's arms, grabbing the side.

David steadied her and sat up. "Oh no."

"What?" Yanna searched the darkness for anything that might match his tone.

Her blood turned to ice in her veins. Not fifteen feet away cruised an oceangoing freighter, churning up a wake that could overturn their rubber raft. And behind it, maybe a mile behind, she made out the outline of yet another ship.

"I drove us into a shipping lane!" David climbed to his knees. "What was I thinking?"

"That you wanted to save us from the bad guys?"

Apparently that wasn't a good enough answer, because he turned away from her and grabbed the outboard motor. He affixed it to the back panel, sat back and gave the ripcord a yank. "I obviously left my brains in the States, because this op has been one stupid mistake after another."

Like saving her?

The motor sputtered, died.

"C'mon!" His outburst shook her. Never, in all her years of knowing him, had he raised his voice in anger.

Then again, maybe she didn't know David anymore. The real David.

He yanked it again. The motor coughed and again refused to engage.

Another wave rocked the dinghy, throwing its passengers to one side in a tumble.

"Get over to the other side, even out the weight. This thing could flip if we both land on the edge."

Yanna crawled to the opposite edge, holding on to a rubber handle. *Please.* She didn't want to go back into the water.

David unscrewed the primer and pumped it. "Please have gas, please have gas." Then he closed it and yanked on the cord again.

The motor gave another feeble effort and then died completely.

Silence preceded another wave. This one she rode by throwing herself across the side, counterbalancing David's weight.

See, she was an asset.

Except David wouldn't even be in this mess if it weren't for her, would he?

David sat back on his haunches. "We're going to have to paddle." He didn't look at her when he said it, almost as if he were talking to himself. He reached under the lip of the dinghy, into the folds, and surfaced with a folded paddle. Snapping it open, he turned and braced his knees against the bottom. "Hold on. This might get bumpy."

He turned the dinghy into the next wave and Yanna held on to the front as seawater sprayed her face, running down her shirt.

In the distance, lights from shore mocked them as the next ship bore down, on course to run them over.

Whoever had decided to lean on Vicktor's doorbell at two in the morning, driving shards of noise into his sleep-hazed brain had better be bleeding from his or her ears and in dire need of help, or they soon would be. Vicktor's bare feet froze against his cold linoleum floor as he yanked open his door. Roman put a hand on his chest and pushed him back inside.

"Don't…hurt…me." He drew in heavy breaths, as if he'd run all three kilometers from his apartment to Vicktor's.

"You do have a telephone at your place, right?"

"Get…your…gear…" Roman leaned against the wall, his breath less fierce now. "Yanna's in trouble."

"What?" Vicktor turned on the hall light, bathing the foyer in harsh luminescence. Roman wore a pair of black jeans and his leather jacket. Vicktor felt a little stupid bare chested and in his sweatpants. "What do you mean in trouble?" He turned and headed for the bedroom, yanking his jeans off a hanger in his wardrobe.

"She has dual tracking devices. One is still working—her phone—but she was supposed to call me twelve hours ago. I didn't panic until her GPS—the one she's wearing—went dark about two hours ago."

"And you didn't tell me?"

"I'm telling you now."

Vicktor yanked a T-shirt over his head. "What kind of GPS was she wearing?"

"A pair of diamond-studded earrings. It's got global GPS and a panic button. She texted me from Korea, said she'd checked in. We were both hoping that she'd befall the same fate as Elena, and that she'd be able to connect with her kidnappers. Yanna and I figured that whoever had her would find her phone. But her GPS going dead isn't great."

Vicktor was already tying his shoes. "I'm sorry, did I hear you correctly—you wanted her to be kidnapped, perhaps killed? Because, in my line of work, that's not such a happy ending."

"No—if you'd listen, we believe Elena is alive, and Yanna thought she knew who had taken her, so she posed as one of the girls in the dating service. And, just to be clear, I've hated this plan from the beginning."

"Apparently not enough to stop her. Please, *please,* tell me that you have a backup plan."

Roman looked away.

"Oh, that's perfect, Roma. She's pulling a classic Roman Novik—run off into trouble without a plan."

"Hey, for your information, I *tried* to stop her. I tried to tell her to wait for us. But she wasn't having any of it. She had Elena on the brain and wasn't going to hang around waiting for us to get clearance for Taiwan."

"Like I said, pulling a Roman."

Roman clenched his jaw. "I got clearance," he said finally. "We leave in an hour. Transport to Korea, and from there a commercial flight in."

Vicktor stood in the doorway, an uneasy feeling clenching his gut. And it wasn't just Yanna's disappearance that made him want to hit something. His fiancée, Gracie, had become increasingly distant over the past month, and he'd finally screwed up the courage to ask, beg…plead for her to tell him the truth.

Did she really want to marry him? Yes, theirs had been a lightning-fast courtship, with the kind of life-threatening drama that would push any girl into the arms of her protector. But since then, they'd had a relatively calm, no-one-shooting-at-them sort of relationship, and he thought everything he saw in her beautiful eyes when he'd proposed had been true.

Real.

Only, that had been nearly a year ago, and she still wouldn't set a date, still wouldn't give him the faintest hint of encouragement to run down to the embassy and apply for a fiancée visa.

He was losing her. And he hadn't a clue why.

He blew out a breath, rubbed his temples with his finger and thumb and let out a cry of frustration.

"*Soglasno,*" Roman said. "Ditto on your frustration."

"No, it's not just Yanna. I was supposed to hook up with Gracie online tonight. We had a fight last time we talked about her living alone in downtown Seattle. I hate being a few thousand miles away, especially when I don't know how to fix whatever is going wrong between us." Her words, from a previous conversation, rushed back at him: *You don't always have to fix everything. Sometimes I just want you to listen.*

Yeah, well, he didn't operate that way.

"She's probably just busy with work." Roman picked up Vicktor's arm holster and tossed it to him.

"Sarai and I go head-to-head about once a month and then I spend the next twenty-four hours trying to get her to talk to me. I've decided that it's a pretty good trade-off for the rest of the month when she's trying to get me to listen. Don't forget your passport."

"At least you know that Sarai is committed enough to live in the same country as you. Gracie doesn't know where she wants to live."

"I thought she was waiting for God to tell her." Roman picked up Vicktor's leather jacket.

Vicktor loaded his pockets with his money clip and attached handcuffs to his belt. "I'm hoping that is a legitimate argument and not just a reason to put off the wedding date. Because I've told her I'd be willing to live in America."

"And she's willing to live in Russia?"

"She says she is. But I don't see her applying for a visa, do you?" Vicktor grabbed his watch from the bathroom shelf, put it on. "She says I treat her like she constantly needs to be rescued. That I think she goes looking for trouble." He looked up at Roman. "I might have said she knows how to find it, but I'm not overprotective, am I?"

Roman gave him a sad grin. "Oh, Vicktor. Do you not know yourself at all?"

He wasn't a stalker, was he? Vicktor shot a look in the mirror. Bloodshot eyes and an overnight beard growth. "You have to admit, she gets into more trouble than most women. And I hate living so far away. I want to marry her, and now. But I'm starting to wonder if that's what she really wants."

"Who can tell with women? I took Sarai's car to the repair shop two weeks ago, and it's still waiting in the lot for parts. She's mad at me because she doesn't have a car. But she seems to think that the 'add oil' light means to drive a little slower. I'd be surprised if it didn't need a new engine. I'm in trouble regardless of what I do. Grab your cell and the charger."

Vicktor swiped it from the table, gave a longing look at his quiet computer. "I've asked her what the problem is. I get a 'Nothing's wrong,' which I know really means, 'You've really bumbled it now, pal, and it's up to you to figure out not only exactly what you did, but how to fix it.'" He pocketed the cell.

One side of Roman's mouth lifted up, but he shook his head. "Maybe you should give her what she wants."

Vicktor took his coat from Roman. "What's that?"

"Stop rescuing her." Roman opened the door. "Give her some space. Don't hover. Stop fixing things."

"Like we're doing to Yanna?" Vicktor followed Roman through the door and closed it behind him.

"We're not dating Yanna. Besides, this *is* different. She's in trouble, and the last thing she needs is to be out there by herself."

"I just don't want Gracie to think the same thing."

Chapter Six

David ached from his shoulders to his toes. The early-morning dawn illuminated the shoreline in a jagged outline and he figured he had about an hour before either he landed on shore or Kwan's men discovered their so-called American arms dealer floating on the high seas.

He should have driven Kwan's speedboat straight into shore and made a run for the nearest airport. But no, he had to get tricky.

And it might cost him and Yanna their lives.

They'd finally cleared the shipping lanes, no thanks to his stellar paddling and all due to the generous wake churned up by the freighters that pushed them toward shore. Frankly, he could probably sit back and let the current bring them in. But paddling gave him something to do.

Something to focus on.

Something to get his mind off what he really wanted to do—and knew he shouldn't.

How he'd like to somehow hit Pause and regroup, return to the moment when Yanna was in his arms, looking as if she wanted to kiss him, looking as if she needed him…

And he'd nearly kissed her. When she looked at him like that, searching his face, everything inside him had simply shut off—all the voices from the past, voices of reason that had kept him from doing something foolish over the years, like quitting his job, packing up his life, and moving over to Russia just to be in her airspace.

No—more specifically—he wanted to be in her arms.

And it didn't help that he'd almost lost her, that he'd spent nearly an hour with her tucked close to his chest, that he'd traced her face with his gaze, noticing the changes, the tiny lines of stress around her eyes, the way her hair still looked like silky chocolate. She was so beautiful—more than even when she had been in college—and it had all swept over him in a wave, washing away his reservations, his fears, leaving only desire.

Good thing Someone was watching his back, because he'd felt the claws of temptation dig in, start to work on his brain, take over his heart. One more minute holding her and they would have ended up as shark bait and he wouldn't have complained.

Thanks, God.

Because, despite his attraction to her, despite the

fact that not only did he respect everything about her, from her courage to her brains and everything in that package, they didn't share the same life goals.

Yanna, even though she was a selfless, incredibly giving person, would always see this life as the final destination.

And he had to live for something beyond that. His faith told him that today mattered because tomorrow mattered. Most importantly, his life wasn't his own.

He believed that God cared, really cared, about what happened to him. Even if he might be stuck out in the middle of an ocean with just a paddle.

Which was why, in the end, David counted the paddling and ache in his shoulder a blessing. He'd tried twice more to start the motor, to no avail. Now, Yanna dozed in a quiet ball of slumber in the front of the dinghy, her cuffed hands drawn up as if in the fetal position. He'd get her out of those as soon as he hit land and could rustle up a straight pin.

"David?"

Maybe she wasn't sleeping. In the early morning dawn it was hard to tell. Probably she'd seen him watching her, seen the look of sadness or more, on his face, too. Swell.

"We'll be to shore in a while."

She sat up, pushed her hair back from her face. "Wow. We're really close."

"Yeah. And we're south of the city, so hopefully Kwan's men won't know to look for us here. We'll find someplace to hole up, change our clothes, maybe figure out some disguises, and then I'm on the horn to Roman to tell him to pick you up. You'll be home by supper."

He refused to acknowledge the twist in his gut when he said those words. Despite the danger, he'd enjoyed the brief time they spent together.

How warped and desperate did that make him?

Yanna turned, looked at him and, in the dawn, he made out a pained look. "I'm not…I'm not leaving Taiwan."

Maybe she was dehydrated. "Uh, *yes,* you are." He kept paddling. "Kwan's men will be on the lookout for you—"

"For us."

"For us, yes, but they'll be looking for a dark-haired man traveling with a gorgeous brunette and in twelve hours I plan to match none of that description."

"Good for you, but I'm not leaving. Not until I get what I came for."

David glanced at her, the face she wore when she planned on spiking a volleyball down the throat of the opposing team. Perfect. *Now* she gets ornery. "Listen, Yanna, you can get a great tan in Bali. Or seafood in Singapore. But you're not staying in Taiwan."

"I'm not here on vacation, David." Her eyes sparked.

He wasn't sure why, but that made him feel worse. Because that meant the FSB had sent her into the serpent's mouth, and hadn't had any plans to rescue her. He'd have a few not-so-nice words with Roman about—

"I'm here to find my sister. Kwan kidnapped her. Or at least, I think so."

David stopped paddling. The wind still held a chilly edge, despite the warming sun creeping over the western horizon. Now it touched his skin, raising gooseflesh. "I don't understand."

Yanna folded her hands, looking toward shore. "A week ago, Elena left Khabarovsk for America, to marry some guy named Bob."

Bob?

"She never made it. Her traveling companion, Katya, turned up dead in Korea."

David set his paddle over his knees. "Go on."

Yanna turned back to him, and in her demeanor, the set of her face, he saw the anger, the frustration. And knew exactly how she felt. He'd been up close and personal with exactly those feelings, seeing her handcuffed and bruised at the hands of Kwan's man.

"I did some research on the so-called dating service she used, and I think it's a front to lure Russian girls out of the country and into human slavery." She took a breath, met his gaze. "So I impersonated one of their clients—a girl named Olga. I was intercepted in Korea by men who drugged me and took me to Taiwan. I woke up on Kwan's yacht. And that's when you appeared."

David closed his eyes, his heart thumping, his thoughts torn between wishing he'd put a bullet between Kwan's eyes and the relief that Yanna hadn't been raped.

Because, until this moment, he wasn't sure he believed her. He knew her, knew she prided herself on being tough. Above emotion.

Apparently they both stood guilty of perpetuating that myth.

"My sister might still be in Taiwan, and I'll bet Kwan knows where." Yanna stared at her handcuffs. "I'm not leaving until I find her."

David stared at the cuffs, at the welt across her pretty face, at her crazy leather boots. "You were nearly killed."

"No, you nearly had to watch Kwan kill me. But you didn't, and I'm here, safe."

"But what if it wasn't me standing there? What if some other creep, a real creep—the kind that *does* take Kwan's bribes and sells weapons to terrorists and hurts women—had walked in? Do you think he would have thought twice about letting Kwan slit your very pretty neck?"

She blinked at his harsh words. Her eyes narrowed. "You're assuming I would have let him."

He stared at her, disbelief choking his voice to nearly nothing. "Yanna, you would still be on that ship if it weren't for me."

Her mouth opened and a laugh that contained humor escaped. "Listen, sea dog, like I said, you'd just shown up. If you'd given me a little time, I would have figured something out. I'm not a total wreck as an agent."

"Did you just call me a sea dog?"

"You look like a pirate."

He glared at her. She smiled, not nicely.

"For your information, Little Mermaid, you would not be okay. Kwan had every intention of killing you, and still does. In fact, I'd say he's even more committed. So, you'll hop a plane like a good little AWOL agent and let me look around for your sister."

"Not on your life. And what makes you think I'm AWOL?"

"Roman would never let you—"

"Roman drove me to the airport."

David stilled. "I'm going to kill him."

Yanna watched him, her eyes dark. "Last I checked, I went through survival school, too. I know a few tricks. Like the fact that Roman is right now tracking me through the GPS I'm wearing."

"You lost your phone, sweetie."

"You must think I'm an idiot."

He clamped his mouth shut before he really destroyed their friendship. As it was, he wondered just how long it might take before she ever answered his e-mails again.

"I'm wearing GPS earrings."

He raised an eyebrow. "And they work in water?"

She seemed to want to speak, but when no words came out, she glared at him.

"I'm calling Roman first thing we get to shore. And I'll keep you in those cuffs as long as I have to in order to get you on a plane and to safety."

Yanna's gaze never wavered, and if he wasn't

already chilled to the bone, he'd be an iceberg at her look. "We'll see about that."

Contrary to current popular belief, Gracie Benson didn't go looking for trouble. But as she pulled up to the Hotel Ryss, an incarnation of ancient Russia here in the seedy side of Seattle, she knew Vicktor's accusations were probably, reluctantly, true.

She knew how to find it.

Or maybe, she just couldn't ever leave well enough alone. Like, for example, her offer to meet Yanna's sister—her absent sister, Elena—at the airport. When the woman didn't show up, Gracie had spent half the day camping out at the airport, hoping she might have caught a different flight. What if she'd just missed her? Just to make sure, she'd spent the rest of the day waiting…hoping. Gracie cringed, remembering her phone conversation with Vicktor. What if she'd made him panic for nothing?

And now, she'd gone and poked her nose into the disappearance of Ina Gromenko, a teenage girl from her weekly Bible study. Not that Gracie usually tracked down AWOL teens, but she'd seen Ina at a local mall just the day before.

Shopping for rings.

With a man who looked about ten years older, wearing the creepy and identifiable garb of a Russian Mafia thug—black pants, black silk shirt, squared-off shoes. Ina had introduced him as her boyfriend, Jorge. However, when Gracie had pulled the girl aside with a few words of caution, the look the man gave her made her feel as if she'd been transported back to Khabarovsk, Russia, and was again trying to dodge the crosshairs of a serial killer.

Apparently, she still had more work to do with her therapist to drive suspicion from the corners of her mind. Still, she didn't have to have her paranoid-o-meter set on high to know that something was terribly wrong when she visited Ina's parents' home this morning.

The entire complex had seen better days—a row of fourteen townhomes built in the eighties. Wrought-iron railings bracketed concrete steps, and wooden siding with lime-green paint flaking off below the windows. A blanket hung over the front window, and on the steps a clay pot imprisoned a sopping wet tomato plant, wilted from the abundant rains. The front yard had been dug up and furrowed, and the potato plants growing in the patch of earth sprouted green and healthy on their mounds.

Venturing into this section of town prodded memories of her stint in Far East Russia, with storefront signs written in Cyrillic, and the yards all furrowed into kitchen gardens.

The house looked vacant, but then again, with the blanket over the window…

At Gracie's knock, the door cracked open.

The woman, maybe in her early forties, with age around her eyes, barely opened the door. *"Privyetst-vooyou,"* she said in typical Christian greeting.

Thankfully, part of Gracie's training here in Seattle had been language based. While trying to figure out her future, she'd joined up with a program helping Russian immigrants transition to their new land, find jobs, learn English and eventually blend into society. But with the little Russian village set up inside Seattle proper, with radio and television stations broadcasting in their native language, with the newspapers and schools catering to only Russian-speakers, she had to ask why anyone would make the effort to change languages if their world adapted to them?

Not that she didn't like Russia. In fact, Gracie was one of the few program managers who still longed for Russian food, Russian songs, Russian people. She even attended a Russian church, hence the Bible study with a group of Russian young ladies.

Sadly, the influx of Russian culture included the occasional Russian gangster, which had driven Gracie and her curiosity to Luba's front door.

"Privyet," Gracie responded, reverting to Russian. "Luba? Remember me, I'm Gracie Benson, from the church? I lead your daughter's Bible study group."

Luba looked away, behind the door, lowered her voice. "Ina isn't here." But something on Luba's face said more.

Gracie heard shuffling. Footsteps.

"Where is she?" Gracie asked, feeling Luba's panic. Something wasn't right—

"She's gone. Left with…that man."

"Jorge?"

Luba nodded. "I have to go—"

"Where might they go, Luba, do you know?"

The door closed with a slam.

Gracie stood there, swallowing back the fear that had perched, right in the back of her throat. Yelling came from inside. She stood there, listening, but the words came too fast, too muffled.

Then, everything went silent.

Gracie heard only the beating of her heart, banging like a fist against her chest.

She backed away from the house, nearly tripping down the cracked steps, wishing Vicktor were here, hating the fact that her brain always ran to him for comfort.

When would she learn that a guy on the other side of the ocean couldn't always come to her rescue? Besides, the way their relationship was going, they might never get married.

Not that he didn't want to. But with the political scene in Russia turning back toward the days of the KGB and Cold War status, sometimes she wondered about the wisdom of getting married.

Besides, could two people truly know each other well enough to commit their lives to each other when they had only sporadic communication? Did they even know each other at all?

Probably she was overreacting. Vicktor loved her, and Ina had simply run away with her new boyfriend. She'd be back—

Behind her, the door to the town house opened. Luba ran out. *"Devochka!"*

Gracie turned at her call of "Girl!" Luba grabbed her arms, her face streaked with fresh tears. "He worked with her at the hotel. Hotel Ryss." Luba's voice broke and she covered her mouth, eyes wide. Her voice dropped to a whisper. "Please, can you find her?"

Please, can you find her? Oh, brother. Vicktor would be ever so thrilled that, staring at Luba and her desperation, Gracie had promised with a reckless *Yes!*

Gracie now stood outside the Hotel Ryss, thinking that next time, maybe, she should think before she opened her mouth.

She'd been in a few dives before, especially overseas, but this seedy so-called hotel located in the forgotten part of the downtown business district, with its ancient carpet that smelled as if it had been installed in the seventies, the outdated velour chairs, and the giant chandelier in the center of the lobby, reminded her of a badly decorated movie set. The place lived up to its name, because it looked exactly like something she might have found in old Russia, a relic from the so-called glorious communist years.

She approached the counter to be greeted by a young woman with golden-brown hair piled atop her head. She looked about eighteen, but wore enough makeup to hope the world thought otherwise. The name tag on her polyester green jacket read Anya.

"Zdrasvootya," Anya said. "Welcome to the Hotel Ryss."

"Hi," Gracie said. "I'm looking for someone—Ina Gromenko."

Anya glanced behind her. "I haven't seen her. She works in housekeeping."

"Do you have a manager here? Someone I can talk to?" Gracie shoved her hands into her jeans pockets and forced a smile. Vicktor would probably flash his badge, demand a lineup of everyone who worked with Ina, but Gracie lived by the "catch more flies with honey than vinegar" philosophy.

And, surprise, surprise, it worked. Anya rang up the housekeeping office. Gracie felt every eye on her, from the man reading the *Moscow Times* in the seating area to the woman holding a bouquet of carnations waiting by the door.

"Can I help you?"

Gracie turned at the voice of the man. Dressed in a suit, dark European shoes and a high and tight haircut, he looked like an older version of the boy she'd seen with Ina.

This was the head of housekeeping? "Kosta Sokolov," he said, crossing his arms. His thumb played with the gold ring on his finger. "Can I help you?"

"I'm looking for Ina Gromenko. She works for you?"

Recognition flickered across the man's face, and he smiled. "I'm sorry, she's not here today. Called in sick."

Gracie blinked back her surprise. "Then how about her boyfriend? He works here, too? Jorge?"

The man's smile dimmed slightly. "I'm sorry, he's

not here, either." He glanced at Anya, who turned away and began working on her computer. "Can I help you in any other way?"

Gracie suppressed the urge to exit the building at a full run. But every instinct inside her screamed *Liar!* and she wasn't going to spook that easily. "Can I at least ask when they worked last?"

The man pursed his lips. "That is confidential information. I'm sorry."

Of course it was. "Thank you," she said. He raised an eyebrow, waiting until she turned away.

Gracie stepped outside and stood on the sidewalk, watching the wind scatter decaying leaves at her feet. Now what? What would Vicktor do?

He'd find Ina, that's what. Regardless of what it took. He'd sneak in the back, maybe interview her coworkers. Or he'd stake out the front, follow Anya home, drag her into FSB HQ. He'd figure out a way to pry the information from them.

He'd spent years learning how to lean on people.

Gracie, well, she had spent years trying to minister to the hurts inside. And she'd seen hurt— or at least secrets—written all over Anya. Gracie walked across the street, fished her cell phone from her pocket and, glancing back at the hotel, dialed the number.

"Hotel Ryss," Anya answered.

"It's me, the lady that was just in the lobby. Listen, I thought…Ina is missing and I'm just trying to find her. If you know anything…"

Silence at the end of the line made her stop walking, turn back toward the hotel. *Please.*

Anya's voice lowered. "She came in with Jorge two days ago. I haven't seen her since."

"You mean she worked her shift?"

"No…I mean, she came in with Jorge, and…I haven't seen her since."

Gracie stilled. There was something about her tone. "Could she still be in the hotel?"

She could hear Anya breathing. Then, softly, "Yes."

Gracie stared up at the hotel, all six stories. Built in the late fifties, it came complete with fire escapes on each floor, and a dark alley filled with Dumpsters. "Held against her will?"

Silence, then a quick, "Yes."

"Any idea what floor, what room?"

"Jorge rents a room on the sixth floor. Number sixty-three—"

The line broke off. Gracie stared at the phone. *Call lost,* it read.

Lost, indeed. Gracie stared back at the hotel, everything inside her screaming to run back to the lobby and sprint up to floor six.

And then what? What if she snuck into the hotel, found Jorge's room, burst in….only to find that Ina had run away? She wouldn't be the first Russian girl—even a Christian Russian girl—to leave home, hoping for a new life.

Gracie stopped outside her car and tabbed the unlock button. Then, sliding into the driver's seat, she cued up Vicktor's number. It wouldn't hurt to ask him to check up on Jorge, but she didn't even have his last name. Maybe she should focus on creepy Kosta, the hotel manager. Vicktor still had friends in America from his internship years ago. Maybe one of them could poke around and see what he could dig up.

She opened her text box. Vicktor would be asleep, and for a second the urge to call him, to wake him up just to hear his voice, pulsed inside her.

Yeah, and it would ignite all his chest-thumping, protect-thy-woman instincts. He'd probably stow away on the first plane to America and get them both into trouble.

She could take care of herself. Hadn't she gotten Anya to tell her the truth? By using her *manners?*

She thumbed in a message. V—Srry. Pls ck name—Kosta Sokolov. Luv U. G.

She pushed Send and had just dropped her cell into her pocket when her door opened. A hand snaked in and yanked her from her car.

Yanna had seen many beautiful sunrises in her life, one off the Kamchatka Peninsula, one from the Caucasus Mountains in Georgia, and one in Vladivostok, the night after she'd won last year's volleyball tournament. But the sunrise creeping over this section of south Taiwan, exploding over the tops of houses and rice paddies to rise glorious, hot and triumphant made her nearly burst into idiotic tears.

And when David maneuvered the raft past a shoal,

and only clear calm water rippled between them and the beach, she wanted to break out into song.

If she never saw the ocean again, she'd die a happy woman. She'd emptied her stomach not an hour ago over the side of the raft—not that there'd been anything in it, but after holding out for nearly twelve hours, she couldn't stand the nausea one second longer. She no longer cared what David thought of her.

Okay, she still cared but she didn't want to. Because she had no doubts their friendship would come to a crashing and ugly end in about thirty minutes when they got ashore. Because he'd have to keep her in these cuffs and maybe toss her over his shoulder to get her to leave Taiwan without her sister.

And she didn't plan on being handcuffed one second longer. She might have been shell-shocked after their *Mission Impossible*–style escape, but all her facilities had awoken with a vengeance when she spotted shore.

Or maybe that had happened when David revealed just how little finding her sister meant to him. He'd *look around* for her sister? Like she might be a basset hound hiding behind a Dumpster?

First thing on her agenda would be to get free. Then she'd simply disappear into some crowd.

Probably that would be the easiest for both of them. If she didn't, she could imagine the fireworks. David was like a dog with a bone; when he dug in, he refused to surrender.

Some might say the same about her. Which added up to two bulldogs in a jugular hold. Pretty.

No, she had to cut David loose, for both their sakes.

"What are you doing?" David asked as she scooted to the back and unlatched the motor, pulling it up out of the water.

"One of my mother's boyfriends used to take me fishing. His motor broke every time he was out." She reached down, clunking her chin on the top of the motor as she did, and groped for the prop shaft. Then she worked her way up to the nut that secured it. "I can't believe I didn't think of this sooner."

She felt around the nut, and finally found it—the cotter pin that secured the nut from unscrewing. She fought with it, turning it, wiggling it. Twice she shook out her hand as it cramped. Finally the pin came free.

She let the motor fall into place and leaned back into the dinghy, holding the pin high in triumph.

David stared at her, a strange expression on his face.

She went to work on her cuffs. Inserting the pin into the place where the arm locked, she pulled it slowly out, pressing against the arm lock.

The cuff clicked open. She shook it off and repeated the process for the other arm.

She held up the cuffs, letting them dangle.

"I would have opened them for you, once we were ashore," David said quietly, turning back to his paddling. The floor of the ocean seemed close enough to touch, clear nearly twenty feet or more down. David set his paddle down, letting the sea take them into shore. Although early, she could make out traffic, scooters and compact cars on the road beyond the beach.

"Where are we?" She dropped the cuffs over the edge of the boat.

David gave her a sharp look. "I could have used those."

"Sorry." She rubbed her wrists where the cuffs had chafed.

"I believe we're just south of Kaohsiung harbor, in one of the suburban villages. I figure we can rent a scooter, or maybe catch a bus and head north to Taipei. I'll call Roman along the way."

Yanna said nothing, staring out toward the beach. On the south side, a small row of kiosks advertised coconut and fruits. And she could smell something cooking, probably fish, from one of the morning markets just beyond the roadway.

"I want you to stay with me. Like glue, you hear me?" David rose to his knees. "I don't know where Kwan's men might be or if they will be able to find us, and I need you to be on your toes."

Oh, she'd be on her toes, all right. But she had no intention of being his shadow, thank you. Still, she nodded. *"Konyeshna."*

Of course? David shot her a look. "I'm not kidding, Yanna. Kwan has men every—"

"Don't worry about me, David." She didn't intend the edge in her voice. Not entirely.

David looked away, obviously scanning the shore for unfriendlies. He dropped his paddle into the boat. "Stay put, I'll bring us in." Then he slid overboard and into the water.

I'm really sorry, David. But she couldn't say it. Not when her voice might break and destroy the veneer of anger she so desperately needed.

David grabbed the edge of the raft and waded to shore, his colorful silk shirt whipping in the wind, the water soaking his jeans.

She couldn't walk into town wearing her wet spiky heels, so she unzipped her boots, pulling them off. She flexed her wrinkled toes.

When the water reached knee-deep, she, too, jumped over. Not as cold as it had been way out in the Chinese Sea; still, the water made her gasp. Thankfully, the blazing sun would dry her in minutes. The waves, not anything like they'd been last night, hit against the back of her knees as she waded in.

David let the raft go and followed her to shore. The sand mortared between her toes and she stood there, just inside the rim of water, watching David. Although he'd been up all night, paddling to keep them afloat, he looked energized, even fierce, as his long hair tangled in the wind. An ethereal force buzzed around him that both fascinated and frightened her.

He scanned the beach briefly before he reached out and took her hand.

"C'mon. We'll have a better chance at the market."

Da, she would. She followed him, letting him hold her hand, strong and confident in hers. Sand kicked up behind them as they walked the twenty or so feet to the grassy edge, and finally hit the pavement. Two lanes of traffic piled tight and they waited at the light like two vacationers who'd been strolling the beach. Tourists…with ocean-crusted clothes and sporting a couple nasty bruises.

"I thought you said this was a village." She had expected rolling countryside, perhaps an occasional house, dogs running, a central pump and a train station like her village of Georgivka. But no, this so-called village seemed a sort of extension of the city, with three-story buildings side by side along a main street that ran as far she could see on either side. The smell of exhaust mixed with the ocean and the faintest scent of meat cooking somewhere. Oh, lead her to it, her stomach begged, now feeling like a cavern.

Scooters jammed the road, some with one passenger, many with two, along with the occasional car. Riders wore face masks in bright colors over their mouths, one set of dark eyes after another. Beside her, at the light on the sidewalk, a short, elderly Taiwanese man in black polyester pants and a short-sleeved shirt glanced at her. She smiled. He smiled back, his teeth bathed bloodred.

"Betel nut juice," David said softly. "It's like chewing tobacco. Don't panic."

She kept her smile but beneath it muttered, "Phew."

"It's really not that bad," David said, and winked at her. "But you'll really like the fried frog burritos." He nodded at the building across the street. "Tastes just like chicken."

Yum. So maybe she wasn't quite as hungry as she thought.

Although her ability to read Mandarin—or rather pinyin, the Latin-alphabet translation—was rough, she guessed that she correctly read the word *market* above the long, low warehouse-style building. Despite David's descriptions, the smells were enough to make her stomach do cartwheels. Worse, her mouth felt on fire. She needed a drink, and soon. But nothing bloodred, or made from amphibians. "Do you think we can find a Coke somewhere?"

David glanced down at her as they waited for the light to change. "Can your stomach handle that?"

She made a face at him. "Sorry you had to see that."

He lifted his shoulder in an easy shrug. "Feeling better?"

"Are we on land?"

His hand tightened over hers. "We're going to make it through this," he said quietly.

She looked up at him, swallowed, forced a smile. No, in fact, they weren't.

Chapter Seven

"I've never understood this airport. I always get turned around and end up in the Korean section, ordering kimchi." Vicktor stood in the center of Incheon Airport, or at least what he thought might be the center. The place seemed as large as his hometown with a concourse that stretched from one end of Korea to the other. And to make matters worse, not only was it divided into two sections—the inner and outer court, but also by culture—Asian and Western. And Russia fit, where?

"Do you have any clue where we are?" He walked over to Roman, who stood staring at a giant multi-colored map of the airport. Written in Korean.

"Yanna said her sister was registered to stay at the hotel in the airport, Incheon Gardens. I say we pay them a visit." Roman tapped a point on the map.

"Lead on."

Aside from the bright lights that never dimmed,

regardless of the hour—which was around five in the morning—the Asian music, the funky styles of dress, the orange and red neon from the stores seemed so foreign from his world in Russia it jolted Vicktor right out of foggy and into annoyed. Or maybe his nerves had just switched to overdrive after being rattled and shaken on the cargo flight Roman had secured for them. He made a mental note to never let Roman make his travel arrangements.

Vicktor dodged a tiny woman wheeling a three-wheel cart loaded with luggage. Incheon Airport always seemed packed. A hub of Korean and Asian airlines, from here, flights arrowed inland across Asia, west to India and Thailand, and south to the Philippines and the Micronesian islands. Vicktor wished he might be on his way to Bali. With Gracie.

In fact, more than once, she'd said her dream vacation would be somewhere warm, with year-round sun and a sandy beach. And if she couldn't have that, she'd take the mountains, some tiny cabin tucked away. She'd even sent him an online site for a retreat in the shadow of Mount Rainier. It had a crazy name, Paradise or Wonderland or something completely fairy-tale romance. What he did remember was the fishing…something about fresh salmon. It had made him hungry for smoked salmon, which he'd purchased that night at the market and shared with Roman.

See, he could remember the things important to her. In fact, Gracie hardly left his mind, and not because he worried about her. Or not *only* because he worried about her. He missed her candor, and the way she didn't pull her punches with him. She wasn't afraid to stand up to him, from the first moment she'd met him and kicked him in the shins, thinking he might be a murderer. She was honest. And refreshingly hopeful. And faithful.

And beautiful.

Most of all, she loved him.

Or he desperately hoped so.

He fished his cell phone out of his pocket, calculating the time change. According to his math, it would be around dinnertime, the day before. He lifted the phone out, searching for a signal. He got the smallest of blips, and his phone beeped.

He jogged to catch up with Roman. "I have a text message."

"Maybe it's from Yanna." Roman dug into his own pocket for his cell and held it up to catch a signal. "Hmm. Nothing."

"I'll bet the message is from Gracie," Vicktor said, dialing. He waited, holding it to his ear, frowned and looked at the screen. "I lost it."

"It's probably because of the airport. It's hard to get a signal. Taiwan is up on all the latest technology. You can probably find an Internet café and chat with her from there."

Vicktor pocketed the cell, frustration knotting his chest. He just wanted to hear Gracie's voice, tell her that whatever he did, he was desperately sorry and that he'd never even think those thoughts—whatever they'd been—again.

"Maybe she just wants to tell me she loves me."

Roman jumped on a moving walkway. "Yeah. I'm sure that's it." He checked his watch. "I should call Sarai. I didn't tell her I was leaving last night when I said goodbye."

"Did you two have a date?"

"Took her to see *Sleeping Beauty* at the theater. She cried."

"I saw it, years ago."

"I think I'm going to ask her to marry me." Roman curled his hand onto the railing, not looking at Vicktor.

Vicktor couldn't suppress a smile. "Every time you go to a theater or a circus you have this urge to propose. You should have done it thirteen years ago in Moscow, when you first wanted to."

Roman said nothing, probably reliving the moment he'd let the woman he loved walk out of his life. Thankfully, she'd also walked back into it about eight months ago. And it had only cost him a couple of broken ribs and a stint in gulag. But they were making up for lost time in a way that made Vicktor long for Gracie. He held up his phone again.

"Leave it, man. Gracie can take care of herself. She managed to live in Russia for two years and, I might add, also escape a serial killer. I think she can stay safe on the streets of Seattle. Calling her every night is not about letting her know you care. It's about you wanting to do her thinking for her. About you not letting go and letting God be in charge of your relationship. "

"Ouch. Listen, I worked those streets when I lived in Seattle. This *isn't* about me losing her. Or even needing her to need me. It's about me knowing that she is still dealing with post-traumatic stress disorder and wanting her to feel safe." Vicktor got off the walkway and followed Roman toward the lobby of what looked like a restaurant. Inside, at a counter, Roman stopped. Flashed his FSB credentials.

"I'd like to speak to your manager," he said.

Vicktor leaned against the wall, arms folded. Maybe Roman was right. Maybe he did need to stop worrying about Gracie. He tapped the cell phone. *I love you, too, Gracie.* Enough to back off and let her decide their future. His words to Roman were honest—he didn't want her to need him—well, yes he did, but he mostly wanted her to love him as much as he loved her.

He touched his chest where it tightened, right above his heart.

"Can I help you?" The voice came from a slight Asian man, well-groomed in a beige silk suit. Why hadn't Vicktor grabbed his own suit instead of a pair of faded jeans and an old T-shirt? He leaned up from the wall and tried to look clean.

"We're looking for a friend of ours, an Olga Rustikoff. She was supposed to check in here two nights ago?" Roman dug "Olga's" picture from his wallet. "She's in her late twenties."

The manager, who introduced himself as Mr. Choi, studied Roman's and Vicktor's credentials for a moment, the picture, and then opened his listing of guests.

"She checked in, but never checked out." Choi wrote down the time. "We book by the six-hour blocks, and she used one block of time. When she didn't check out, we charged her for another block. Housekeeping notes say they checked in on her room during the third shift, but it was vacant. Did she make her flight to America?"

Roman glanced at Vicktor. "How did you know her destination?"

Choi looked about forty, but with a youthful tan and little facial hair. "We take all the flight and passport information, in case they haven't checked out an hour before their flight. Sometimes, patrons oversleep."

"So, you never saw her leave?" Vicktor asked. He wasn't sure why, but places like this that rented by the hour always made him feel as if he might be walking into a back-alley brothel. Despite the manager's three-piece suit and the welcome-to-Korea smile.

"Not that I recall. Her account says that she had dinner in the restaurant shortly after she checked in. I'll ask my staff if they remember seeing her." He handed Roman a card. "If you will write your phone number, I can call you if I have any further information."

Roman scribbled down his cell number. "Can I see the room she stayed in?"

"It's been cleaned numerous times since her visit."

Roman glanced at Vicktor. "We have a couple hours to kill."

Vicktor turned to Choi. "I think we'd like to see the room."

They followed Choi down a long orange-and-lime-green hall, passing through another long corridor until he stopped at a door. He opened it with an access card.

An Asian double-size bed jutted from an alcove beyond the bathroom. Vicktor followed Choi and Roman inside. The room smelled of stale air and artificial room freshener.

"It's a sleeping room. Most guests use it while waiting for international flights, like your friend Olga."

"The only way in is with the key card?" Roman asked. He stood at the door, holding it open with his foot.

Vicktor stared at the television, a queasy feeling in his gut. What would he do if it were Gracie who vanished?

She was fine. Hadn't she texted him? He needed to listen to Roman and trust Gracie. He acted as if she was going to get kidnapped or murdered. He'd clearly let their history with the Wolf go straight to his head.

"I told you there was nothing here," Choi said. He had turned to go, just as a housekeeper came pushing her cart down the hallway. Roman darted out to catch her.

Vicktor held the door, blocking Choi's exit.

"Ma'am, do you clean this section of hall?" Roman asked in English.

The woman, a middle-aged Korean, with a wide face and short, dark hair, stared at him. She glanced at Choi. Vicktor followed her gaze and saw nothing written on Choi's face.

"We're looking for a friend who stayed in this room. A young Russian woman, long, dark hair, traveling alone. Did you happen to see her?"

The woman glanced again at Vicktor, but he stepped in front of Choi. For a second, she looked surprised. Then, shook her head, frowning.

Probably she didn't understand a word he'd said.

Then, in a voice barely above a murmur she said, "No see. Sorry."

Roman frowned, stepped back toward the room. "Thank you."

The woman continued down the hall. Roman turned back to Choi, still trapped behind Vicktor. But as the woman reached the next hallway, she stopped and looked back at Vicktor. And deliberately pulled something from her pocket.

She let it drop onto the floor. Then she pushed her cart around the corner.

"Let's go. There's nothing here," Roman said, but Vicktor cast him a look.

"Stay here. Be right back."

Vicktor took off down the hall, but by the time he got to the corner, the woman had vanished. At his feet, however, was a small silver locket.

He picked it up, ran his finger over it. And everything inside him went very, very still.

David lost Yanna in between the fried squid on a stick, the fresh tilapia fish still gasping their last breath, the hedgehog-looking, horrible-smelling durian fruit, a vat of sweet potatoes and a woman making Ba Wan that had him so distracted with the smell, it was no wonder Yanna easily ditched him. And because she was smart, as well as sneaky, the woman had waited until right after he'd purchased her a fresh papaya and a bamboo sack filled with rice.

At least he didn't have to worry about her starving as Kwan tortured her to death. Super. Could this day get any worse?

He turned, looking for the leggy Russian brunette, but of course every other person in Taiwan also had long dark hair, wore a size four and moved as if they were late for work or, in her case, running from the man who'd saved her life. Thankfully, she also stood about half a foot taller than every woman at the market. However, not a woman Yanna's height was in sight. He wove past a table of vendors selling fish heads, and toward a booth of sushi. "Yanna!"

Of course, his voice carried about as far as the star fruit vendor's in the din of the market, and hum of the street traffic. Morning market always reminded him of the Philippines, where he had attended boarding school, while his missionary parents worked in Japan—the din of the crowd, the smells of fresh vegetables brought in from the villages, people on bicycles and scooters weaving through foot traffic.

He stood, surveying the heights of the patrons. Yanna had a good six to eight inches on the average Asian woman. Only he'd also purchased her a pair of flip-flops, which cut his advantage severely. He almost longed for her spike-heel boots.

Clothes. She needed a change of clothes. And it was then he realized she would have also lifted his wallet. He checked his front pocket, where he'd slipped it just as they were walking into the market. Nice, very nice. She'd probably nicked it when he was arguing with the Ba Wan lady about which dumpling he wanted.

So, Yanna had his wallet and his cash, leaving him high and dry while a murderer hunted them down. Apparently she had a short memory when it came to people saving her life.

Then again, when Yanna wanted something, especially something near and dear to her heart, she usually got it. Stubborn. Blunt. Capable. Qualities that had netted her respect in her FSB department but managed to scare off every man on her side of Siberia.

He had to wonder, perhaps, if she did it on purpose.

The only thing that scared him about Yanna was the fact she so easily shrugged off her own safety for the good of the people she loved. Which meant that if she hung around David for any length of time, it meant pain and sacrifice. Because Kwan would find him. And when he did, people would get hurt.

The second he found Yanna he'd handcuff—no,

hot glue—her to himself until he shoved her on an airplane to Russia. She might hate him when they were finished with this, but he couldn't look himself in the mirror if he let Kwan hurt her.

Contrary to what Yanna might think, he didn't intend to leave Elena high and dry, either. But first stubborn Russian woman first.

David turned for a moment in the middle of the market, gathering his bearings. Like a maze intended to trap customers, the tables of food—from nuts in bags, to dried seafood, to raw meat suspended from hooks, to fresh vegetables—stretched as far as he could see under the low-hanging metal roof. Beyond the offerings of food, kiosks filled with kitchen utensils, plastic wear, cheap aluminum pots, rice cookers and woks, and an electronics store ringed the outside entrance to the market.

Which reminded him that he should probably ditch his current cell phone, grab a new one.

Oops, one normally required *money* for that.

He headed out the back entrance, toward the clothes vendors. Styles in Taiwan ranged from skimpy to spandex, with most of the women wearing their size-two crop pants low on their hips, their blouses tight, their skirts avert-his-eyes too high. And the colors—bright and gaudy seemed the fashion of the hour. He should be able to spot Yanna in her boring white blouse, leather skirt. Beyond this alcove of kiosks, the street jagged down along the coast, littered with buildings lit with vertical neon characters in Mandarin, again, in all colors. Exhaust fumes, meat and rice frying in a giant wok and the cloying smell of women soaked in perfume seasoned the too-warm air.

He dodged a man riding a bicycle and ran across the alley to a kiosk filled with women's lingerie.

"Foreigner?" he asked in Mandarin. An oversize woman sitting on a bench looked at him and shook her head. In the next booth overflowing with shoes, a woman pointed toward the center of town.

"Shei-shei," he said, thanking her, dodging marketers and more bicyclists. He clipped a stand of durian fruit, scattering them on the ground. The vendor came screaming out of his booth, but David didn't slow. Why, Yanna, can't you just trust me?

I'm here to find my sister. Kwan kidnapped her. Her quiet words, torn with emotion and spoken as they drifted to shore, replete with images that made him wince, laced his thoughts. What if it were his sister who'd been gulped into Kwan's world of slavery? They'd have to sedate him probably and even that would only slow him down. In fact, he'd shown up— or asked pals around the globe to show up on her behalf—for nearly a decade, most recently during a coup in the center of Siberia. It wasn't easy keeping track of a woman who put the welfare of her patients miles ahead of her own.

No, he wouldn't leave his sister in the lurch. And he could hardly blame Yanna for acting the same way.

Once she got clothes, where would she go?

He stopped at the intersection, waiting on the light, or at least an opening in traffic. Beyond this street, he saw signs for lodging.

The bus station.

The first thing she'd do would be to get back to the nearest big city—Kaohsiung—and regroup, maybe fire up some of her electronic gizmos, see if she could get a bead on Kwan.

David, for one, planned on camping out at Kaohsiung Harbor until Kwan resurfaced.

The light changed and David followed the crowd across the street. She couldn't be that far ahead of him, and he jogged past a clump of betel-nut-juice-spitting taxi drivers. "Bus station," he asked, and they pointed him beyond the hotel and across the main thoroughfare. He didn't wait for the next light, just darted out into traffic, dodging cars, the horns, the Mandarin that couldn't be welcoming.

Across the street, up on either side of the sidewalk, scooters lined up like dominoes, one squashed next to the other, helmets perched on their seats. A two-foot-wide channel separated the rows and David quick walked down it, eyes on the end, where the busing kiosks began.

There. The woman in the brown-and-orange shirt, halfway down the row of scooters. She looked over her shoulder and he ducked his head. The minute she spotted him was the minute she'd vanish into some kiosk. The coast seemed clear because she continued walking quickly, her dark hair shimmery down her back.

He picked up his pace, breaking out into a trot.

Then his foot caught the exhaust manifold of a shiny red scooter. Like a waterfall the bikes began to tumble, one into the next into the next, dominoing down the row. He gave a halfhearted attempt to grab one, stop the wave, then surrendered to a full-out run.

He dodged the scooters—thwunk, thwunk, thwunk—and cringed as the entire block-long row tumbled over.

Yanna turned and, for a second, their eyes met.

Hers widened, and then she began to run.

His pants leg caught on the fender of a scooter. No! Behind him, he heard shouting and a glance over his shoulder told him that at least one irate owner had spotted him.

He yanked free and charged toward the buses. Way to tick off the entire country.

The woman in brown had vanished into a bus terminal. The Taiwanese busing system ran out of individual storefronts, each destination and bus line operating inside a street-side lobby. David read the signs overhead, looking for the Kaohsiung sign, scanning each passenger who sat on the outside vinyl seats, waiting for the bus.

A bus pulled up beside him and he sounded out the

destinations on the side—thankfully the Mandarin had been transliterated into Western characters.

Taipei, Taichung, all north of Kaohsiung. He broke into a jog—how could she simply vanish?

Behind him, another bus pulled up. He turned around.

There, the woman just climbing aboard.

He sprinted back to the bus terminal, pushed through the line to the counter. "One, to Kaohsiung," he said, and reached for his wallet.

No. *No!* He stared at the woman as she printed out the ticket. Backed away from the counter. Perfect, just perfect.

He wrestled his way back out to the sidewalk. The bus driver had exited the bus, was taking tickets, stowing luggage.

David beelined to the bus, aiming for the stairs, and plowed aboard.

Yanna sat slouched in the backseat, looking out the window, her head down, hair over her face. Her blouse might be clean and new, but she looked wrung out. As if, maybe, she'd spent the past twenty-four hours lost in the ocean. Windburned. Hungry. Tired.

"Yanna!" he shouted down the length of the bus.

A hand grabbed his arm. He whirled, but whoever the bus driver had been in a former life, he knew to duck. David stumbled, and the driver yanked him down the aisle and gave him a heave-ho onto the sidewalk. He scrambled back to his feet, but the driver had already closed the door. As the bus coughed and grinded into gear, David looked for Yanna.

He found her in the somber woman who gave a feeble wave as the bus pulled away from the curb.

Chapter Eight

"That's a decent-size goose egg, Gracie." Mae Lund replaced the bag of frozen peas. "Are you sure you don't want to see a doctor?"

"I'm fine, Mae."

"So after you bonked your head on the door, and Bad Kosta had you by the jacket, then what did you do?" Mae Lund, recent retiree from the air force, sat back on the hardwood floor of their apartment living room, and leaned against the overstuffed sofa, her knees pulled up to her chest, her face alive. Gracie had wondered over the past month how Mae's recent move out of military life and into the private sector would change her. Hopefully, it would also calm Vicktor down to know that Mae would be moving into Gracie's extra room, although she didn't know why he was so paranoid. Okay, maybe that wasn't fair. After today, she did. It would probably be good for all of them since Mae was currently short on allies.

After Mae had hopped aboard a C-130 transport to Russia and flown an outdated tin can across protected airspace in order to save her friend Roman from execution, it was either resign or face discipline. Although she'd easily landed a job as a SAR pilot for a local Emergency Services crew, she had to miss her life of training and commitment. Still, maybe the move would be good for her. She looked comfortable in civilian duds—her brown crop pants, the green T-shirt. Then again, tall and slim, Mae looked good in just about anything. She'd let her hair grow, and the curly mane of auburn only made Gracie wish she hadn't let herself be duped into cutting her straight blond hair short, nearly into a pageboy.

Next to Mae's easy style, Grace felt like a refugee in her old jeans, sleeveless tee, and with the purpling goose egg over her eye.

Now, Mae acted as if Gracie might be telling her a campfire ghost story, all wide-eyed and wearing disbelief on her face.

Probably exactly how Gracie had looked as she'd driven up to her brownstone and stumbled up the three flights of stairs, banging the door open and slamming it behind her, dead bolting it. Good thing Mae was already inside unpacking, because Gracie planned on barricading herself in.

"I don't know, Mae, I just lost it. I guess I was right back there in the past, with the Wolf dragging me out to his getaway plane, about ready to blow me up, and I just reacted. My therapist says that it's normal to feel you're right there, for the smallest things to trigger a memory, and that—"

"What did you do, already?"

"Oh, I stabbed him with my keys. Right in the hollow place in his neck. Then I went for broke and kneed him, just like I learned in self-defense, jumped in my car, locked the door and floored it home."

Mae sat back in her chair and stared at her, a new admiration in her expression. See, she wasn't helpless. Mostly.

"Do you think you were followed?"

"I doubt it. It was a pretty crazy drive home."

Gracie lowered the peas, touched the bump on her forehead. "Think I should tell Vicktor?"

Mae got up and went to the pile of boxes in the corner. She opened one, began to dig through it. "Want him to lose it? Because he will. He'll be on your doorstep by morning. Well, for the few seconds before they deport and/or jail him."

Gracie made a face. Yeah, that pretty much summed up her fiancé.

She put the bag of peas on the ground, began to break up the ice chunks that made sharp edges under the plastic. "I think I need to go back there."

"You need to go to the police is what you need to do. Right now." Mae returned, holding a hand mirror. "You might think you're fine, but take a gander at this." She handed Gracie the mirror.

Gracie held it up, grimacing at the black-and-purple swelling on her forehead. She touched it gingerly, wincing. But as she put down the mirror, she shook her head. "And what do you propose I tell them? That I think a young girl is being held at the hotel against her will? How do I even know that? Do you know how stupid that sounds?"

"It's not stupid if we can get her parents to file a missing-person's report." Mae picked up the bag of peas and pressed it again to Gracie's forehead. "Her parents' testimony, combined with your Rocky Balboa-size bump—maybe you can get someone to listen."

Gracie let the words sink in, looked again at her wound. Smiled. "See, I knew I'd enjoy having you for a roommate."

"I'm getting my keys. I'm driving to Ina's house, and I'm going with you to the door, because I might look skinny, but I did take a few how-to-take-a-man-down classes in the army, you know." Mae grabbed her jean jacket, slipping it on.

"Wow, my own bodyguard," Gracie said, climbing to her feet. Her head did a slow whoosh and she grabbed the sofa, closing her eyes.

"Methinks one with a near concussion shouldn't be so sassy," Mae said, and looped her arm through Gracie's.

The Gromenkos' town house seemed dark and quiet as they drove up, the blanket in the window sending a clear leave-now message, especially when combined with the absent outdoor light. Gracie noticed that the tomato plant had fallen from the stairs, cracking, the mud spilling out onto the stairs and the walk.

They sat in Mae's Jeep Liberty, staring at the house. Down the street, a dog barked, then another in response. Ten feet farther, a streetlamp pooled light on the pavement, but Mae had parked far enough away that it didn't splash against the black of her Jeep.

"They don't look home," Gracie said, remembering the last time she'd knocked. But they'd surprised her then, and maybe Luba was in there, in the dark, not sure what to do, needing a friend.

Gracie toggled the car handle. "Let's do this. Before I go home and climb into my bed and hide under my down comforter."

Mae turned off the car and reached past Gracie to open the glove compartment. She grabbed a small silver can. "Pepper spray."

"Oh." Of course Mae would be prepared. Gracie got out, rounded the car and took a breath. The fragrance of rain tinged the night air, and down the street, one of the dogs had begun to whine. Shouting came from another house. Somewhere in the distance, a car started. Gracie's heart thumped, threatening to climb up her throat and maybe lodge there for safekeeping.

"This is silly." But memories of the day in Russia when she'd stood outside her best friend's apartment, creeping inside only to find her worst nightmare, rooted her feet to the pavement. She swallowed, but her throat tasted of bile.

"I'll go first. Or maybe you should just stay here," Mae said.

Gracie nodded, then followed Mae as she crossed the street. Sometimes, probably more than she wanted to admit, she wished she were like Mae. Tall, red-headed, graceful. Mae knew how to fly a plane, and wasn't easily rattled. More importantly, she'd been Vicktor's first love. Although Gracie had never viewed Mae as competition, she couldn't help but compare.

And in all her measurements, she came up lacking. She even stood at least four inches below Mae's chin.

What did Vicktor see in her, or worse, was she just the consolation prize? The girl who couldn't take care of herself?

Mae stopped at the steps, looked at the plant, then the front door. She put her hand out to stop Gracie. "The front door is ajar."

Gracie came up behind her. Sure enough, the front door hung open by an inch. Mae started up the steps, but Gracie touched her arm. "I know them. Just in case someone is home, maybe I should go in first."

Mae moved aside. "I'm right behind you."

Relief rushed through her. She might not be as tall and beautiful as Mae, might not be able to fly C-130s, but she could speak Russian, and most of all, she could be just as gutsy as Mae. Really.

"Luba?" She pushed the door open. *"Zdras-vootya?"*

The small, shadowed entryway opened into an eating area, and then the kitchen. And running right up from the front door, a stairway led to blackness. "Hello?"

A blue light flickered from over her shoulder. Mae, with a penlight on her key chain, scanned the room.

Now why hadn't Gracie thought of that? Obviously she'd have to work on her sleuthing skills. That, and maybe talk her legs into moving a bit farther into the house. Mae even gave her a nudge. "Let's check upstairs."

Somehow, Gracie found herself moving upstairs. "Luba? It's Gracie Benson, I was here—"

"Did you hear that?" Mae grabbed her arm. "Shh."

Gracie stilled, straining to hear above her thumping heart. A Dr. Seuss rhyme from her old *Cat in the Hat* books filled her head: *They should not be here when Mother was not. They should not be here, they should not!*

She held her breath.

Moaning.

"Luba?" Gracie ran up the stairs, felt for a hall light, found it and flicked it on.

The luminance bathed the destruction in the hallway. Books were scattered on the floor, a picture lay shattered. And in the doorway beyond, whimpering.

"Luba?"

Mae panned her light toward the door. In the

bluish glow, Gracie barely made out Luba hunched over a still form.

"Oh, no." Mae rushed past Gracie. She flicked on the bedroom light.

Yakov lay in a heap, blood oozing from his ear, his face cut and bruised. Luba sat above him, rocking, her hair loose and disheveled, her shirt torn.

As Mae checked for Yakov's vitals, Gracie pulled Luba away. "We need to call nine-one-one—"

"*Nyet.* No militia!" Luba practically screamed. "*Nyet!*"

"Okay, okay," Gracie said, glancing at Mae. She was probing Yakov's head for wounds, her hands covered with blood. She gave Gracie a grave look.

"What happened?" Gracie asked.

Luba covered her mouth with her hands, shaking her head, staring at her husband. One side of her face had already turned purple. Someone had hit her, and hard.

"*Ya neznaio, neznaio—*"

"She doesn't know?" Mae translated, although Gracie got it. "What does she mean?" She looked up. "He's still alive and breathing, but he needs medical help, right now."

Gracie pushed back the hair from Luba's face, grimaced. "I think she was hit, maybe knocked out." Mae translated this theory into Russian, and Luba nodded.

"Did you get a look at who hurt you?" Mae asked in Russian.

Luba stared at Gracie, eyes wide. Then she closed them, and began to sob. *"Da, Da."*

"Who, Luba? *Kto?*"

Gracie had no idea how to translate her answer. Ina.

Yanna's tough inner super spy must be malfunctioning, because she sat on the bus to Taipei crying as if she'd just lost her best friend.

Which, for all practical purposes, she had.

The look on his face when David had boarded the bus, panic, and even desperation, had made her feel like a water slug.

He'd only been trying to help.

Yeah, sure he had. Help her all the way back to Russia, leaving her sister to who-knows-what fate.

Yanna leaned her head back against the tall red cloth seats. Overhead, on a tiny television no larger than her toaster back in Khabarovsk, a ninja movie played, complete with subtitles in Mandarin.

All of Taiwan seemed one big sprawling city, separated not by rolling countryside, but smaller buildings, two and three stories high. Instead of vacant lots, rice paddies filled every spare inch of land between apartment buildings. The green rows in glistening brown water reminded her of dacha country—every hectare of earth used to mound potatoes. Storefronts advertised in glowing neon and brightly colored Chinese characters, and commuters filled the streets, wearing the ever-present patterned face masks.

Right before every stop, the driver would call out the name. She'd let Kaohsiung pass by, her destination Taipei and the international airport. She'd gotten a good look at the two thugs who'd brought her into the country, and guessed that she wasn't the only woman they'd trafficked in through Taiwanese passport control. She'd camp out, waiting for them to show up, then follow them to Elena. Meanwhile, Taipei just might have what she needed to fix her GPS earrings. And she could start nosing around brothels.

Elena, where are you? The thought of her sister, who didn't have a David or even the few kung-fu abilities Yanna possessed, captured by Kwan and his men… Yanna put a hand over her stomach, in case the rice packet decided to make its way back up.

So she'd been right about Kwan. In fact, she probably had tidbits of information that might help David and his undercover adventure. But no, David wouldn't allow her to be an equal partner. She had to be the damsel in distress, he the dashing hero. What was it about him that always had to save the day?

Yes, she'd been handcuffed to the chair, helpless and had a knife to her throat, but she would have figured out something.

Really.

Yanna wiped away another tear.

She didn't need him, and already regretted the briefest of moments she'd depended on him. This leaking was precisely why.

She had to face it—he *wasn't* going to help her—
not if he thought her life was in danger. He'd promised
to help, but she'd experienced his promises before.

Men were all the same—disappointing.

She could find Elena on her own, as she planned
to do.

She didn't really have to track down Kwan. She
just had to let him know she was still alive. He'd do
all the work.

And next time, she wouldn't be the one who ended
up with a blade to her neck.

The bus stopped again, and she looked up,
checking out the embarking passenger. She didn't
really think Kwan could have tracked her down
already, but…

A man climbed the stairs, holding his little black-
haired maybe four-year-old daughter, bows in her
hair holding up two wispy pigtails. He appeared
about forty, with a leather bag slung over his shoulder
and strong arms around the girl. She looked around
the bus, then back at him with adoring eyes as he
found their seats.

Yanna swallowed, her throat suddenly thick. Apparently fatigue also made her susceptible to painful
longings buried deep inside, because she was right
there with that little girl, adoring the man who held
her in his arms.

She hadn't been sure if he was boyfriend number
two or three, but Boris had been the man she'd
wanted to be her real father. Older than her mother,

he seemed to love both Yanna and her mom. He had worked at the local bread factory and perhaps her mother had seen in him someone stable, even kind, when she brought him home to live in their two-room house. He didn't drink—well, not much at least—and loved Yanna like she might be his own. Yanna remembered his smile, the long walks in the park, the stuffed monkey he'd given her one year for New Year's Eve.

"*Papichka,* will you be my daddy and stay with me forever and ever?" she'd asked him once, right before first grade, as he'd picked her up from kindergarten. Even at six, she knew that not all daddies stayed. Boris had knelt right there on the sidewalk, tugged her long, dark braid wrapped with brilliant red ribbon, and said. "*Ya obeshaio.*"

I promise. She knew all about men and promises. Perhaps not all men broke promises, but the ones she loved did. Over and over and over. Like Boris, when he left them only three months later, simply disappearing into the night after a ferocious fight with her mother. Yevgeny, then Slava, had promised, and left. Some of her "daddies" she'd silently begged to leave, especially when they promised to make her life very, very difficult if she told her mother what they did to her when she wasn't home.

After a while, she didn't care who promised what.

Until, of course, she'd met David.

Why was it that every time she let a man into her heart, he tore it to smithereens? *Especially* David.

Because once she had let him close, she'd never really gotten him out of her system, as evidenced by her gigantic lapse in judgment on the boat. She could hardly believe she'd nearly kissed him.

She closed her eyes, willing herself not to sleep, but feeling tired. So very tired.

Which was when the memories usually surfaced. *"This time, you're going down, Yanna!"* David's voice found her, and she frowned, knowing that if she followed the memory long enough it could only churn up hurt. Yet, as if pulled by some ethereal force, she lost herself in the briny smell of the sea, the feel of hot sand beneath her bare feet, the sun overhead, the shouts and laughter of children running into the surf.

"Bring it on, Yankee," she retorted, dusting off her knees and glancing at Roman behind her, ready to take their friend Mae's serve. The sun overhead left its mark on blond David's fair complexion, turning his nose red, his shoulders a deep russet-brown and lifting from his skin a field of freckles. He'd taken his shirt off, and she'd refrained from telling him that he was only asking for trouble. Because, though she was his friend, she also had plenty of appreciation for his physique, toned from hours at the gym and playing street hockey.

Behind her, Roman taunted David in Russian. "It's the 1980 Olympics and finally you're going down, Yankee!"

"Game point," Mae said, twirling the volleyball in her hand. She'd pulled her curly red hair back into a ponytail, and wore a pair of beach shorts and a sleeveless shirt. Yanna had preferred wearing her bikini, and even David had given her a long once-over, trying to hide it of course, when she emerged from her room at the Black Sea Resort. It wasn't hard to figure out that calling them "just friends" hadn't made him immune to her.

Perfect.

Because with David leaving in about five short weeks to head back to America, and possibly out of her life for good, she wanted him to remember her for a long, long time.

She flicked her hair back, shiny and dark in the sun. David's gaze squared in on her. Mae tossed the ball and served it over the net.

Roman met it with a bump, setting it up. Yanna sent it over. David scooped it up, Mae set it and David jumped high to spike it. Yanna saved it low with a bump and Roman got under the ball, setting it high.

"Drill it!" Roman said. Yanna jumped high, spiked it hard.

David dove and bumped it right before it hit the sand. Mae set it up high for him again. This time, Yanna paralleled him to block it. But David was going for broke, and he jumped, drew back and arrowed the ball over the net.

It slammed Yanna square in the face. Blood spurted as she dumped into the sand. She cupped her nose, eyes watering, face smarting.

"Yanna!" David ducked under the net and skidded

in the sand to her feet, horror replacing the triumph in his voice. "Yanna, I'm sorry!"

Roman had torn off his sweaty shirt. He thrust it at David, who tried to get Yanna to move her hands. She pinched her nose, tipping her head back. She took the shirt, bunched it under her nose.

"I'm fine, I'm fine," she said, but tears ran down her face, her nose burning, the pain making her dizzy. She even put a hand out as she fell back onto the sand.

"I'm taking you back to the hotel," David said, and before she could protest, he had scooped her up into his arms.

For a second, the briefest of seconds, she let him. Just stayed right there next to all that sweaty, golden-red skin. And then she came to her senses. Because, well, she'd never been a pansy, and especially not in front of Roman and David.

"Put me down!" But David was already walking across the sand, Roman behind him. "I'm fine!" She kicked, struggling, blood spurting from her nose as she pushed against him.

He put her down. "Knock it off. I'm just trying to help you."

"I don't need your help." Yet, as she took a step, she had to hold out her hand for balance, the earth spinning.

"Uh…I beg to differ." David grabbed her around the waist, taking her sandals from Roman. "We'll meet you back at the dorms."

Roman jogged back to Mae, who had begun to

collect their things. "We'll track down Vicktor and get a place in the café!"

Yanna barely heard them, focused as she was on staring at the sky, trying to stop the flow of blood.

David threw down her sandals. Guided her foot into one, then the other. "I'm fine," she said again, sounding much like she might be talking through a tunnel.

"Sure you are." David took her by the elbow. "I'm really sorry. I thought you'd block it."

"I did block it," she said, almost tripping on the curb.

"Yeah, with your nose. I thought you were supposed to use your arms or your torso."

She glared at him—not so easy while holding her nose—and walked through the parking lot to the four-story sanitarium. They'd found the resort, as Mae and David called it, through friends of Vicktor's mother, a nurse in Khabarovsk, Far East Russia. Fifty acres of beach and wilderness, with a spa, a cafeteria, segregated dorm rooms, and plenty of Black Sea beach. The five friends had taken this last break from Moscow University for a final hurrah before graduation.

David slowed and Yanna did, too, looking down for a moment to find the sidewalk.

David took her elbow. "I'm not going to let you fall, I promise."

Yanna stepped up, took her hand away from her nose. Looked at it, and Roman's sweaty, blood-soaked shirt. "I think it's stopped bleeding."

David tilted her chin up and surveyed her nose. "Maybe. It might be broken."

She didn't want to confirm that it felt like it might be broken. Because, then he'd go all horror face on her again, and possibly treat her like she might be pitiful or weak.

And Yanna didn't do weak.

Only, she suddenly didn't care about her nose. Or that she had blood all over her hands, or down her chest. She only saw the concern in his blue eyes, the ones that could turn her into some sort of sappy schoolgirl. She didn't even protest when he said, "Let's get you cleaned up."

Nor did she protest as they walked in, past the *storge,* the dorm mother who sat at her desk. The old woman, built like a tank, raised an eyebrow as she handed Yanna her room key, dangling from a giant wooden knob.

"Volleyball accident," David offered.

Yanna smirked. David never took his hand off her elbow as they walked up the stairs and down the hall. Yanna noticed how her heart had started to thunder, how her pulse felt hot, everything inside her aware that he walked beside her, tall, amazingly handsome, with arms that could carry her, with a smile that made her forget her own name. This incredible American she'd known for two years, the one who had protected her when she needed it, and even when she didn't.

In fact, she didn't recognize this Yanna, not really, because this Yanna didn't depend on men, didn't let them see her crumble.

But this Yanna loved David Curtiss.

Probably had since the day she'd met him, in that dark alley off of Red Square.

They reached her room, and she stood there, suddenly shivering as she opened the door.

"You cold?" David asked, his hand, his *hot* hand, on her shoulder.

"It's just the blood loss," she said, smiling up at him.

He looked at her and his smile dimmed. She watched him swallow.

And then she opened her door.

He followed her inside the tiny room, where two single beds were shoved up against opposite walls. A thin rag rug lay on the floor in front of a long wooden night table. The bathroom door hung ajar.

"I'll get a washcloth," he said, turning, the strangest tone to his voice.

She watched as he wet a towel and brought it back to her. She held out her hand, but he took her chin in the cup of his hand, lifted it, and began to wipe the blood from her nose, her chin, her lips.

She put her hand on his arm.

He stilled, then looked her in the eyes. And right then, before he could blink it away or hide behind that perfect smile, or his righteous exterior, she saw it.

He loved her, too.

Or something like it, because suddenly he bent down, put his hand around the back of her neck and kissed her. And it wasn't a gentle, I'm-sorry-that-I-just-gave-you-a bloody-nose kind of kiss, either, but urgent and needy and nothing like she would have expected from Mr. In-control David Curtiss.

But, well, she didn't mind. She put her arms around his broad shoulders and stepped close, curling herself into his arms and kissed him back. Just like she meant it.

His arms tightened around her and pulled her tighter against him, and he leaned down, deepening his kiss. She could feel his heart pounding against hers, and even heard a little groan in the back of his throat, as if he might be losing a battle he'd been so long in fighting.

Me, too, David. Emotion swept over her. Finally. After two years of waiting, hoping…her eyes closed and she lost herself in his arms, letting him kiss her over and over, and—

He tore away, his eyes wide, a look of horror on his face, so much like the one at the volleyball court for a second she thought she might be bleeding again.

But no. It was she who'd wounded David this time, because he stepped back, disentangling himself from her arms, breathing harder than she thought was necessary. After all, they were just getting started.

Or, not.

"I'm so, so sorry, Yanna. I don't know what came over me—"

She smiled, "That's…fine, David. I'm not complaining." She inched closer, but he grabbed her by the upper arms, stopping her, his eyes so dark it scared her.

"No, it's not okay." He looked down, away from her, although not letting go. "I shouldn't have—"

"It's just a kiss, David." Now she felt cold. She stepped away, shaking free of his grasp. Her voice lowered. "It's just a kiss."

He shook his head, still not looking at her. "No, see, that's the thing." And when he looked up, the guilt on his face, in his eyes, now red rimmed, rocked her. "Not to me, not where my mind was going, it wasn't just a kiss."

Oh. Yanna wasn't sure what to say, what to do. She didn't feel any of the wretched guilt so clear on his face.

Which only made her step farther away from him. Apparently, what was okay for her wasn't okay for David, which made her…what? Dirty?

"Is it because I'm Russian?"

His expression changed, and for a second, real anger flashed across his face. "What? No! Is that what you think?"

She shrugged, hating the fact that her eyes began to burn. Oh, she would *not* cry in front of him. Never. She turned away, grabbing the first item of clothing she could find—her silk robe—to cover herself. She put it on, hitching it tight around her waist.

"No, Yanna, I…" He ran a hand through his sun-streaked blond hair. "I feel everything for you that I put into that kiss. I just can't…"

She rounded on him. "Kiss me? I didn't know that was so…taboo."

He tightened his jaw, but his gaze didn't leave hers.

"It's not…about the kiss." His voice dropped as he looked away. "We're not married."

Her voice lowered to a harsh whisper. "One kiss, and you already have us in bed?"

He closed his eyes, and she saw the faintest tint of red. He shrugged. "It's hard not to," he said softly. "You're so beautiful. And I…I'm sorry I thought that."

Her throat burned. But she wouldn't give him the satisfaction of knowing that, yes, she'd thought that, too. Even, for a split second, hoped it.

But that was the difference between her and David. David thought beyond this moment. Always had. Always preached about eternity, and doing the right thing because "life mattered beyond right now."

Well, right now was all they had.

She let out a laugh that had nothing to do with humor. "Oh, I forgot. God and the church would frown on it."

David opened his eyes, looked at her, pain in his expression. "My heart would frown on it."

Ouch. She took a breath, fighting her voice, and the way it quaked. But inside she felt the old Yanna returning, the one who didn't believe in sappy love stories, and storybook promises. She turned away. "Get out."

"Yanna—"

"Get out, David. Now."

She heard him open the door.

"I'll be down later, after I get cleaned up."

He said nothing.

"Don't—" she hated herself for the hitch in her voice "—don't tell anyone."

David sighed. "No…I won't."

He shut the door behind him as he left. And Yanna climbed up on the bed, pulled her legs tightly to herself and heard her heart fall to the floor and shatter.

See, even David broke his promises. Still, even in memory. Even her dreams couldn't change that.

"Yanna?"

She roused, and shook herself out of the memory, aware suddenly that her eyes felt gritty, hot. She blinked and saw that shadows filled the bus. A slight sweat slicked her, and oh, no, was that drool on her chin?

She put a hand to her face, looked up.

And yes, David stood there, all windblown and sweaty, leaning over her looking like he'd just caught Moby Dick.

"Welcome to Taichung."

"The locket is Yanna's, which only proves what she said when she texted me—that she'd made it to Korea. And I think whoever took her sister also took her, right from the hotel." Roman stood in the passport-control line behind Vicktor, his voice just above a whisper. "And I think Choi is a part of it."

Vicktor didn't look back at Roman, just observed the people standing in line. Like the short dark-haired woman and her four-year-old son, who hung on her leg as she balanced a huge floral bag and a suitcase on wheels. And the stick-thin Asian coed plugged into her iPod, chewing gum and toting a dark backpack.

Or the two Asian men standing beside three teen-age girls who seemed as if they'd traveled for days on foot from the interior of Mongolia by the way they stumbled forward in line. He lifted his chin, caught eyes with Roman.

Roman nodded. "Could be that Yanna came right through here, drugged to the eyeballs, courtesy of our friend Choi. Who knows what kind of operation he's set up?"

"I can't believe that traffickers would bring people through right under the noses of the government."

"In some countries, passport officials are on the payroll. And once victims are in the country, their passports are taken or burned, and even if they do have the courage to escape, if they're found without a passport they are sent to prison. Human trafficking is the third largest industry in the world, right behind arms dealing and drug running."

Vicktor moved forward in line. "If Yanna is here, I'm going to find her."

"Me, too, pal," Roman said with the same tight emotion in his voice.

Vicktor pulled out his cell phone and turned it on. But reception didn't kick in. He pocketed it and held out his passport and visa to the Taiwanese official. She looked him over and stamped it. Vicktor passed through to the receiving area of the airport.

Outside, although still twilight, darkness pressed

against the windows, seeping into the dirty linoleum floor, across the rounded vinyl seats set up in rows. He dug out a handful of rubles and headed over to the money exchange.

Roman came through moments later.

Vicktor took the brightly colored Taiwanese money as it passed through the little drawer. "Now what?"

"First, flash her picture around passport control, see if we get a hit. Then we find someplace where we can set up shop, and pray that we can get a signal on her laptop. The last location I had for her came through Taipei, and then headed straight out into the ocean, which means there is a boat in our near future…" He trailed off, watching as the Asian men came through with their party of women. "Or…"

"Yeah, I'm thinking the same thing."

Vicktor watched the group pass through the lobby, through the grimy double doors, out to the street where they piled into a grimy white-sided Toyota Liteace van.

"I got the license plate," Roman said.

Vicktor watched them go, frustration rising in his chest. "What if we're too late? We may never see or hear from her again." He tried to keep the edge from his voice. "Why did you let her go to Taiwan in the first place?"

Roman said nothing, pressing his lips together. "I already know I'm an idiot."

"I doubt it."

"We'll find her," Roman said, heading for the office at the far end of passport control.

Vicktor had turned to follow when, from his pocket he heard a beep. He pulled it out, smiling as his reception kicked in. Gracie's text message. He connected, opened it.

V—Srry. Pls ck name—Kosta Sokolov. Luv U. G.

He slowly deciphered her words. At least she was still talking to him. He released the smallest breath at that. Sokolov.

"Vita, c'mon, the passport chief wants to talk to us. He'll let us interview his people."

"Sokolov. Ever heard that name?" He looked up at Roman.

"Maybe. Sounds familiar. Why?"

Vicktor pocketed the phone. "Gracie asked me to check on it."

"Later." Roman pulled out Yanna's picture. "She's not the one who's in trouble."

Chapter Nine

"Sit down or get off, but I'm staying on this bus until I get to Taipei," Yanna snapped.

Sometimes Yanna acted just like his sister, Sarai, stubborn to the bone and like a three-year-old. She even had the toddler pout nailed. She crossed her arms over her chest and drew up her knees. "How'd you catch me, anyway?"

"You don't want to know," David said, grabbing her arm and hauling her to her feet.

"Ow. Hey! What's your problem?"

"Oh, honey, don't get me started." He pushed her out into the aisle in front of him.

"David, *perestan!*" She made to round on him, but he pointed her the other direction.

"No, *you* knock it off. We're getting off this bus, right now. Playtime is over."

She looked back, and he should have ducked,

because the glare she gave him hit him square in the heart.

He refused to flinch, however. "Get moving, sweetheart." He raised an eyebrow, like a dare, and she read it just fine, because she pursed those pretty lips and moved to the front of the bus.

But just as she got to the entrance, she moved to the side and tried to trip him.

He caught her move at the last second and grabbed her by the arm. They tumbled off the bus together, and he managed to clip his skin on the stairs. He barely caught his balance as they hit the pavement.

Apparently the bus driver had had enough of his tourists because he closed the door behind them.

"What did you do that for?" Yanna snarled, pushing away from him and sitting down on a padded vinyl chair. "You could have broken my neck."

Oh, yeah, never mind his. Or the fact that he'd broken about a hundred and ten laws between Kaohsiung and here, starting with the theft of a motor scooter. He'd have to track down the owner and send him a hefty check. He got up, aching a little on his leg where he'd left some of his skin inside the bus. He shot her a look, something loaded with everything he wanted to say and knew he shouldn't, and plopped down next to her.

They sat in silence, as if reading each other's defeat. He hoped she also heard the sound of airplane doors closing behind her as she flew away from Taiwan, and danger.

"I'm not sorry I ditched you."

"I didn't think you were."

"And I *am* going to find my sister."

"And I'm going to put you on the next plane to Russia."

"You can really be a jerk, you know that?"

"Right back at you, honey."

He looked at her, at the way she crossed her arms over her chest and suddenly hurt, right down the center of his sternum. He sighed then turned in his chair. He laid his arm along the back of her chair. "I *will* find your sister, Yanna. I promise."

She shot him a look, one eyebrow high.

"I just can't think when you're here. You're… distracting."

She rolled her eyes. "Get a hold of yourself. Roman and Vicktor work just fine with me."

Roman and Vicktor hadn't kissed her. Hadn't thought of her nearly every day for ten years. Didn't live to see her e-mails in their in-box.

Or at least, they better not.

He sighed again.

"You know, my phone might still be aboard Kwan's yacht…if I can track down the signal, maybe I can find him…and then we'll have another shot at finding Elena."

Now she had his interest. "You can really do that?"

"Please. Give me some credit for knowing what I'm doing."

He glanced down at his bleeding shin. Back up at her. She smiled.

"I'm taking you someplace where you'll be safe while I hunt down Elena, and while you're waiting for Roman to come and get you."

Her smile vanished.

Taichung looked like every other Taiwanese town, with scooters cramming the streets and bright neon signs littering the thoroughfare, turning the pavement red or blue, orange and yellow against the night sky. He'd ditched his stolen ride and rented a bright red scooter. Yanna climbed on behind him, not afraid, apparently, to hold on and wrap her arms around his waist as they zigged in and out of traffic. Driving in Taiwan reminded him of surfing—he just had to let the traffic wave take him along. They drove through downtown, and he glanced at a KFC and a T.G.I. Friday's. He'd bet there wasn't one frog leg on the menu.

This late at night, the shops were gated, and now musicians and teenagers roamed the streets, their music loud. Men with leggy women riding behind them in short skirts and helmets, glanced over at him, smiling. Apparently, Yanna caught more than a few eyes.

Then again, he'd never been able to take his eyes off her, either. Distracting…that just might be the understatement of the century. Which was why, with her pressed close to him, her arms around his waist, he had to think of anything but how much he longed to simply keep driving into the night, away from all this.

But that wouldn't solve any problems. He'd walked

over that line, nearly trampled it once before, and it had taken years for him to earn his way back into her life.

No, her friendship, her trust meant too much to risk it again by taking her in his arms. What he really wanted, more than her friendship, even more than her arms around him, was her arms around God. Letting Him love her past all those hurts she buried so deep. So deep, in fact, she thought no one remembered them.

David motored through another light.

But he did. Remembered the stories she'd told him in e-mails, the sketchy tales of abuse and neglect, and everything inside him hurt at her words, imagining what she left out. Sometimes, after their e-mails, he sat in the darkness of his apartment back in the States, stared out the window and simply prayed that God wouldn't let her be alone.

"I'm wondering if you're going to feed a girl," she said into his ear at the next light.

"You're not the only one who is hungry," he said over his shoulder. "Because this fella had no cash."

"She might say she's sorry if he took her someplace."

"And not run away?"

She tightened her hold on him. He'd take that as a yes. He got into the right lane, turning onto a side street. In fact, he knew just the place.

They drove though the neighborhood streets of three-story apartment buildings and homes, past gated entrances to tiny courtyards, and little garages that held shrines to Buddha and other gods. Worshippers had left flowers and jewelry and food. Burning incense evidenced their prayers.

He turned left at a 7-Eleven, and Yanna covered her nose at the smell seeping from the building. "What is that? It smells like rotten eggs soaked in gasoline."

"Tea eggs," David said, pulling up next to a sweet potato stand, turning off the bike. "They're a specialty, and all the 7-Elevens here sell them. They boil the eggs in soy sauce all day. They're supposed to be delicious, but I can't get past the smell."

Yanna climbed off the back of the bike while he parked it. "I might have lost my appetite."

"You'll find it again in a second." He reached out for her, grabbed her hand. She looked startled.

"Just so you won't be tempted to go on your own private excursion."

"Why, sea dog, don't you trust me?" She grinned, and he narrowed his eyes at her, trying to stifle a smile.

It seemed the city never slowed, regardless of the hour, and the hum had long invaded his pores, become a part of him.

He pulled Yanna toward an open-air stir-fry café. Around a horseshoe-shaped counter patrons sat, watching the cook in the center fry their food on a giant wok the size of a kettledrum.

Yanna settled on the wooden stool. "I don't know how to order." She looked at the menu glued to the countertop. "It's all in Mandarin, and, well, I'm not fluent in cuisine."

"Look at the picture and point to the item you want. They'll figure it out." David caught the chef's attention and pointed to item three. Shrimp in fish sauce.

Yanna ordered the same and watched with a sad smile as the chef flipped her food with a flourish. "Elena would love this." She put her hands on the counter. They were dirty and chapped from the seawater. David resisted the urge to cover one with his. Because she wasn't his captive at the moment. "She loves to travel." She ran her hands through her long hair, closing her eyes when it caught on a snarl. "Why did she think she had to be married?"

David had no answer to that. He'd never even considered marriage—his career, his commitments to his job left little room for relationships. But sometimes, when he returned home from an assignment to an empty apartment with dead plants, he wished for more.

Even his partner, Chet, had a girlfriend. He didn't know who, but it certainly hadn't hurt his will to live.

Maybe if Chet could figure it out, David could, too.

He lifted his hand to cover Yanna's, then put it down. Had he lost his mind? Yanna and he could never be together.

And not just because they lived on different sides of the world.

The chef served up their bowls of shrimp, noodles and bok choy, and handed them each a set of chopsticks.

Yanna stared at them. "Uh, and how am I supposed to work these?"

David peeled the paper off. "Hold one chopstick

stationary against your thumb, the other moves against your pointer finger." He demonstrated.

She stared at him. "I'm too tired for this."

He motioned to the chef. Thankfully, they kept forks below the counter.

"Vakoosna," she said, halfway into her meal. The next time he looked over at her, she'd finished.

"Did you inhale it?"

Yanna held up her bowl, looking at it longingly.

"Don't lick it."

She put it down. "Thanks. That was delicious. I guess you're not entirely a jerk."

"Oh, yes I am. But I'm a jerk who feeds you." He finished the last of his noodles. "Let's get you to the safe house. By the way, I'm still waiting for an apology."

She simply grinned at him. He refrained from holding her hand on the return to the scooter, but kept her close enough to grab if she should decide to make a dash for it.

Surprisingly, she didn't. And wrapped her arms back around him when they got on the bike. "I might be a little sorry."

They rode in silence through the streets, David's mind on Kwan and his whereabouts. He knew of Kwan's contact on Taichung—he'd start there, and see if he could find out where Kwan had holed up.

David had no doubt he had a target on his head. But perhaps that could work in his favor. Like Yanna said, if Kwan had taken Elena, then eventually, perhaps, he could lead them to her.

And he meant to keep his promise to Yanna. He *would* find Elena.

He reached down, clasped her hand and squeezed.

Leaving the main road, they drove back through the alleys and streets of a neighborhood. The safe house sat back from the street, a three-story apartment once used by missionaries. An office building acted as camouflage for the various people who moved in and out of the complex.

David drove around back and secreted the scooter in a metal shed.

A palm tree cast blades of shadow over the courtyard. Overhead the sky was clear, stars bright, the moon full and too illuminating. David grabbed Yanna's hand and pulled her to him under the palm tree. "Wait."

She stood there, quiet beside him as he watched the house. Lights on the second-story windows reflected in elongated squares on the grass. The outside lights bathed the front walk and the opposite street. "They know we're coming. They'll turn the lights out, then we'll go in."

Yanna tucked herself in close to him, her hand behind him propped on the scaly bark of the tree. "How do they know?"

David scanned the windows, looking for movement. Strange. When he had spoken with Bruce, he'd said he'd have the lights off by ten.

Reaching into his pocket, David pulled out a cell phone. "Bartered for it on the way up."

"Bartered—is that what you're calling it?"

David slipped it back into his pocket. "They'll be reimbursed." He knew his job demanded creativity, but he couldn't help but feel as if he might be losing his footing. Ever since he had shot Chet it seemed as if his moral lines had blurred, smudged by frustration and urgency.

Instead of wanting to see Kwan and his operation captured, the web of weapons smugglers and suppliers destroyed, he just…he just wanted to see Kwan dead.

And he didn't like that feeling, not at all. Or rather didn't like the fact that, yes, he did.

Sometimes, David longed not to be him. Not to be the guy who lived by an invisible set of rules that seemed foreign to the rest of the world.

Not to be the guy who wouldn't put his arm around the intoxicating woman beside him and kiss her like he had ten years ago…only this time, not stop.

Sometimes it felt…and he hated to say it, hated to think it, hated that it felt like betraying everything he stood for, but…sometimes it felt, indeed, like good guys finished last.

How could one man, by doing what was right, have even a smidgen of hope to slow the rampage of evil in the world?

So maybe he hadn't always done what was right.

He blew out a breath.

"You okay?"

David ran a hand through his long, grimy hair, over his scraggly beard, wishing all that gone, too. The lights flickered off in the upstairs windows.

"Yeah. Let's go—"

"Someone's coming," Yanna whispered.

He leaned back against the tree, his breath low. He reached for his weapon, which of course, he didn't have.

So, he snaked his arm in front of Yanna, put her behind him.

A man appeared from around the side of the house, out the darkened side entrance. It didn't take David long to figure out that this man wasn't Bruce's contact. Maybe it was the clothes—all black and dressed for stealth. Maybe it was the way he stopped at the edge of the house, looking back, checking for a shadow.

Or the way he then edged out into the lawn and vaulted the fence.

"I have a bad feeling about this, David."

"Me, too," David said in a barely audible voice. "Stay put, I'm going to check on—"

"*Nyet.* I'm on your tail like glue, like you said before."

Of course she was. "Quickly, then." He went to the gate, punched in the four-channel code, and it opened. Sliding through, he left it ajar and ran for the house. Yanna, true to her word, stayed one step behind him. He reached the back door, opened it and went in first, pulling Yanna in his shadow as he froze in the entry, listening.

The moon filtered in through bamboo window slats, across a terra-cotta tile floor and wicker furniture. Beyond this room, he spotted the kitchen and, even farther, stairs.

He pointed to the stairs. Yanna nodded.

They were across the room in seconds, and he took the stairs on his toes, crouching at the top.

Moonlight streamed out of one of the upper bedrooms. The other, on the opposite side of the hall, contained only darkness.

He glanced at Yanna.

She wore her fight face, the one that said, *Don't mess with me, or someone's getting hurt.*

He should have heeded that warning long, long ago.

David stood, crept down the hall toward the moonlight-bathed bedroom, the one they'd been watching when the light went out.

He froze at the door, a word he rarely used on his lips. Their contact lay on the floor, hands bound, throat slit from ear to ear.

David turned, grabbed Yanna by the elbow. "Go. *Go.*"

"What—?"

He was pushing her now. "Go!"

Yanna whirled and headed for the stairs, her feet thundering as she ran down. David took the steps two at a time, then pushed her toward the front door, grabbing her up before she could run out onto the lawn.

And good thing, too, because whoever he was must have anticipated their rapid exit.

David yanked Yanna back just as a form

launched at her. David caught a dark flash of light right before the assailant took him down onto the tile floor.

"He nearly killed you!" Yanna snapped as David pulled her by the shirtsleeve away from the heavy drama and mess inside the so-called safe house. Her mind reeled, sorting through what had just happened.

"But he didn't, so move!"

But she couldn't, caught in the moment they'd nearly been ambushed by a knife-wielding bad guy who would have stabbed right in the center of her chest had it not been for David's quick thinking.

Instead, David had taken the hit, or *nearly* taken the hit, because with all that Black Ops, or whatever training he had that made him faster than a speeding bullet, he dodged, and managed to land on top of said bad guy.

Who, sadly and inconveniently, also landed on his own blade. David had given him about ten seconds of sketchy medical intervention before he jumped to his feet, turned and pulled Yanna out the door behind him.

She noticed that he had confiscated the knife.

"Through the gate. C'mon!" David opened the gate, pulled her through and yanked open the garage door. Climbing onto the seat, he pulled the scooter upright and started the motor.

He backed it out. "Get on."

Get on? Her brain seemed to be stuck in slow motion, but thankfully her body still responded to commands. She leaped on behind him, and it was a good thing she had a decent hold because he gunned it without her even seated.

Apparently, Mr. Cool was a little freaked out, too.

She hunkered down, her arms around his waist, feeling the beat of his heart against her chest. Yes, definitely rattled.

They sped through the streets, cutting through alleys, down obscure streets, David barely slacking his speed as they took corners. He finally braked in the shadow of a Buddhist shrine.

He cut the motor, then just sat there, breathing. In, out, in, out.

She felt his hand grip her arm. Then he pulled her off the bike and around to face him.

The light from the still-flickering candles inside the shrine illuminated his face. "You okay?" His voice sounded rough, as if just barely holding back emotions. And truly, his eyes said it, too, that their close call had shaken him. It was moments like this, when she saw a chink in his cool exterior, when all those carefully guarded emotions simmered right below that layer, that she realized how much she loved him. Loved him for his passion and his control, for the good that seemed so much a part of him. Loved him for his strength and his friendship, and even loved him because he couldn't seem to let her go. It took her breath away.

It didn't help in the least that the past two hours had almost felt like a date. Had she really raced through the streets of Taichung, with her arms wrapped around David, leaning against his strong back, feeling for the first time in days, no, probably years, safe?

With his scruffy beard and his long hair, he appeared downright dangerous, rough and anything but safe. But the way he looked at her, concern in his blue eyes, she knew without a moment's doubt that he would have given his life for her.

Then why didn't he love her? At least the way she loved him?

She reached out to touch him, and he grabbed her hand. "You're okay?"

She nodded. "You scared me."

"Yeah, me, too." His words came out clipped. "I'm starting to see a connection to my activities and Kwan's ability to ambush me."

"How do you think he found us?"

"I think I've been trusting the wrong person." He rubbed his forehead with his hand. "I think I found the so-called CIA mole, and his name is Bruce. Or rather, I knew it and tonight just confirms it." He gave her a look that seemed connected to whatever scenario played in his head. "We need to get someplace safe."

"I've heard that before."

He pulled her close, arm around her neck, more of a relief hug than anything. And she put her arms around him. "I'm sorry, David. Really sorry."

His embrace tightened. "That's enough of that," he said. "It's not your fault—"

"No," she said, pulling away. "I'm sorry that I didn't trust you. That I took off. That I didn't listen to you."

He touched her cheek, ran his thumb along her chin. His eyes fixed on hers, and her breath clogged in her chest. She traced his face, and remembered, oh, how she remembered, what it felt like to be in his arms, kissing him with everything she felt inside. Probably she betrayed that memory in her captured breath. And maybe even he was there, too, in the past, because he swallowed and his jaw tightened. "I forgive you, Yanna. After all, what are friends for."

He let her go. "Get on. I'm going to call Roman."

She tried not to show her disappointment as she climbed on behind him. For a wild second, she'd hoped that maybe the concern in his eyes was more than simply concern. That he still loved her like he had years ago.

But maybe he hadn't really loved her then, either. Distracting, he'd called her.

As in, distracting him from what he really should be doing—saving the world.

In fact, it was worse than that. Regardless of what language was spoken, "friends," meant "just friends."

"Here's hoping my new phone has an international calling plan." He dialed Roman's number and she wondered at how he had it committed to memory. How many times did he call Roman, really? Because, and she shouldn't forget, Roman was David's *friend,* too.

"You're not going to believe where I am," David said into the phone. "Or who I have with me."

Yanna sighed, closed her eyes.

"You're kidding," David said with a laugh that Yanna couldn't interpret. "Then I guess I don't have to kill you. Now, tell me you have someplace safe for Yanna and me to hide."

"Apparently, one of us is a righteous man, because our prayers have been heard and answered, my friend," Roman said, snapping the phone shut. "You'll never guess who that was."

Vicktor stood away from where he'd been holding up the wall in the passport-control office, showing Elena and Yanna's pictures to various control agents. So far, they'd had no hits, but with the traffic that came through in a twenty-four-hour period, no surprise there. They did confirm, however, that both Elena and "Olga" had entered Taiwan.

And vanished, of course.

Until…now? "I'm tired, Roman. Too tired for games." Vicktor desperately wanted to talk to Gracie. He kept looking at the clock, wanting to wait until at least six in the morning before he woke her. But everything inside screamed to call her now, just to hear her voice.

Just to tell her that he loved her, too. And that he'd back off. But calling at four in the morning certainly would communicate "giving you space" loud and clear, wouldn't it?

He hated time zones and distance and even, at the moment, his cell phone.

"That was David," Roman said.

"You're kidding me."

Roman stood and turned his attention to the director of passport control, who'd had an eagle eye on them for the past two hours. "We found her," he said, reaching out his hand. "Thank you."

"We *found* her?" Vicktor eyed Roman who shot him a smile. He followed Roman out of the office. "We found her?"

Roman headed into the lobby. "I gotta make a few calls."

Vicktor grabbed him up by the jacket. "You're going to have to fill in the blanks for me, Roma."

Roman dialed, held the phone up to his ear. "I don't know how David got into all of this, but he has Yanna. And needs a safe spot to stay while he— ·*Zdrasvootya*, it's Roman. Can I talk to Pastor Yee?"

Vicktor moved away while Roman waited, lifting his own cell out of his pocket. He plugged in Gracie's speed-dial number, waited. Then, couldn't stand it and pressed Send.

The phone took an eternity to connect. Vicktor closed his eyes, imagining Gracie turning on her bedside light, groping for the phone. Maybe hitting it and it falling onto the floor. He smiled at the image of the woman he loved all tousle haired and sleepy eyed—he couldn't wait until they were married and he woke up every day to that. The phone rang once and clicked over to voice mail. Vicktor hung up, then pressed redial. Maybe she was on the other line.

Voice mail, again. Vicktor shot a look at Roman. He was off the phone. No, redialing. Roman looked at him, grinned, as if amused.

Vicktor didn't see the humor. Roman's girlfriend lived in Russia, where he could see her every day. It was true that Vicktor did let his everyday life spill out into his worst nightmares. It was hardly likely that Gracie, safe, conservative Gracie was going to get into trouble of the sort he saw every day. Maybe, occasionally, she'd lock her keys in her car, but the girl he knew and loved didn't go looking for trouble.

Even if she found it more often than most—which gave him enough reason to worry. She didn't deliberately put herself in danger, however. A girl who had stared death by serial killer in the face and won didn't take risks with her life.

Which meant that when her phone shifted over to voice mail the third time, he opted not to say any of the crazy things that had plagued him, simply hung up and slipped the phone back into his pocket.

Roman motioned him over and, by the time he joined him, Roman was thanking whoever was on the other line. He snapped his phone closed. "Okay, Yanna is headed to a friend's house, courtesy of my Chinese friends at church. Apparently, they have members who have cousins in Taichung. She can land there and we'll go pick her up. Meanwhile, that name you gave me earlier has been bugging me, so I called a pal back at HQ who looked it up." Roman glanced outside. "Did you get a hold of Gracie?"

"No." Vicktor gave him a smile that said, *So what, yes, I called her.*

"Call her back. That guy, Sokolov, that name is familiar. There's a mob boss out of Seattle who's on our radar. He makes trips in and out of Russia to see so-called family. He's been on international watch lists for years—for human trafficking, child pornography, the works. He's got family everywhere, especially in the big Russian hubs—Florida and New York. Seattle." Roman shrugged, but his eyes didn't match the no-big-deal body posture. "Tell her to steer clear."

Vicktor pulled out his phone, wrapped his hand around it, and that old, painful feeling returned to the center of his chest. The one that said, *You idiot, why aren't you married already?* He opened the phone and hit Redial, glancing at Roman. "I'm going to find myself the next flight out of Taiwan for America."

"Viktor, you can't just get on a plane—"

"I'm going to America, Roman. Today."

Was it so much to ask that his son obey him? Kwan rose from the pool in the private room of the Ming Shan spa, the room so filled with steam from the natural spring, it seemed to seep into his lungs, his eyes. As he rose, dripping from the square, tile-lined pool, his skin barely recognized the difference between water and the humid air. A towel, slightly damp, lay folded on the floor, next to the bucket he'd used to wash himself. As he sat on the edge, exhaustion wrung him out, the water sapping his strength.

Or perhaps he should blame his fatigue on his son's failure, again. The fact that yet again, he'd put them all at risk. He couldn't believe that twice now, Curtiss had gotten away, and this time, with a Russian spy who could only put a snarl into his operations.

Kwan picked up the towel, wiped his face, then his hair. Out of all the Asian customs, this treasure nestled in the Taiwanese mountains, used in secret by people of his position, ministered to him the most.

That, and the masseuse waiting in the next room, hopefully with a tray of sea bass baked in lemon sauce. He stood, wrapping the towel around his waist.

The woman in the next room stood beside the door, her head bowed, waiting.

He smiled, but his attention cut to his cell phone, vibrating in his pants pocket, folded over the chair. Debating a moment, he wrestled it out of the pocket.

"I thought I told you not to call me on your—"

"This isn't my phone. It's safe."

"You're a fool if you belie—"

"Father—"

He gritted his chin against the Mandarin—why had he spent years teaching the boy English if he planned on never using it?

"I only want to know that our problem has been taken care of. No more mistakes."

Silence. Then, "He got away from the safe house. But I found a way to find—"

"Finish it. And then I will talk to you." He hung up, turned his phone off.

Tough love—wasn't that what they called it in America? Thankfully, his other son, the one stationed on the other side of the ocean, understood the importance of obedience. He was a son a man could count on.

He slid the phone back into his pants pocket, next to his diplomatic pass, and smiled at the woman waiting to ease from him the stress of his position. Obedience, was that so impossible?

Chapter Ten

David had very few dreams. He had goals—like fix up the 1967 Mustang in his storage unit, or learn to paraglide, but the dreams, the ones he'd sacrificed a decade ago when he signed on the dotted line committing his life to Uncle Sam, he rarely even took out to regret. He liked his life, the challenges, the travel, even the friends. It suited him.

Or had. Until lately. Until his friends had started getting married and he was the guy at the party petting the dog, or seated next to the other single person in the room. Until he preferred to spend his Friday nights at home, with his laptop computer, connected to a chat room with Volleygirl on the other end. And until he walked downstairs into the kitchen of the simple Taiwanese three-story home Roman had directed them to last night and saw Yanna in the kitchen, apron around her waist.

Cooking.

Cooking?

David stopped on the stairs before she could see him, and just watched. He had to admit surprise last night when, after Roman had called him back and sent him to an address in Taichung, his knock at the door had opened to a Chinese man…and an American woman. Cho Yung had married Trish, a student from Taiwan University, and settled down to teach English as a second language to the students in Cho's church where he was a pastor.

David had a long moment of misgiving when he saw Trish's slightly rounded belly. He'd stood on the stoop, flicked off the overhead light that Cho had turned on and asked, "Did Roman tell you—"

"You're safe here, under God's watch," Cho had said, and touched his elbow. "Come inside. We're happy to help a brother."

Oh. Something full and overwhelming had filled David's chest at that—he'd nearly forgotten what it felt like to be among people who thought like he did. He'd been sniffing around the scum of the world for so long, blending in, watching them prosper, his frustration tightening like a noose around his neck. The feeling of fresh air seemed to almost hurt.

Still, he had drunk it in. Especially as he'd watched Trish welcome Yanna, lead her upstairs to draw her a bath, and give her all those girly things a woman needed.

It surprised him how much Yanna had taken to Trish and her ministrations. As if, perhaps, Yanna wasn't beyond mothering, or perhaps in this case, sistering. Possibly, he didn't know her as well as he thought he did.

Or maybe he only looked at the things he wanted to see. Because if he thought of Yanna as a woman, sweet-smelling, soft and gentle, well, there went another layer of defenses.

Which was why, as he stood in the stairwell, spying on Yanna as she made...pancakes, it shook him right to his core.

She looked good, *really* good. Fresh and clean, with her hair pulled back in a ponytail, highlighting her regal face, and those pretty dark eyes that could swallow him whole. Like they nearly had last night in the candlelight. He'd come so close, again, to forgetting why they were here....

Until he remembered that she'd nearly been killed. And then it rushed back to him, and all he could think about was keeping her safe. He had to wonder at God's timing that Roman might be in Taiwan, armed with hints to help him accomplish the keeping-her-safe part. The only reason David let himself step over the threshold into the Yungs' home was that he felt pretty sure Bruce, and thereby, Kwan, didn't know the Yungs, or even that David and Yanna might still be alive. Yet.

At least David had found the mole. Because if he did the math, only Bruce had known—twice now—where David would be. Only Bruce had known that he'd be meeting Kwan.

Fool him once, shame on Bruce. Fool him twice, well…somewhere in David's list of things to do was to have another face-to-face with Bruce and make him *painfully* aware of everything he'd nearly cost them.

Yanna looked at Trish and laughed at something she said, her face lighting up, her eyes twinkling. It made a sort of explosion in his chest, and he had to ease back into the shadows lest he make a fool of himself by breaking into tears.

In every buried dream, every unlikely Norman Rockwell photo, Yanna was always front and center. And for that very reason, David had stopped dreaming.

Why bother trying to find it with someone else, when it would only be a sorry substitute? He was a one-woman man. He'd known it for years, and watching her in the orange apron as she poured batter into a pan only confirmed it. No, he didn't want a housewife, but seeing her had him conjuring up two little dark-haired boys hanging on her apron strings.

"You okay, pal?"

The voice, coming from above him, made him jerk. David looked up, and yes, he must be dreaming, because there was Roman, sitting on the top steps, giving him a small shake of his head.

Of course, his voice made Yanna look up, but David ducked up the stairs and into the relative safety of the next flight. "Shh. You trying to get me busted?"

Roman grinned, but it wasn't a grin of triumph. He, better than anyone, knew about unrequited love. Only, his love had finally been returned. While David's…

He shoved those dreams right back where they belonged, in never-never land.

"You're a sight for sore eyes. When did you get here?"

"This morning. Early. Took a bus from Taipei. Vicktor's in the shower."

"He's here, too?"

Roman looked like he'd been up for about a week, with circles under his eyes, a two-day beard growth, and his hair matted on his head. David guessed he didn't look much better, although his shower last night had at least made him feel human.

Roman confirmed his assumptions with a sorry look. "You need a haircut."

"I don't want to talk about it." He rubbed a hand down his face, sat down next to Roman. "Tell me everything you know about Elena and her disappearance."

Roman filled him in on the details. "Truthfully, I think Yanna knows the most."

"Which is painfully little," David said. "For all she knows—really knows—Elena was kidnapped by someone else, or is even still in Korea. Or ran off with *Bob* to Maui."

"No, she's here. Elena passed through passport control over a week ago. And the fact that she used the same dating service, stayed at the same hotel and ended up in the same country, well, I'm thinking that Yanna's at least warm."

"Great. I was really holding out for Maui."

Although David could have guessed that Yanna wouldn't be that far off the trail.

"I probably shouldn't ask what you're doing here, huh? Something about top secret, and special forces?" Roman scratched his beard, making a face.

"Something like that. But it's all gone south, and my partner's been shot—"

"Chet?"

David nodded.

"Who shot him?"

"See, that's why you don't want to ask."

Roman raised an eyebrow and wisely said nothing. Finally. "How are we going to track down Elena?"

"We're going to track down Kwan, that's how." Yanna stood on the landing on her way up the stairs. "If you think I can't hear you then you must think I'm stupid. I'm going to track down the GPS I left on the boat, and see if I can find Kwan."

Roman got up and gathered Yanna in his arms. "You really scared me." He let her go and dug into his pocket, pulling out what looked like a necklace.

Yanna took it and held it to herself. "Where'd you find it?"

"At the hotel. A maid found it."

David looked up at Yanna, saw that her eyes glistened. "What is it?"

"It's my locket. I wasn't sure where I lost it. It must have been ripped off when they snatched me from my hotel room. My sister has one just like it," Yanna said, opening the locket. She handed the picture to David to look at. A girl who resembled a younger version of Yanna, without as much verve, stared back. He gave it back to her.

"She is very pretty."

"Thanks for coming after me." She backed away from him, looked at them. "I find it extremely eerie that here I am, in Taiwan, with two of my best friends—"

"Three. Vicktor's in the bathroom."

"Three—when I need you the most. Thanks."

David saw emotion flicker into her beautiful eyes, and his throat tightened. He knew what it cost her to say that. He touched her hand. "We're not the only ones on your side, you know. I think you might need to chalk this up to God's providence. Maybe He's trying to tell you something." Please, *please*, Yanna, listen.

Her smile fell and she stared at him, her face unreadable. Roman glanced at David, then back to Yanna. "It smells great down there."

"Pancakes. American-style." She lifted the apron, swayed with it. "Like my new outfit?"

David took a breath and said nothing.

The door in the hallway above them opened. Vicktor came out, trailed by a gust of steam.

"Any hot water left?" Roman asked, rising.

"Hey, Yanna," Vicktor said, but David wasn't sure if it was relief or a question his tone held. "I'm glad to see you. How fast can you get me a visa to America?"

"First, stop hovering. Second, you're acting like I haven't the foggiest idea what I might be doing. Go back to your corners and let me work." Yanna opened up the laptop computer Roman had brought with him and entered her password.

The breakfast dishes had been pushed away, and she hadn't felt this full in—actually, she never let herself eat as she had today. And being here with Vicktor and Roman and David, watching them interact…it felt like college again.

It felt like maybe, yes, everything would be okay.

"So you work with computers?" Trish said, coming to sit beside her. Slim—except for her cute little belly, with short brown hair and hazel eyes that seemed to pick up more than Yanna expected, Trish hadn't even asked last night—just instinctively known that Yanna needed privacy. Some time to sit in the bathtub and…cry.

And stupid her, she was crying just as much for herself as for Elena. While she knew she should have every thought focused on finding her sister, Yanna couldn't help but wish, with everything inside her, that David loved her. That he'd hijacked a scooter and flagged down a bus and jumped in front of a thug with a knife because he couldn't live without her.

But even last night, when she'd all but begged him with her eyes to kiss her, he'd simply done the *I'd hate to lose a friend* act.

So this morning, when Trish handed her an apron and wire whisk and asked her to stir, she'd decided it would be fine to let him see what he might be missing.

It was his loss. She made good pancakes.

"Yanna runs the IT department in Khabarovsk," David answered for her.

She did more than run it. She had single-handedly brought the lot of them into the twenty-first century. *And* she made pancakes.

"Tell me your brilliant plan," David said, apparently not listening to a word she said about hovering. Then again, when did he ever? Like his comment about God. Thanks, but she wasn't going to take some good fortune and start proclaiming revival. Even if she did believe there was a God, she'd done just fine on her own.

She simply didn't need someone else letting her down.

"Hopefully Kwan still has my cell phone. Even if it is off, the GPS is working. We can use it to track down Kwan, who will lead us to Elena." She looked over at him. "So, you see, this isn't over—not by a long shot." She smiled, real big, at the men in the room. "Brilliant."

"You do surprise me," David said, smirking. He glanced at what was left of his pile of pancakes.

"Tracking down Kwan isn't necessarily going to lead you to Elena," Roman said.

"How do you even know this guy was a member of the Serpents?" Vicktor asked, turning away from the window. "Maybe he was just a human trafficker."

"His ring," David said. "We've discovered that all the major players in the Serpents are given a ring, usually with a snake emblem. Kwan had one on his middle finger."

Yanna's hand went to her cheek, where said ring had left a bruise. "That brings me to brilliant plan number two," she said. "What if Kwan were to see *me,* the girl who got away. And I'll be wearing another tracking device, but now that you are in the country, I let myself be captured again and—"

"No way. Not on your life." David cut her off, shaking his head as if maybe she couldn't understand him. "I'm not letting you near him. He'd kill you, and laugh while doing it. No way. Uh-uh. Nope."

"Okay, okay, I got it. I just thought maybe you'd be hiding in the bushes, and do that thing you did last night."

"What did he do last night?" Roman asked, shooting David a look.

"Someone jumped us. Tried to kill Yanna."

"I don't think he really cared who he stuck his knife into, as long as he started with one and ended with the other," Yanna said with a shake of her head.

Silence filled the room.

"Okay, David's right, there's no way you're getting near Kwan." Roman wore a strange look as he glanced at David. "I'm really sorry, I should have never let her go alone."

"Oh, that's not the half of it, Roma," David said in a dark tone. "I haven't told you about the boat, or the ocean or her stealing my wallet. She's lucky I haven't wrung her neck and sent her home in handcuffs."

"Which I'd just take off."

"And throw in the ocean."

The silence in the wake of their words made Yanna realize she'd been yelling. She glanced at Trish, who was staring at her coffee. Yeah, nice one, David. Now she sounded like some gangster in front of this sweet woman. She directed her attention back to her computer program, and her GPS system and what she did best.

There, lit up on the screen, was her signal. "I found Kwan, only he's not in Kaohsiung." She looked up at David. "The signal's here, in Taichung." She pointed to the screen, then zoomed in to the street name. "It's not on his boat at the harbor, which means he has it with him. Why would Kwan hang on to my cell?"

"Maybe he's using it."

"Maybe it's a trap." This from Vicktor, who came back to life from where he stood at the picture window. "Maybe he knows you'd try and track it down. Maybe he wants you to find it. And him."

"He's right," Yanna said, but Vicktor's theory had David's attention. She turned to him. "We're going after that blip."

"*I'm* going after that blip. You're staying here. Aren't you supposed to be getting Vicktor a visa?"

"It'll be ready in a day or so," Yanna said, trying not to be terse. They acted as if she was a glorified secretary. She did have combat training. And even knew how to use it. Sort of.

Trish and Cho had gotten up from their places to lean over Yanna. "Where is that?" Trish asked.

"It's an address downtown." She read off the address in Mandarin.

"I know that spot. It's a teahouse. I've been there a few times." Trish set her cup down. "What would this Kwan man be doing there?"

"Some traffickers use businesses to warehouse women en route because they're high profile, an unlikely target," Roman said. "Our team in Vladivostok raided a casino filled with Korean and Chinese women on their way to inland Russia."

Trish put her coffee down. "Well, I think I need some tea."

"Trish—" Cho said, his tone dark. "Don't—"

She rounded on her husband. "No, you listen. While I'm there, Yanna can have a look around. She can pretend to go to the bathroom or something. I won't get hurt."

"You could get hurt," Yanna said.

"I'll be fine. Besides, I want to help. I've been in the country long enough to know about this problem, and to feel frustrated by my inability to help. I'm doing this." She turned to Cho. "I'll be fine, I promise."

Yanna looked at David. His expression broadcast his feelings loud and clear.

Cho took his wife's hand, his expression mirroring David's.

In the corner, Vicktor sat down on the sofa, sighing so loudly that he sounded as if he might have had something terrible to eat for breakfast. And she'd made the pancakes, so— "What's wrong?"

"It's just driving me crazy. Now that I know Yanna's okay, I can't get her out of my mind. If I could just get a hold of her, know she's okay..."

She didn't have to ask who. "Going to America is a really bad id—"

"I need to be Dr. Vladimir Zaitsev. Today."

"Vicktor—" Roman started. "That's a forty-eight-hour medical pass. That's barely enough time to hail a taxi. If you get caught with a fake visa, you'll be deported, and then you'll never get back to America, and you might as well kiss marrying Gracie in the States and living happily ever after goodbye, because they'll take your visa application and use it for dart practice."

"Who's Vladimir Zai—" Trish started.

"You're assuming that I'm the kind of guy who just twiddles his thumbs while the woman I love is in trouble."

"No, we're assuming that you didn't dump your brains in the Pacific on the flight over and can see that a few missed phone calls doesn't a national emergency make," David said.

"Vladimir Zaitsev is a, let's say, friend who lets Vicktor borrow his identity...occasionally, for sudden trips into the U.S.," Yanna said quietly to Trish.

Vicktor got to his feet.

"In Vicktor's defense," Roman said, stepping between David and Vicktor. "Gracie's been acting weird, and he can't get a hold of her. She might be mixed up with the wrong fella." He turned to Vicktor.

"Still, you can't go running off to America every time she doesn't answer the phone."

Yanna stood up. "Vladimir Zaitsev has a forty-eight-hour pass from Russia to America. I can make that happen for you, keep it under the radar and have you pick up your visa in Taipei. But you have to promise that you'll leave the States in two days or you're not the only one who will be chipping ice off the sidewalks if you screw up. An FSB agent going AWOL—"

"Not just AWOL," Roman interrupted.

"In the United States," Yanna clarified, "is going to raise more than a few eyebrows in Moscow. And Washington."

"What she's saying is that we might all be writing to each other from various correctional facilities around the world," David said.

"Gracie needs me," Vicktor said, and the expression on his face, filled with so much agony, or perhaps fear, was enough for Yanna to sit back down at her computer and start digging around her records.

Because, deep inside, in the places she didn't want to visit, she desperately wished that David might look and say that about her someday. And come running.

Instead of always running…away.

"I must have lost my mind. There seriously must be a fracture of some sort in my head where there is gray matter leaking out because, never in my wildest dreams, in any scenario did I ever see myself agreeing to letting Yanna and some untrained American citizen put their lives on the line while I sat in a battered van, watching from across the street." David put down his camera and looked over at Roman. "Check. Do I have liquid running from my ears?"

"They're going in," Roman said from his place beside him. "We have about ten minutes before Yanna goes into play."

The teahouse, located in the center of the city, flanked on one side by a courtyard and a professional office building, and on the other by a clothing store, looked like something David might see in an Asian tour magazine, all crisp lines and lotus flowers, with a typical pagoda-style roof and columns beside the doors. Scooters lined up on the sidewalk outside the building, and Cho had to circle the block for an hour before he could find a spot this close to the door. Even so, it would take them roughly twenty-three seconds to go from the white English-school van to the front door, and that was barring any traffic. Way, way too long.

"If this goes south, you have my permission to beat the stuffing out of me."

"I'll take you up on that," Roman said. "Yanna, can you hear me?"

"Everyone calm down," she whispered. Her voice reverberated through the cell-phone speaker. "We're in, and being seated." They heard her interact with the reception staff, sit down, heard the waitress hand her menus. David had been inside a teahouse once on this op. He knew they could be upscale places with Oriental music and hundreds of different teas served in individual pots. Personally, his taste buds had been so hardened by gut-rot coffee he didn't understand the fascination.

He heard Trish and Yanna putting in their orders.

"I hate myself," David whispered.

"She'll be fine," Roman whispered back, his hand over his mic. "You forget that she is a trained agent. She really can handle herself."

Roman's words held resonance only in the fact that the gizmos that allowed them to talk to Yanna had been created by Yanna herself from parts she'd found at the market—cell phones, some wax, wire and lots of creativity. Yeah, she'd earned David's respect.

But respect wasn't the issue here.

"It only takes one second, the wrong place, the wrong time."

David shoved his hands through his hair, which thankfully, he'd gone ahead and cut short and dyed back to its natural blond color. At least when he looked in the mirror he wouldn't hate the face looking back. Well, not if everything went well.

He might still have that urge. "I can't erase the moment from my mind when I saw her sitting on Kwan's boat, looking up at me, as if I might let Kwan kill her." He sucked back the emotion that threatened to enter his voice. "I was…scared."

He looked at Roman, but his friend didn't meet his gaze, just stared at the salon.

"It's no secret how you feel about her, David. We all know that."

He froze. "She knows that?"

"Not unless you told her." Roman looked at her. "You didn't tell her, did you?"

"You think I want to feel this way? To have her inside my head, inside my heart, right there, reminding me of what we don't have, what we can't have? I have tried, *really* tried, to get her out of my system, but it's like she's lodged there for all time."

"You're still praying for her."

"Every day." David couldn't count how many hours he'd logged on his knees for Yanna, practically begging God to show her how much she needed Him.

"Sometimes, Roma, I'm so close to giving up." He looked at him. "I have to tell you something, but you cannot say anything. Not one comment. On pain of death."

Roman looked over at him. "Now you're scaring me."

"I mean it."

David's throat tightened, no, his entire body tightened. "Remember what happened at the beach, all those years ago?"

Roman nodded.

David looked at him. Raised an eyebrow.

"I'm trying to keep my promise. Yes, I remember." Then Roman's face darkened. "You guys didn't…I mean, I know what a little stress can do to a relationship, but David—"

"I know, Roman." David scrubbed his hand down his face. "Sometimes I love her so much it just hurts, right here in the center of my chest, and I want to scream. I nearly pointed my scooter north last night, and rode away with her. The urge inside me was so powerful, it scared me. And then in the boat—"

"What happened in the boat," Roman said softy, the slightest edge of warning in his voice.

"Yeah, the boat. There she was, shivering, and the wind was cold, and she was crying a little."

"What happened in the boat?"

David looked at him. "It would help if you'd stop jumping to conclusions. Nothing happened. I promise. But not because I didn't think about it. And that's the problem. I'm sitting here telling you that, yes, I have issues. I thought this would have been out of my system by now."

"Because you're a…man of steel? I mean, I know you're a superhero and all—"

"Knock it off. I'm as red-blooded as you. But I'm not twenty-one anymore. And I'm past a lot of the temptations I had then. At least I thought so." He groaned. "Until I see Yanna, and then I'm right back there holding her, and—"

"Okay, we might be bordering on too much information than is good for me."

"I'm just saying that seeing her makes me hurt, because…" He took a long breath, "The fact is I'd marry her in a second, but I know in my heart I wouldn't be enough for her. I'd do something stupid,

and let her down, and then, she'd see me the same
way she saw every other man in her life. The same
way she sees God. And I know that would be it.
She'd never ever let God into her life. And we'd be
separated for all eternity. And that would be far worse
than never having her here, on this side of forever."

He turned back to the teahouse. "But what if, what
if she never ever believes? What if I'm wasting all
this time for nothing? What if I could be the man for
her, and I refuse to be because I'm holding out for
something that will never happen?"

The thought of never having her in his arms again,
well, he thought he'd resigned himself to that. Or
maybe he'd just been fooling himself; otherwise why
would he spend every off-duty hour thinking about
her, or chatting with her or writing to her…yes, he
definitely had been seriously pulling the wool over
his eyes, because he still longed for her with every
cell in his body.

"But what if you're right?" Roman said in a
whisper. "What if you're not supposed to be her
husband, but be the man who loves her enough to
let her go?"

"I think I hate you. You weren't supposed to speak."

"On the other hand, what if you're supposed to be
the one who shows her that God is on her side?"

David stilled. "Now you're just confusing me.
And I'm really tired and probably cranky. Are you
saying that I should tell her how I feel?"

"Not necessarily. But I am saying that maybe,

someday, you should and you will, so don't give up. And by the way, it's never a waste of time to pray for someone's salvation." Roman looked at him, finally. "Who do you have in heaven to fight your battles?"

David frowned at him. "God."

"And who on earth?"

"Obviously, God."

"So, the point is, God is on your side, in heaven, and here. And He knows your heart for Yanna."

Roman looked back at the building, lowered his voice. "And as for the other thing, you're not going to fall, David. Because you're a man of integrity. Of honor. And in your moment, God is not going to forsake you. And He's not going to forsake Yanna, either."

Oh, I hope not. Because, God, I long for her even more to know You. To know Your peace. Your healing.

"I'm going to use the restroom," Yanna said to Trish and the two men in the van, from inside the teahouse.

David watched the building, listening to Yanna as she gave them a play-by-play so softly he had to lean close to hear it. But his own words hung in his mind.

Yanna equated God with men. And she'd never get past what the men in her life had done to her.

Sometimes, it made David want to put his fist through the wall, remembering the stories she'd told him, her knees drawn to her chest, her voice tiny. College had been gentle, he realized, because the real truths, however guarded, came later. Over e-mail. And online chats.

In a way, the Internet had given her a way to share herself without risk.

Now, suddenly, they were face-to-face with that risk. How David wanted to fix it, make her past better, help her see hope. Be the man who didn't let her down.

But until this moment, he'd forgotten the real danger they faced. Over the Internet he was a name, a friend.

Face-to-face, he was just another man.

Another *disappointing* man.

And although he really wanted to believe Roman's words about himself, about his integrity, lately, he'd felt himself slipping.

His heart was going first. And after that, well, he didn't trust himself. Not at all.

"We're going to find Elena if I have to track Kwan down and pry the information out of him with my bare hands," David said to no one but himself. And then maybe she'd see that—*please, God*—all men weren't the same.

In fact, maybe she'd wonder if perhaps she had it all very, very wrong.

Chapter Eleven

And He's not going to forsake Yanna, either.

Yanna heard Roman's words, spoken into the cell phone a second before she decided to get up and meander to the back of the teahouse, in so-called search of the restroom.

She wasn't sure she agreed with him—after all, she had little, if any, proof that God even knew she existed, but somehow those words ignited the dying embers of courage inside her.

Because if God hadn't forsaken her, in all her doubt and disbelief, then maybe He wouldn't forsake Elena. She certainly deserved Him. After all, it was Elena who had faith in people.

Then again, look what trouble that sort of naiveté had landed her in.

See, it was a good thing to be a steely-hearted, man-wary, *just-friends* kind of gal.

Yanna rose, smoothed the crop pants that Trish

had given her. Although Trish stood a good three inches shorter than Yanna, the pants fit her well, as did Trish's silky black sleeveless shirt. Yanna felt nearly normal, as if she belonged in this posh tea-house, in this surreal world where women sipped herbal teas while Taiwanese music played and woman talked in Mandarin, probably about their children, their husbands, their homes. Orange sprays of bird-of-paradise flowers and white orchids stood on tall marble pedestals around the room, decorated with busts of Buddha. Their waitress, a woman who looked about a size one, with chopsticks in her hair and a high-cut sleeveless metallic dress, approached, holding a tray. Atop it sat two teapots, each capped with an inverted teacup. She smiled and raised a thin eyebrow as Yanna approached her.

"Restroom?" Yanna asked in Mandarin. The waitress inclined her head and motioned toward the back.

Yanna smiled at her, looked at Trish, who barely raised her eyes to meet hers. But Trish did check her watch. If Yanna didn't return in five minutes, then she was to simply leave.

Yanna resisted the urge to glance outside, but Roman's voice in her ear felt strangely reassuring.

"Be careful," Roman whispered. "No fancy stuff—oy!" From the muffled sounds, some sort of struggle for the mic was happening and she fought to keep her face from betraying the chaos in her ear as she headed back to the bathrooms.

"You see any sign of Kwan and I want you out of

there, no hero stuff, you hear me, Yanna?" David had obviously won the battle.

What did he want from her, a *Yes, sir!* right here, in front of all these patrons? "Mmm," she said.

"I'm serious, I want Kwan as badly as you do— probably worse—and I know you want to find your sister, but I'm not going to lose you."

She smiled at another waitress. But oh, how she wished those words might be real, and not about her getting in the way of his mission. Because they both knew that as soon as she found Elena, it was back to separate sides of the world and the occasional Friday-night chat—if he was still talking to her.

Another set of rooms angled off through an arched doorway. She glanced back at Trish, and noticed the waitress had left their teapot and vanished. Instead of entering the restrooms, Yanna slid into the adjacent hallway.

A doorway at the end of the hall beckoned, and she opened it.

A closet, filled with table linens and silverware, a broken black wooden chair. She bit back her disappointment, closed it, then returned to the hallway. Another hallway, sectioned off by dangling black beads, hinted at more doors. Passing through the beaded doorway, she continued through the narrow hallway to the end, where she opened another door.

Another closet. Supplies lined the walls, from towels to silverware and dishes. Frustration shot through her as she turned to leave.

Voices entering the hallway stopped her and she shut the door, leaving it ajar only a crack.

Two attendants came down the hall, waitresses carrying tea to the private rooms. They knocked on the doors before they entered. Yanna didn't want to guess at the activities in those rooms.

"What's going on, Yanna?"

David's voice in her head shot a tremor right down to her toes. "Nothing. I'm coming out—wait."

As she'd turned to open the door, she saw that the closet shelves didn't extend to the edge of the wall. She closed the door behind her, flicking on the light. Yes, the shelves had stopped, leaving room for a small door. "I found something. A door."

"Be careful."

She moved to the door and found that it locked from her side. She unlocked it and, checking to make sure it wouldn't lock behind her, she opened it.

It led to a cement hallway, a loading zone, really, but cement stairs ran up the back, to another landing.

"I'm going upstairs."

"Be careful."

"Will you stop saying that? I'm being careful."

"I can't help it. I don't like this, and I don't want you—"

"Shh!"

She knew in her brain somewhere that no one could hear him—in fact, she'd tested that fact in Trish's house, with the earpiece in Trish's ear and Roman nearly shouting. However, it felt exposing and she didn't need any distractions as she crept up the back stairs and into another cement hallway. It contained a door, parallel with the one below. She tried the knob, but it was locked.

"I need to pick this," she said, wishing David, for once, could see her. This was why she'd had field training, for moments like this. And for when she was handcuffed in the middle of the ocean on a rubber dinghy. As she pulled out the lock-pick kit she'd taken from Roman, that old adrenaline, that idealism she'd had when she first joined the FSB, rushed through her. Too many years with buzzing florescence in the dungeons of FSB HQ had made her forget that she had other skills than just how to write computer programs and create surveillance devices.

She worked the lock and opened it easily. "Going in."

"Be careful."

"There's a hallway, like before. I can smell rice, or something cooking. There's a door at the end of the hall." She moved toward it, her heart thundering, and she resisted the urge to hold her breath to listen.

"What?"

She also resisted the urge to rip the earpiece from her ear. She put a hand on the door, eased the handle open.

Swung it in.

Her breath caught. It was a house, or a dorm or something, because whoever had been here had slept on the uncarpeted floor, on pads. And in the center of the room, a rice cooker, with bowls stacked up, the rice in the cooker half-eaten.

"What? Talk to me, Yanna!"

"There's a room. It's empty. But someone was here, not long ago." She moved around the room, lifting the pads, the silky bedspreads perhaps used as blankets. "Whoever was here, they're gone."

She stopped, her heart cold inside her. "Oh, no. Oh, no—"

"Yanna, what is it? What is—forget it, I'm coming in there." Somewhere in the back of her head, she heard muffling, Roman's voice yelling, the sound of the van door opening.

But that was all drowned out by the increasing siren going off in her head, the one making her sink to her knees, reach out and pick up the silver locket, lying smashed on the floor. She curled it in her hand. "Oh, no—"

Somewhere deep inside, she'd hoped this might all be some sort of nightmarish misunderstanding, that Elena would call and say, *Hey, sorry, sis, my plane took a detour to Bali. But it's all good, and I'm in the States.* Better even would be, *I decided not to marry Bob, and I'm on my way home. Throw a party.*

But as Yanna opened the locket, peeling up the cutaway picture of her taken only a year ago, something inside Yanna gave way. Something huge and holding back the last layers of hope and self-control.

Which was right about the time David rushed in, finding her there, crumpled on the floor. She looked

up at him, at the expression he wore, his don't-get-
in-my-way face, and she didn't even want to imagine
the scene he'd made downstairs and who might be
behind him. But it didn't matter. All she knew was
that he was there and she needed him, oh, how she
needed him.

"Oh, Yanna," he said.

She held out the locket, and he took it from her.
He stared at it, and the agony on his face told her that
he got it. "She was here. Your sister. She was here."

Yanna didn't answer. Just, for the second time in
twenty-four hours, let herself buckle into his embrace.

And friend that he was, he held her without saying
another word.

If anything, the discovery of Elena's locket only
fueled David, solidified the panic that had been a
sort of radioactive buzz in his chest into a nuclear ball
of rage, of purpose.

If he had ever needed a reason why he did his job,
he found it written on Yanna's face as she sat on
Trish's sofa, running her thumb over the broken,
crushed locket. They'd found Yanna's destroyed cell
phone parts in the alley behind the teahouse. Yanna
had scrounged up the parts, hoping to figure out why
Kwan might have used it.

But apparently, the cell phone was the last thing
on her mind at the moment.

"She's alive, I know it, deep inside."

He wanted to touch her, to hold her hand, to wrap

his arms around her. Instead he kept working on her computer, trying to access his online files about Kwan and his contacts. "We're going to find her, Yanna. I promise."

Her face changed at that, her expression hardening. She looked up at him, nodded. "I believe you."

With everything inside him, he wanted to stand up and shout, *Hoo-yah!* But it only sent off explosions of fear inside him. What if they didn't find Elena? What if Elena had already been gobbled up, swallowed by Kwan's organization?

Where would that leave his promises?

Sometimes, he just wanted to live outside his body so he could wave himself off from making stupid statements. What he should have said was, *While I have breath left in my body, I'll help you find Elena.* That promise he could keep.

Yanna reached up and wiped her cheek with the heel of her hand. He couldn't take it anymore. David got up and came over to sit beside her. She didn't look at him.

"Elena used to be the homeliest thing I'd ever seen, all big eyes and greasy hair. When we were little girls, I never let her forget that she was annoying. When she was three, I made her sit in the bathroom when my friends were over, just because she couldn't stop talking and annoying us."

David could almost see Yanna like that, eighteen and just as gorgeous as today, only perhaps less jaded because of her job, with more laughter in her eyes, hungry for life to begin. He wished he could have known her then, but perhaps that would have only started his agony four years sooner.

"She was about nine when she came to live with me. I was just out of university—"

"I remember. You were heading into the academy. You wrote to me."

Yanna lifted her gaze to his. Smiled, only it didn't quite reach her eyes. "Yeah, I did. I guess you remember then how Elena and I fought over the years. When she became a teenager, she always had boyfriends, as if she were desperate for a man."

"And you hated that." He reached out and took the locket from her.

Yanna looked up at him. "It made me angry. Because out of both of us, she was the one who should have been happy. She had a father who loved her, doted on her…"

He lifted his hand to touch her hair, then settled it behind her on the sofa.

"Yanna, could it be possible that you, uh, might have been…jealous? I mean, your sister had all these boyfriends…."

Yanna recoiled as if she'd been slapped. "Are you suggesting that I couldn't get a man?"

"What? No—"

"Because I have news for you, David Curtiss, there are men who come to see me play volleyball from across Russia, I have men flocking outside the locker room and—"

"Calm down, that isn't what I'm saying." And no, he didn't need to hear about other men; in fact, he had a sudden sick acid in his chest. "It's just that your sister has a different outlook on life, and like you said, she had this good relationship with her father, and maybe that let her trust men a little more, and…"

David didn't know whether to flinch, maybe duck, and he certainly didn't know why he'd said that—it just came out. But it was suddenly so clear to him what this was about all along.

Yanna was *still* jealous. Her sister had clearly made abysmal choices. But at least she'd tried. At least she'd made room for love, or the hope of it, something Yanna would never do. And probably wouldn't now.

He ran his hand down his face. "I'm sorry I said that. I just thought that maybe that was why you never dated any…other…"

But Yanna looked up at him, the strangest look on her face, and in a blinding second of pain he realized why she'd never made room in her life for any other men.

Oh, no. His chest tightened with a strange but frightening explosion of joy.

She'd been waiting for him. All this time, *him*.

Oh, Yanna.

He swallowed, as the truth whammed him right in the chest and took away his breath.

"Yanna," he said, lifting his hand to her cheek. She

stared at him, all her emotions suddenly right there, in her beautiful eyes, the eyes that haunted him, that never left his dreams, his memories.

He could hear the voices in his head starting to warn him off, even feel some ethereal force pulling back, reining him in, but she was so beautiful, and he didn't even realize he was putting his arms around her until they already were, and then, just like that, before he could stop himself, and just like he always feared, and always hoped, he was kissing her.

It was like fireworks and confetti, a flood of emotions that knocked him off his feet. She melded right into him, as if she belonged there, as if they had been made for each other. She was so beautiful and strong, and he was so proud of her, and scared at the same time, knowing that she'd do anything for the people she loved. So he kissed her, wove his fingers into her silky hair, letting his heart right off its leash.

And like before, she kissed him back, as if she, too, had been waiting for this moment—*please let it be true*—for over ten years. She tasted like tears, so sweet and gentle, so willing.

He pulled her close, put his other hand to her cheek, and she made a little noise in the back of her throat, like she might be crying.

It was that sound that snapped him out of it, made him take a breath and pull away, his heart thumping. She stared at him, all wide-eyed, blinking, and he knew...

He was a jerk. A huge jerk. He had no business

kissing Yanna when he had no intention—despite the desires of his heart—to tell her how he felt, maybe make anything permanent.

And he hadn't a clue how she might feel. Hadn't even asked.

"Yanna, oh, I'm sorry. I'm so—"

Her face instantly hardened. "Oh, my—I can't believe this." She shook her head. "I am not going through this again." She put up her hand. "Stop speaking. Right now."

Right before him, as if she might be some sort of shape-shifter, she morphed back into that tough FSB agent. Clearly, he wouldn't have to ask how she felt about him. She backed away and lifted her chin. "I know you think I'm upset—"

"That's not it—"

"And I know I've been a little needy and emotional lately, but it's only because I'm a little tired—"

"Yanna—"

"And I know that you're still pretty freaked out, and I might have given you the wrong impression when I collapsed into your arms back at the teahouse, but the thing is, I'm good now." She smiled up at him. "I don't need any more…uh, comfort."

David raised an eyebrow, even though he felt skewered straight through. "Comfort?"

She patted his knee. "It was nice. Thanks."

Thanks? Nice? His heart was still trying to reboot and she was getting up, going to the computer, logging on, as if they'd had a nice *chat?*

David stared at her.

"I have an idea about Kwan. Didn't you say that you had a file on him? Why is he here in Taichung? Just to pick up his girls? And why did he hang on to my cell phone, then ditch it at the teahouse?"

"Wait—Yanna, I just kissed you."

"Yeah, I know." She turned to him. "It was nice, but I won't tell anyone."

Just like that, he was back at the resort, seeing her face as he walked out on her.

She met his gaze. Didn't even blink.

His throat burned. So much for her believing in him. Trusting him. Way to go, champ.

He nodded in response to her words.

"So, while I try and read the SMIM card on this cell, tell me everything you know about Kwan. I want to see if I can figure out what he's got next on his agenda."

It took him a second to regroup. Especially since, while she might have ice in her veins, and be able to hop up after that rather steamy—from his point of view—kiss, he was still trying to figure out how to take a full breath.

He could hear voices outside. Roman and Trish were returning with Cho after they parked the van in the garage down the alley. He got up, sat next to Yanna at the desk, all smiles and lies when Roman walked in.

"Hey," Yanna said, looking up. Roman glanced at David, then back at Yanna.

"So, what have you found out?"

That David wasn't at all the hero Roman made him out to be? That deep inside, he was still that creep who'd made Yanna feel cheap and unwanted? Worse, he had done it this time when she felt vulnerable and broken.

Yeah, a real man of integrity.

He cleared his throat. "There's something that's been bothering me since I met Kwan. He just doesn't fit the part. Kwan's reputation precedes the birth of the man I met on the boat by about twenty years. The Twin Serpents is an organization that is passed from father to son, and the torch passed to Kwan two decades ago, at least. My gut says that the man we saw was a decoy."

"Or an heir. Maybe you met Kwan-in-training." Roman sat down on the sofa while Trish went to the kitchen.

"Tea?"

Roman lifted his hand in response. Yanna, too.

What David wouldn't give for an espresso. Something to wake up his brain, maybe keep him out of trouble.

"So you think the real Kwan is grooming his son for the job?"

"The Twin Serpents is an international operation. To run a tight ship, they keep family in all the top slots. If Kwan has a son, or more than one son, they're being groomed for leadership."

"So, we find Mini-Kwan, we find Kwan," Yanna said, taking the tea Trish offered her. "Thanks."

Trish delivered Roman his tea.

"Why is this Kwan in town?" Roman asked.

"We know he has a house here. He also has a house in Taipei, only that one is for his mistress, and when he goes to the symphony."

"The symphony? Kwan doesn't seem like the symphony type," Yanna said, not looking up from her keyboard.

"I think his mistress likes it—maybe. Or maybe he's just a man of hidden tastes. But according to our sources, he's been to the symphony and the opera a number of times."

"Did you say opera?" Yanna put down her tea, punching in addresses. "The Taipei opera is playing tomorrow night in Taipei. You don't suppose…"

She looked at David. "I've never been to a Taiwanese opera. And I look great in an evening gown." She smiled, as if he hadn't just had her in a clinch, as if he didn't have the foggiest idea that she'd look downright breathtaking in an evening gown. "Anyone want to take me to the opera?"

Roman glanced at David. "You're going to look great in a tux."

Chapter Twelve

Gracie felt like a spy, a supersleuth, just like Vicktor. Only, with her heart beating in her throat and her hands slick against the rubber handle of the housekeeping trolley, it was a wonder that everyone who passed her didn't stop, point their finger and scream, *Imposter!*

Maybe Mae was horribly right—she was only making things worse. And she'd dragged Mae right into trouble with her.

Of course, once they got Ina's parents to the hospital, sat with them all night, long enough to know that Mr. Gromenko would live, and finally had a coherent conversation with Ina's mother, Mae had all but led the charge to track down Ina.

"Jorge has a cousin, Kostov. He's Mafia, and runs the Hotel Ryss, where Ina worked. There are people who saw that Kosta takes girls and kidnaps them." Luba's voice had lowered to a wisp. *"Sells them."*

Luba's words had chilled Gracie clear through,

and it had been Mae's tight voice that had responded. "Is it possible that the men who hurt Yakov weren't doing it because Ina wanted them to, but to scare her? To remind her of what she could lose if she didn't obey them?"

Luba's expression told Gracie she'd already gone there, already worked that scenario through her head, because although tears ran down her face, off her chin, she looked at Mae and nodded.

That was all it took for Mae to join league with Gracie and even concoct this harebrained idea to track the girl down in the suspicious Room 68, on the sixth floor of the Hotel Ryss.

Gracie felt as if a thousand tiny bugs crawled over her skin as she pushed the housekeeping trolley down the halls. The hotel, outfitted with lime-green wallpaper, a smelly shag carpet and a radiator at the end of the hall that clicked on and rattled, smelled like it hadn't been updated since the seventies and should offer hourly rates.

But no one, not even the men who walked past her dressed in Mafia black—where was she, Moscow?—even gave her a second look.

Mae had obviously gone overboard with the padding, the wig, the makeup that made her look about fifteen years older than her current age of twenty-six.

She stopped in front of a room as another Sergei in black walked by, and bent her head as if checking the list on the clipboard.

Please, Mae, be waiting at the elevator like you promised.

So far, their supersleuthing plan seemed to be going off without a hitch—other than the fact that they hadn't indeed found Ina. But Gracie hadn't had to dive off any buildings or climb out of any windows or even slam her cart into the knees of some greasy thug and take off for the stairwell.

It was true that her imagination had done that already half a dozen times. But who was counting?

Mae had taken a room on the fourth floor and Gracie snuck up the stairs into her room. After Mae had swiped a housekeeping uniform and a cart—Gracie hadn't asked, and Mae wasn't telling—Mae had added a couple sweaters for padding, zipping up the uniform so tight Gracie started to sweat before she even left the room.

Then again, that might have had nothing to do with the extra padding.

Mae had then gathered her hair into a net and put on a hideous black wig that smelled like it had been in mothballs for sixty or so years, yet covered up her now black-and-green bruise.

"You act like you might know what you're doing," Gracie said.

"I watch a lot of television," Mae said, then held out a small white card. "All the rooms are accessed by this, the master key." Mae had held out the card to her. "The lady who had it is gone on lunch break, so we have a ticking clock here. I'll be right behind you, and if I see anyone on to you, you won't even have to blink, I'll be there. But running is always a really good option."

Gracie took the key card, shoved it into her pocket. *Ina, here I come.* For a second, she'd felt downright heroic.

Now, she'd never felt more stupid. Good thing Vicktor wasn't here to see her. Her cell phone battery had died at the hospital, and she'd left it in Mae's hotel room to charge.

This phone-tag communication system she and Vicktor had going made her want to scream.

But maybe she should count her blessings that Vicktor wasn't here to give her one of his signature *what are you thinking?* looks.

Maybe she *did* know him. Or at least the protective part of him.

A door opened down the hall. She turned into her cart, crouching, checking her supply of towels. *Head in the game, Gracie.* But she could feel her courage begin to dribble out. The man passed, and Gracie stopped at Room 68 and knocked. When she didn't get a reply, she inserted the key card into the electronic lock.

Of course it couldn't be this easy, that Ina was still here, after all these days, that Gracie might just open a door, find the girl watching television…

Ina looked up from where she sat on the bed, wearing a pair of sweatpants and a T-shirt. Her golden-brown hair hung limp and greasy, and she was barefoot. Her mouth opened, disbelief streaked her face.

Oh, c'mon Gracie had a better getup than that, didn't she? Apparently not.

"Gracie?"

And that's when Gracie saw the black eye, the bruised, swollen lip.

"I *knew* it." Gracie closed the door behind her, latched it. "Get your stuff."

Ina's eyes widened, and she appeared as if she might cave in on herself, simply vanish right there in the middle of the mussed double bed. "No, I can't."

Gracie picked up her tennis shoes, plunked them on the bed. "Now. We're leaving—"

"You don't understand…." Ina's voice came out in a whisper. "I can't."

"Your parents are safe."

This seemed to make a difference because Ina's entire face changed. She went from scared and withdrawn to the Energizer Bunny. Grabbing her shoes, she opened them and shoved her feet in without socks. "Where? What do you mean? How did you find me?" Tears rushed out, and she brushed them away the palm of her hand. "How's my papa?"

"He's going to be okay. And they're safe. I promise. But they're worried about you." Gracie reached out to help her from the bed. "We need to leave."

But Ina didn't move, or maybe couldn't move, caught right then in the memory, the horror. "I…I just *stood* there, while they hit him. And I didn't care what happened to me. I just wanted it to be over." She emitted a full sob now, and covered her mouth with both hands.

Gracie stared at her, not sure what to say. But she knew, oh, she knew *exactly* how it felt to watch someone you love hurt, even dying before her eyes, and not know how to stop it. Yeah, she knew the shock, the disbelief. Her throat tightened. "He understands, Ina. They both do. And I'm going to take you to see them, but we need to leave. Right. Now." She turned to the door.

But so much for their flawless mission, because the lock had already disengaged, and the door clicked open.

"Jorge," Ina whispered.

Gracie simply…reacted, as if on autopilot. She rushed the door as it began to open. Just ran straight past Ina, and with all her strength, rammed both hands into the door. It slammed on the hand of whoever had tried to enter and Gracie heard a howl, and some nasty Russian words on the other side. Retaliation came next, full out and more than Gracie expected because the door banged open, pushing her to the floor, right into Ina's arms.

It wasn't Jorge. Which might have been good news except for the fact that Gracie recognized this man. She'd already met tall, creepy Kosta Sokolov and she desperately hoped he still had a nasty bruise in the well of his neck where she'd speared him hard enough to make her getaway.

Confirming, once and for all, that her disguise hadn't fooled a soul, he smirked. Either that, or seeing his terrified captive cowering behind the housekeeper made him downright giddy.

Gracie hadn't notice before, but Sokolov had silver teeth. Two of them, right where his eyeteeth might have been.

"Going somewhere, Ina?" he asked in Russian.

Surprise, surprise, the girl had some fight left in her because she stood up and spit at him.

Sokolov slapped her, hard, right on all those bruises, spinning her. She smacked against the wall and went down.

Oy.

Gracie looked up at him. If Vicktor decided to walk in right now, she'd never ever again complain about his overprotectiveness.

Some time to see the light. All the same she offered a prayer, something short and to the point, to that effect as Sokolov advanced on her.

Gracie held up her hand—she wasn't sure why, maybe in some feeble gesture to ward off one of those head-pounding slaps he'd just given Ina. The girl still lay crumpled on the floor, holding her now-bleeding face, whimpering.

"Get away from me," Gracie said in English, scooting back, then bouncing to her feet.

Sokolov laughed.

Gracie kicked at him. Yeah, she'd taken a couple self-defense classes when she got stateside—part of her therapy—but this came from pure adrenaline, and two-hundred-percent panic.

It might have worked if Sokolov hadn't taken karate or something of that nature, because he reacted fast and deflected her kick, knocking her off balance.

He brought his hand backward, and Gracie saw jewelry and a fist.

This was going to hurt. Gracie didn't bother holding back a scream.

Wonder of wonders, it worked. Because as Sokolov lunged for her, as she fled, the door opened and there was Mae.

Holding a gun.

A gun?

"Stop!"

Mae got Sokolov's attention—she'd probably gotten the entire hotel's attention with her volume. But mostly she got Gracie's attention because she leveled the gun straight at Sokolov's head.

He glared at her. She didn't even blink.

Mae was Gracie's hero, hands down. She definitely wanted to be like her when she grew up.

"Gracie, come here."

"When did you get a gun?"

"It's mine. I keep it in my car, for emergencies like this."

Emergencies? This qualified. But Gracie didn't move. Because, she calculated all of about six inches on either side of Sokolov and the wall, and even she saw worst-case scenario in that move. She glanced at Mae.

Mae apparently could also read minds. "Get over against the wall and sit down in that chair."

She wasn't talking to Gracie, and Sokolov knew it. Gracie climbed over the bed, rushed to Ina as Sokolov obeyed.

"Get up, get up." Gracie grabbed the girl by the arm, and hauled her to her feet and then they were past Mae and out the door, running. Because, as it turned out, that was really good advice.

Mae caught up to them at the stairwell. "Down, down!"

"Where is he?"

"Probably taking the elevator. Run!"

Gracie tore down the stairs, feeling fat and jiggly and hot in the uniform. She tore off the wig, dropping it in the stairwell. "We can't go out into the lobby!" She heaved open the fourth-floor door, pushing Ina through.

Mae grabbed her arm. "Not our room, either— they'll find it!"

Gracie slumped against the wall and hauled in breaths. Ina still cupped a hand to her bleeding face. "Now what?" Ina asked, her voice tinny.

Mae looked past Ina to Gracie, breathing just as hard. "We're waiting, Brains. Now what?"

Now what? *Now what?*

Gracie's hand went up and rubbed against a little red box secured to the wall. She turned, looked at it and yanked.

Yeah, two hundred crazy, scared guests, sirens

and enough noise to peel the lime-green wallpaper from the wall would effect a very slick escape, if Gracie did say so herself.

Ina looked at her with wide eyes.

Mae gave her a smile.

"Now we find someplace safe," Gracie said.

Do you trust God, David?

The question came to him last night as David had sat on the roof terrace of the Yungs' three-story home. The breeze had been warm, rustling the spider plants draping from the terra-cotta-and-blue plastic pots. He'd put his feet up on the solid cement railing that ran along the deck, leaned back in the wicker chair and stared at the stars. He knew that he didn't deserve God's trust.

Not after the way he'd practically pounced on Yanna. All these years of cultivating their friendship, of showing her how much he cared about their friendship, and he had to blow it in a moment of… weakness.

Lord, I told You that was why You needed to keep Yanna on the other side of the world. Because every time I'm with her, I'm just angry and frustrated and—

Sometimes, he wondered why God even bothered with him. He only made things worse.

I'm sorry I kissed her.

Boy, was he sorry. Because if he ever hoped Yanna might see a hint of God's love for her in the way David treated her, the way he respected her, he'd trampled that hope into tiny crumbs. Her expression, the cold lilt of her voice as she'd told him…thanks? *It was nice?* Ouch. Only, it had told him exactly how much he'd hurt her so long ago. He felt like crawling back into the hole from whence he came.

Do you trust God, David?

He'd traced the sky, identifying the stars in this section of the world, smelling fried dumplings and rice coming from the nearby houses.

Did he trust God? Enough to let Him have His way in Yanna's life without interfering?

He'd closed his eyes. *I'm sorry I counterfeited Your love for Yanna, that I didn't wait for Your yes. I'm sorry that I didn't trust You enough to love her more than I love her. Please, help me not only keep her safe, but show her Your love.*

He'd heard footsteps then, and a door open. His friend handed him a bottle of lemonade and sat down in an adjoining chair.

Roman sat in silence, staring at the stars with him. Finally, "You know, when I asked you that question about who is for you in heaven and earth? That's not my brilliance."

"I know," David said. "It's from one of the psalms."

"Yeah. Psalm 73 to be exact. I love that psalm because it's about defeat. King David knows God is on his side, but he looks at the world and all that people have, and he wonders if he's kept his way pure in vain."

David said nothing as he drank the lemonade. It contained just enough bite to make him wince.

"These thoughts sap his energy, and confuse his focus. But then he goes to the house of the Lord, and suddenly, he realizes. He's been looking at this entire thing from an earthly perspective. There is an ending, and guess what—God's on the winning side."

David began to peel the lemonade sticker off with his thumbnail.

"'Surely their way is slippery', David says, meaning that someday, those who are opposed to God are going to fall. Hard. And permanently. And then King David realizes that even though he's stumbled into all this negative, false thinking, and probably done a few things he's not real proud of because of it—"

David didn't look at him, just took another drink. But it burned all the way down.

"—Yet God was still on his side. David calls himself a brute beast—and then says that, even so, God held his right hand. He was with David even in his dark, cluttered, futile thinking. And he'll be with him all the way to the end."

"He says, 'There is nothing I desire on this earth but the Lord. He will guide me and then bring me to glory.' King David confirms that though he might make mistakes, even die, God was his portion and strength."

David closed his eyes, making himself hear Roman's words. His portion—enough, and everything David needed to help him be the right man. His strength. The ability to stay the course and do what was right for Yanna, for eternity, instead of the now.

Roman's words seemed to be enough, at least

then, to remind David of his higher priorities, give him perspective.

Until, of course, tonight on the way to the opera. In fact, Yanna was surely trying to torment him.

What was worse, he probably deserved her punishment.

Right now, he'd rather be letting Kwan and his goons take their best shot at him than be holding out his hand for the very shapely and devastatingly gorgeous Yanna Andrevka to take as she got out of the taxi to the plaza in front of the Taipei concert hall. It had to be some diabolical plot that her black dress fit her like a waterfall, sliding down her lithe body, revealing exactly what he was trying not to notice.

Hopefully, Kwan wouldn't notice, either.

David didn't like this plan, not at all. But he didn't have a full hand of choices at the moment. Even Roman had agreed to Yanna's plan, reinforcing it by agreeing to follow them to the opera with the scooter. Should things go south, David would have a plan B.

That had clinched it.

But David wasn't going to slip again. He had complete focus on keeping her alive, and he wasn't going to compromise it by getting in the way. Regardless how difficult that might be.

David let go of her hand and paid the driver.

Rain had recently fallen, puddling in the cement, and turning the air fresh as it groomed fragrances from the multicolored azaleas in the lush garden outside the concert hall.

Across the plaza, beyond the booths of hawkers selling trinkets and souvenirs, the Taipei concert hall rose glorious, regal and gleaming with its two-tiered pagoda-style roof, the columns flanked with red sash that ringed the wide hall. It gave David the sense of stepping back in time, to the realm of the great Chinese dynasties, and reminded him that Taiwan and China still fought over who had control, really, of this fourteen-thousand-square-mile island.

Then again, maybe something so lush and beautiful, so exotic and dangerous and fragile as Taiwan could never truly belong to anyone.

Yanna hooked her arm around his. "Reminds me of that time we went to *Sleeping Beauty* at the Bolshoi," she said.

Yeah, he remembered that, and how she'd smelled and looked just as incredible then as tonight. How they'd strolled through Red Square, talking about their dreams and plans. How even then, as the wind had played with her dark hair, he was jealous and wanted to put his arm around her, maybe twine his fingers through all that silk. Tonight, her platinum wig shimmered under the bright lights as they approached the wide steps of the concert hall.

She gripped his arm, not at all unsteady in her heels but perhaps of the task before them.

"You ready for this?" Yanna asked through her smile as she retrieved a program from the usher by the door.

And right then, with the chandelier lights twinkling against the faux-diamond earrings, with her smile so brilliant, her hair like a halo around her, her eyes bright and full of hope, he saw it. Why he was waiting for God's plans for Yanna. Because Yanna might be beautiful now, but when God took over her heart, she'd be radiant.

So very worth the wait.

He took a program. Blew out a breath. Was he ready for this night? Definitely not. Because if he found Kwan, well, he'd have some hard choices to make. Like, did he drag Kwan into a back alley and pry information out of him the old-fashioned way? Or did he do it Yanna's way—tagging the man with the Velcro-backed transmitter she'd concocted from her bag of tricks, and follow him back to his lair, and hopefully, Elena. What if David caught Kwan talking to Bruce? Who did he strangle first?

"I don't know," David said in answer to her question.

Big questions, all of which made him pause as they went inside. Yanna turned toward him, putting her hands on his chest, as if fixing the lapels of his suit. "I don't see Kwan."

He put his hands on her bare shoulders, aware of how smooth and soft her skin felt under his touch. "Nothing to the north, either. Maybe he's already in his box seat."

"It's hard to know what alias he booked the tickets under," she said. "We'll have to search the boxes during the performance."

She finished smoothing his suit. "You look nice tonight, by the way."

He glanced at her, surprised at the approval in her eyes. It made his stupid heart sit up, take notice. "Thanks," he said, trying to keep happiness out of his voice.

"I like the blond hair. I'm glad you dyed it back." She reached up to touch the hard bristles behind his ears. "I'll never forget your pirate look, however, sea dog."

He smiled at that. Yeah, he'd never forget nearly losing her, either. "You're a pretty blonde, too, by the way." Of course, she'd be a knockout even if she dyed her hair purple and green and bedazzled her skin with silver speckles.

She rolled her eyes. "I've always wondered if it was true that blondes have more fun."

"We're not here to have fun—this could really backfire. I'm still trying to figure out why I agreed—"

"I was kidding, David. Of *course* I know why I'm here…but I'm glad you're here, too." Then she lifted to her tiptoes and kissed him on the cheek. "I'm grateful for your friendship and the fact you're willing to help me. I know you and Roman are both worried, but we *are* going to find my sister. And when we do, I know I'll owe it all to you."

From the look in her eyes, he knew she meant it, but it made him hurt a little, too. Because if they found her sister, it would be completely due to the fact that God had intervened, and not at all due to him. Clearly, it would be some sort of miracle if she ever looked past David's mistakes to see that God was on her side.

Still, he had hope. Lots of hope.

"Here's hoping that ten years from now, we're remembering the night we found your sister and took down Kwan's empire."

Her smile dimmed and she nodded, her eyes glistening.

They entered the concert hall, and he let himself be surprised at the elegance, the rows and rows of crushed red velvet seats, the two balconies above. The orchestra was warming up in the pit, and the cacophony of strings and bass added an eerie tone to the moment.

"We were lucky to get these tickets on such short notice. I found these through a scalper online."

Luck had absolutely nothing to do with it, and it was just on the tip of his tongue to say that, but something like shame held him back. See what happened when he took things into his own hands. It affected every area of his life.

"We're on the side, on the second tier. Hopefully we'll have a decent view."

He knew she didn't mean of the stage, however, for a second, it felt like a date, something precious that he'd file away and remember, forever.

He climbed the stairs behind her, and they found their seats. He opened the program, pretended to read the listing of musical scores, written in Mandarin.

"Listen, I'm not kidding. I know you don't want to obey me, but I'm dead serious. If for some reason I tell you to abort and run, I want you to do exactly that, just like we talked about. Just because things went relatively well at the teahouse doesn't mean that Kwan wouldn't hurt you right here, right now."

Yanna picked up the opera glasses she'd purchased at the market. "Now, *dawling,* when have I ever disobeyed you?" She began to scan the audience.

"Funny. I'm serious, Yanna. I may look all cleaned up and spiffy, but I'm still the guy you saw on Kwan's boat, and I'm not afraid to put you over my shoulder and drag you out of here. I care about your sister, but it's not worth losing you."

"That's very sweet of you, but you don't have to worry about me."

"Because you won't do anything stupid? Yeah, tell me about how you ended up here in the first place? I forget…"

She kept her voice light, her smile affixed, but he noted a muscle pulling in her jaw. "You know, you might consider the fact that Kwan was on to you the entire time, and was just using me as a ploy to distract you so he could kill *you.*"

"I have thought of that, by the way. But it doesn't matter now. What matters now is finding—"

"*Tochna.* I found him." She leaned over toward David and handed him the binoculars. "The box across from us, third from the front. Looks like his party has the entire box."

David put the glasses to his eyes. Here David was, dressed in a monkey suit, sitting next to the most beautiful woman he knew, staring at one of the most despicable men he'd ever met. And there Kwan was, wearing a better tux, his hair slicked back, an exotic woman on his arm, a small entourage of goons war-riors watching his cowardly back.

David handed the binoculars back to Yanna, put his arm around her. "Remember, you're going to obey me."

The lights began to dim, and she turned and smiled at him. "Oh, David, you know me better than that."

He stared at her in the darkness, feeling a little nauseous. Because, yes, oh, yes, he did.

Chapter Thirteen

Even Yanna could agree that something or *Someone* was looking out for her, because her plan seemed to be going off without a hitch.

David might not be so happy, however, because Yanna Plan A and David Plan A differed not so much in result, but in process.

Her plan involved her getting up close and personal with Public Enemy Number One while David stayed far enough away for Kwan to walk out and lead them all to Elena.

She'd been cooking up her plot ever since she had slithered into her slinky black dress—courtesy of another stop at the market—and glimpsed the look on David's face. He looked as if he'd never seen her before, or at least this side of her.

Or maybe he didn't want to. Maybe he didn't want to be reminded of what he refused to acknowledge.

Even if his brain didn't want her, his heart did.

Because no man kissed a woman as David had kissed her without having at least a portion of his heart engaged. David never did anything halfway, and his kiss was no exception—strong arm around her shoulder, hand entwined in her hair, kissing her like he'd been waiting, dreaming of her in his arms for…at least as long as she'd been dreaming the same thing.

That had lasted only as long as it took for him to come to his senses.

He simply didn't want her in his world longer than the space of a kiss.

That made her feel oh so wonderful, so cherished.

All the same, it had given her the idea that she now clung to as she followed Kwan's floozy out of the bathroom and toward his private box.

Kwan would look at her exactly the same way David had. Perhaps—even she could admit it was remote—perhaps he wouldn't recognize the beat-up brunette who had jumped ship two days ago. Instead he'd see a blonde who just wanted to have fun.

"We're going to Jin's house after the performance. I'm sure he'll let you come along." Up close, Kwan's girl was slim, and no older than Elena, with short, black bobbed hair. She'd accidentally—or not, thanks to Yanna and an unsuspecting waitress—spilled red wine down her black satin dress during intermission. David had been watching Yanna, and she'd seen his eyes widen as she followed her victim back to the bathroom.

See, Yanna had already discovered Kwan's real name. Jin. David should trust her more.

Once inside the bathroom, Yanna had simply offered the assistance every girl needed—towels and sympathy. Oh, and plenty of *I'm so bored* to go along with her act.

Which conveniently led to "why don't you join me and my boyfriend after the show?"

Yanna had smiled, protested, and finally given in. *Oh, sure, you want me to ride in your limo, back to Kwan's secret lair, so I can wait until everyone passes out, then surprise him out of a sound sleep, preferably with a kitchen knife to his throat? Oh, okay, if you insist.*

The only glitch so far in her ultraperfect plan was when Floozy, aka Ari, invited her to join her in their box seats.

Yeah, that would be trickier. Especially with David standing in the hallway, leaning to one side, holding up the wall and trying to act nonchalant. Not an easy task since worry rippled the air like heat around him. He reached out to catch her as she walked by, but she moved her arm out of the way and shot him a look.

Back off.

Or maybe, *Trust me.*

Probably both, but David reacted like some sort of jilted lover, all dark frowns and glares.

Well, this wasn't about him. Or her. She'd do whatever it took to track down Elena. Even sit in Kwan's box, in the back, next to one of his body-guards, who looked vaguely familiar and stared at her like she might be a nice roll of sushi.

She gave him a wan smile. Ari turned back to her and shot her a grin. Best friends. She wondered if Ari had a big sister and where she might be tonight, if she worried about Ari and the company she kept.

Glancing down at David's seat just as the lights lowered, Yanna saw that he had reentered his box. He now stared up at Kwan with his hands folded over his chest in a very if-looks-could-kill kind of posture.

Loosen up. She could take care of herself. Really. Mostly.

Yanna pulled her silk shawl over her and tried to concentrate on the soprano over the roll of her pulse.

The opera ended long before she had figured out what to do to get Kwan alone, or if—please, no—he recognized her before she could get her hands on a real knife (as opposed to her Barbie knife). By the show's end, she'd turned her program into an egg roll, soggy and unreadable.

The last of the applause died, and the lights flickered on. Yanna stood, aware that Kwan now bent toward his girlfriend, who at the moment was probably informing him of her addition to their party.

Indeed, he turned. Yanna braced herself, smiled, and didn't see a flicker of anything but interest cross Kwan's dark face.

Just what, she suddenly wondered, had her new friend gotten her into?

Kwan's, er—bodyguards? Business associates? pals?—steered her into the hall and down the stairs, protecting Kwan from the press of the crowd as they exited off to the side and down to the front lobby. Yanna glanced around for David, but didn't spy him in the throng.

And then they were outside. The air, fresh and cool, still damp from the rain, swept over her and she gulped it, more for strength than anything else.

Really, she didn't care what happened to her. As long as she located Elena.

But she preferred that whatever happened to her be relatively painless.

That would be better than the scenario currently happening in her mind, the one where Kwan used her cute little knife on her throat, just like he'd suggested on the yacht. Good thing David had confiscated it.

"Coming?" Ari asked, and Yanna climbed into the limousine next to her and across from Kwan, who was pouring himself a highball of brandy.

He offered it to Yanna. She glanced at Ari, who raised an eyebrow. Then accepted the glass.

Kwan poured one for himself, and they toasted to a fine performance.

Yanna tried not to gag as her throat sizzled, her stomach convulsing in on itself. See, this was why she didn't drink.

They pulled away from the concert hall.

Yanna looked out the window to see David standing on the steps, staring out into the parking lot. For a moment, she had a wild urge to wave, open the window, yell his name.

It didn't help that his worried expression made

her think that yes, he had meant everything he'd put into that kiss.

Too little, too late.

Kwan reached across the limo and put his hand on her knee. "So, what is your name?" he asked in English.

David was going to kill her.

Well, once he tracked Yanna down and got her away from Kwan, who at the moment was first in line. Because David knew without a sliver of a doubt that Kwan knew—he *had* to know—that the beauty he'd picked up in his little entourage was none other than Agent Andrevka, the woman who'd slipped out of his hands two days ago.

Nothing else accounted for her easy reception into Kwan's merry band of terrorists.

David felt sick, watching the limo pull away from the curb, a shiny hearse under the bright lights of the parking lot. He refused to look straight at the car, but saw it in his peripheral vision, memorizing the license plate.

He gave the car about fifteen seconds before he sprinted down the curb, found the scooter Roman had left in the dark shadows of the lot. Plan B.

Again.

He leaned into the ride, into the rain, his anger about all he could feel. He'd known she had something cooking in her sneaky brain. A smart man, a man who knew Yanna like he did, would have kept a better grip on her, at least kept his arm around her waist.

Instead, he'd let her wander out into the crowd. Never to be seen again.

He gave himself points for not hauling both Yanna and Kwan out of Kwan's box for some elbow room, and then getting down to business with Kwan.

But like Yanna, who should *trust* him, he also wanted Elena found. And Kwan had too much padding around him for any sort of snatch-and-run to work.

So Yanna, of course, knowing this, apparently decided to employ her own version of hero.

Why couldn't she trust that David meant what he said? They *would* find Elena, they just needed to do things *his* way.

The thought zeroed in on him and only made him drive faster, spraying a puddle onto himself. His monkey suit clung to him, his face slick and grimy with rainwater. But he had eyes on the limo and Yanna.

Please, God, keep her safe.

They drove through Taipei, past the downtown markets, the bright neon lights. In the distance, Taiwan's tallest building, Taipei 101, glared down on the wet streets from its glowing, lofty heights on the soggy peons below. David kept three lengths away from the limo, and tried desperately not to let his thoughts wander.

He most definitely didn't need to imagine what Kwan might be doing right now to the shapely blonde in the clingy dress.

He should have made her wear a parka.

The limousine cut north, toward the mountains,

and he had to hang back as they wound into the hills. Houses here had broken away from their foundations, sitting in rubble from the last earthquake. The air here smelled fresh, out of the smog of the city, rife with evergreen, umbrella-shaped banyan trees, and the bombax flower, which resembled a lumpy tree.

The road began to bend, the traffic thinning, and he held back even more, finally deciding to drive without his lights. The last thing Yanna needed was Kwan alerted to his presence.

David pictured an ugly repeat of the drama on the boat.

But when he rounded the curve, now high enough up to see the city stretched below him, Kwan's car had vanished.

David sped up, barely avoiding the edge of a long and ugly careen down the side of the mountain. Turning on the lights, he saw nothing ahead. Another mile and he knew.

Kwan had lost him.

And David had lost Yanna.

Chapter Fourteen

She could do this. She could. Absolutely. Because Yanna was a superagent, double-oh-seven…

Oh, who was she trying to fool? She was *not* a field agent. Someone needed to write that on a glowing neon sign and hang it over her head.

These moments were exactly why she preferred to sit in her office with all her humming CPUs.

Yanna fabricated a smile for Kwan as she took his slimy, too-smooth hand and stepped out of the limousine. He slipped his arm around her waist, held on. Everything inside her wanted to seize up and hurl at his touch, but she kept her mind on Elena, pasted a smile on her face and giggled.

Maybe she did have some latent undercover skills, because she didn't recognize the smiling, supposedly drunk woman now flirting with Kwan. But a superspy would have remembered to bring the transmitter with her, not leave it with her partner, who right now might be sitting outside the concert hall, wanting to wring her neck. Why had she ditched David? She must have been out of her mind, because she'd reconsidered about ten minutes into the trip, and had been sending him silent SOS's ever since as they drove into the hills toward Kwan's place.

Kwan might be playing at treating her like an American, but she felt sure, right to her bones, that the little smile Kwan gave her had nothing to do with delight at her presence and everything to do with the fact that she'd walked right back into his clutches. He recognized her, even if he hadn't said it. Which meant that not only had she been deluding herself, but instead of finding Elena, David would find Yanna's decapitated, mutilated body.

She wanted to scream and take off in a hard sprint when Kwan opened the door to his digs—a two-story cement-and-stone monstrosity nestled into some Chinese-style gardens with bright lights turning the place into a garish display. Torches on either side of the door, worried by the breeze, gave off an eerie effect, as did the giant red Buddha that stared at her with glassy eyes as she followed the entourage into the house.

Kwan hadn't quite figured out what world he fit into, evident in the Asian sprays of orchids and a small fountain that was centered in the entryway and separated the main room from the dining room. The European Kwan showed in the animal skins on the floor, the black-and-chrome furniture, the flat-panel television above a gas fireplace. Beyond that, a steel stairway led to a second floor, one that overlooked the main room and hinted at numerous bedrooms.

It reminded her of the yacht, and she pressed her hand against her stomach, which might give way any second.

Kwan motioned them toward the main room, picked up the gas remote and lit the fireplace. Yanna stood at the edge of the sunken living room, frozen as Kwan sat down on the sofa, used the remote to turn on music—*not opera*—and put his arm around his girlfriend. Ari leaned back against Kwan, pulled her legs up on the sofa, kicking off her heels.

"Join us," she said to Yanna.

"I need to use the bathroom," Yanna said, serious now about the lurching stomach. In fact, maybe she should run.

Kwan smiled at her—not a nice smile—and motioned down the hall. Near the kitchen.

The kitchen…maybe this might work…

"Shei-shei," she said, and walked down the hall, locking herself in the bathroom, flicking on the light and staring at her sorry self in the mirror.

She looked scared. In the wide eyes, the platinum-blond hair, the too-red lips. Flushed skin, all the way down to the edge of her dress, and a heartbeat tattoo-ing at the base of the neck told her that Kwan must be in the next room laughing.

Laughing.

Laughing. At her fear. At her hopes of finding her sister.

At the fact he'd lured her to his house, to do…
who knew what?

Laughing.

Nyet. She took another look at herself, and everything inside her went very still. Kwan might think he
had lured her here, but here she was, just as she'd
planned. And she wasn't leaving until she had found
out where he was hiding Elena.

Even if she had to get messy.

She took off her high heels. Hopefully the music
that reverberated through the house would cover her
footsteps, but just to be on the safe side…

Flicking off the light, she cracked open the bathroom door, slipping out into the hall and closing
the door behind her. She tiptoed into the kitchen.
Stainless-steel surfaces around a main island reflected the outside terrace lights. She moved
quickly, easing out the drawers until she found a
butcher knife.

Footsteps advancing down the hall made her suck
in her breath. She shifted toward the alcove that hid
a closet or a pantry.

Just as she'd hoped, Kwan appeared, filling up the
door. He stood there for a moment, then moved to
turn on the light.

Yanna felt an arm snake around her waist and a
hand clamp over her mouth. She was yanked into
the closet.

"Don't move," a voice whispered directly into
her ear.

She gasped, but the human gag over her mouth, as well as the raucous music, muffled her noise. Yet, she didn't even dwell on the how or why, because David had followed her, snuck into Kwan's house and stopped her from doing what she had come to do.

Because that was what David did.

"Let me go," she tried to say, but it came out completely unintelligible.

Kwan flicked on the light. It didn't matter, because David had already closed the pantry door, sealing them inside.

"Don't…move."

Yeah, not with his arm clamped around her like a vise. She still had the knife in her right hand, and for a long moment, she debated using it. As if reading her mind, David's hand closed around her wrist.

She stayed there, pulled tight next to him, smelling the rain and sweat on his skin, his whiskers rough against her cheek, his wide chest solid against her back. His heart thumped against her spine and she knew he'd probably saved her life.

Again.

He caught the knife before she dropped it.

"Shh," he said, softly so only she could hear it. But his lips brushed against her ear, and a ripple of pure electricity went through her.

Not fair. Didn't her heart pay any attention to her brain?

Kwan turned off the light—Yanna saw it flick out

from under the door. She relaxed, poised to move out, but David held her tighter. "No, he may be waiting."

"He didn't see me come in," she said, but David didn't let her finish, clamping his big hand over her mouth again.

She pulled it away but stayed quiet. In the pitch darkness, she heard only the swish of her heartbeat.

Then, after what seemed like forever, she turned in his arms, putting her arms around his waist, whispering directly into his ear, trying to keep emotion from leaking from her voice. "Why did you stop me? I could have made him tell—"

"Stop." His voice was so soft, so urgent, it made her heart skip. "Trust me, please." She felt his lips move against her neck. He smelled like rain and the dampness from his shirt seeped through her dress.

"He's right out there," she whispered. "We could go out there, jump him."

"I'm not a superhero. There are three guys in there. Let's be smart about this—"

"But he has my sister!" She bit her lip to keep her voice down, but he held her even tighter.

"I know that, Yanna. C'mon, I haven't forgotten." He pulled back and looked at her. Her eyes had adjusted to the light, and she saw his, earnest in hers. He ran his hand down her cheek and it was trembling. "Just trust me. I put a transmitter on his limo. According to the *plan*. He's not going anywhere without us knowing it."

They heard voices outside the room, shouting.

"Apparently they're starting to think that Elvis has left the building."

Huh? She frowned at him.

"They know you're missing. We need to lie low for a bit. Then I'm getting you back to Taichung."

"You're not listening. I'm not leaving here until I know where Elena is." She started to turn, but for a nonsuperhero, he sure had superhero arms that were even now tightening around her.

"I know you want to find her, Yanna, but this is the best way. We can't go charging in there with three armed men. I did some visual reconnaissance during the performance and those boys have enough hardware on them to defend against an attack from China. So we're going to trust that God has our backs on this one, and pull back to a safe distance."

God had their backs? "David—"

"Yanna, I know you don't think this, but I promise, God knows and cares, and He's going to get both of us, and Elena, home safely. We have to believe that."

Confidence, bold and unwavering, thrummed in his voice. It found her bones, her cells, and filled them with hope.

She put her hands on his chest. "How'd you find me?"

He paused for a moment, as if thinking about just why he'd had to track her down. She made a little face. "Sorry, by the way."

"Yanna, I'm telling you, you're going to give me a heart attack."

She lowered her forehead into his shoulder, her fingers angling into his jacket lapels.

"I followed the limo out of the parking lot. I nearly lost you out on the road, but thankfully, I picked up the limo right about the time the lights went on in the house. Then, I parked up the road a bit and worked my way through the back gardens, so conveniently lit up like high noon. I didn't know you were going to sneak into the kitchen and try and serve him up for dinner, but I have to admit, I'm glad it's you and not one of Kwan's pals,who came in to get a late-night sandwich."

"Me, too."

Her voice was so soft, she didn't think she'd said it. But at her words, she felt him catch his breath, felt his arms tighten around her. "Don't ever do that again. That took a lot of spine, I'll give you that, but you…you really scared me."

Tears burned her eyes, and she blinked them away, angry. Did he even have an inkling what words like that did to her? The sooner she could get back to Russia and back to a safe chatting distance—like a couple hundred thousand miles, over the Internet—the better. The man's tenderness was like shrapnel on her heart.

All she wanted was him to love her. Like she loved him.

She closed her eyes and, for a moment, let herself be there, in the counterfeit embrace of his arms.

"Okay, I think it's safe. Let's get out of here."

But she had to disagree. *Safe* wasn't a word she would ever use with David again.

He didn't want to tell her how close he'd come to losing it, just breaking down, right there in the closet, overcome with relief.

Kwan hadn't killed her. Because again, God had intervened and shown David a door he could easily jimmie open, and given him the perfect hiding place to pull Yanna to safety.

And not a second too soon. Because David saw the scenario that would have played out. Lights up. Action. Yanna with the knife, then Kwan with a gun, or maybe just his bodyguards rushing to intercept her and—*what had she been thinking?*

Maybe she hadn't. Like David had done when he'd seen her on the boat and every moment since then, Yanna had simply reacted. Panic drove her actions and she'd risked everything she'd come to Taiwan to do.

It scared him sometimes how much he and Yanna thought alike. No, reacted alike.

But perhaps she had felt that knee-buckling relief, too, because she clung to him.

Yanna, oh, Yanna. He'd leaned his head into her hair and let his relief roll over him. *Thank You, Lord.*

The house seemed eerily quiet as they stepped out of the closet. Too quiet.

"Let's go." He pulled her back toward the door

that entered the kitchen from the garden. He'd opened it for her to go through, and flicked off the terrace lights when he heard voices.

Kwan and another man. Arguing.

"Do you hear that?" she said, putting a hand on his chest, stopping him from shoving her out the door and to safety.

He stilled and nodded, but he had more important things on his mind, so he pitched his voice as low as he could. "Get outside and stay down beside that palm tree in the yard. I'm right behind you."

He didn't know why he'd expected her to obey him. Because, as usual, she didn't. In fact, to make matters worse, she stepped toward the conversation. He clamped a grip on her arm, but she neither shook him away nor moved to his pressure. "Shh…I understand what they're saying."

No, he didn't want to shush. In fact, everything inside him wanted to throw her over his shoulder and run.

"They're talking about me."

Of course they were. He gritted his teeth and pulled her toward him, but she yanked her arm out of his grip. Perfect. "C'mon," he ushered.

She put a hand on his mouth, not looking at him. "The other guy is mad at Kwan, that he brought me here. And—" she glanced at David, her eyes suddenly big "—they're expecting you."

Him? His hand closed around the knife handle. Maybe Yanna had been correct in her impulse to take out Kwan, here, now… He leaned into the conversation, willing his heart to still.

"They don't want you dead—" She was still staring at him, only not at him, but through him, as if trying to see what Kwan might value in him.

He could name a few things, the framework of his undercover operation being at the top of that list.

"He says you know the other Serpent."

The other Serpent? Perhaps he should be paying more attention. But just as he took a step closer, David winced as he heard a crack, skin against skin.

That was enough. David took her hand. "We're outta here—"

Grabbing Yanna by the hand, he pulled her behind him through the door, keeping low and near the brushes as he sprinted along the house. Outside, he heard more voices, and then heavy thuds along the groomed lawn.

He pulled her through a sculpted garden and leaped a tiny decorative stream, searching for his scooter. There, hidden under a lush banyan tree. He yanked out the scooter and started it. Yanna was already on the back when he hit the gas.

They'd have to have a decent head start to outrun the limo.

Or, maybe—he turned north, away from the complex, away from town. "Hang on!"

She clamped her hands around his waist and dug her knees into his thighs. He motored up the mountain a mile or less, then cut the engine and pulled the scooter far off the road. Yanna got off and he hunkered down beside her.

"I have the tracking device on the limo. They'll give up and leave. And we'll be on their tail."

Crouching beside him, she was breathing hard. "They knew you, knew you'd come after me. And they think you know something."

"I have no idea what they're after," he said, his mind scrolling through the megabytes of information he'd digested about his op. "And it didn't sound like whoever was with him was too happy."

"He said that you know who the other Serpent is. What is he talking about? What did he mean by the other Serpent?"

"It's the other leader, the other Twin Serpent—we don't have a fix on who that might be." And he was looking forward to the bonus round of this op, another Kwan for him to hunt down. And after that there'd be another, then another. The world seethed with Kwans and his types.

David's adrenaline began to dip, his breathing calming. Yanna's hair had come down and now wisped about her face. "You know, that means that Kwan wasn't duped a second by your little disguise." Some disguise, too. It was hard not to appreciate the way she could still look amazing after a sprint through the garden, the slightest glisten of perspiration at the base of her neck.

He took off his jacket and put it over her shoulders. He'd kept on the dark jacket, not needing the white shirt to announce his presence as he crept up to Kwan's estate.

That's when he noticed her feet.

Her bare feet.

Now cut and bleeding.

He sat and began to untie his shoes. He didn't need both wingtips *and* socks.

He pulled off one sock and handed it to her. She took it, a strange expression on her face. "What is this?"

"Your feet. Put it on."

"David, they stink."

He pulled off his other shoe. "Your feet are bleeding."

"Do you know how often Russian women walk around in pain? We live in pain, every day of the year, with our feet jammed into high heels and spike boots." She wrinkled her nose. *"Nyet."*

He handed her the other sock. "Just put it on. I don't know how long it'll be till we get home or get you decent footwear. Humor me."

She made a gagging sound as she put on the socks. "I am never telling anyone about this." She looked up at him. "And you'd better not, either."

He supposed it was designed to make him laugh. Except it didn't, not when those words hung out there, mocking him.

"Yanna, about what happened back at the Yungs' when I kissed you…"

Her smile dimmed. "I told you, I don't want to talk about it."

But he had to talk about it. She had to know. "I haven't kissed anyone since…well, since *you,* ten years ago."

She blinked at him. Her mouth opened, closed, opened again. "I don't understand."

"I just wanted to let you know that while I might have a sorry habit of just grabbing you and kissing you, that behavior is rather, uh, out of the ordinary for me. And I'm sorry. And I respect you."

"I know that." But she looked away, down, as if she didn't. As if maybe his words had sunk in. Rattled her.

"And I don't want our friendship to be destroyed because I'm stupid. You're one of the best friends I've ever…the truth is, I don't want to lose your friendship."

Suddenly he saw that he'd made it worse. All worse. She clenched her jaw, looked away from him.

Yet maybe if she understood more…. "And I haven't even dated anyone—you know that—and I don't want to, with my job—" Liar, liar, why couldn't he just tell her the truth? That it wasn't about his job. Maybe it once had been but now it was only about him knowing that he would be in the way of her seeing God, and that it would just get complicated, and that some things were bigger and more important than what he wanted—

"Stop, David. I know." She put her hand on his cheek.

And just like that, his emotions reached up and grabbed him around the throat, choked him, sucked away his breath. There must be something wrong with him, because he wanted to kiss her again. And it seemed so utterly unfair that he couldn't take her in his arms and show her, oh, to show her exactly how much he loved her.

But Roman's words rushed back to him. Not his assurances that he was a man of integrity, but rather the ones that told him that God hadn't forsaken them.

He was with him, even now, watching. Loving Yanna even more than David did.

So, instead, David swallowed and forced a smile. "Okay," he said. "Good." But his voice came out all croaky and raw.

And of all crazy things, that made her smile. Light even came back into her eyes, the light that had always meant things were sweet and easy between them. She tugged on his stinky socks.

"For your information, I haven't dated anyone, either." She pulled on the other sock. "And not because of my job, although that's what I tell people."

He looked up the road, toward Kwan's camp. Then back at Yanna although she was hard to look at without laughing, sitting there in that evening dress, his black socks up to her knees, bagging at the heels. But he couldn't ask why.

"I never found anyone that believed in me…like you did."

Oh. He wasn't sure what to say, or why his throat tightened, burned. But suddenly he could hardly breathe.

"You always listened to me, and made me feel as if I mattered—"

"You do matter." He could barely make out his own words, speaking through his sandpaper throat. She touched his arm.

"I know." She met his eyes. "*Really,* I know."

He nodded, unable to speak.

"But I never had anyone that mattered to me—that was family like you and Vicktor and Roman and Mae. When I met you guys, I felt as if I had…I don't know, siblings, maybe. People that I could count on. And then you walked out of my life—"

She held up her hand to stop his words.

"And Elena took that place. She became my world, my best friend. I want to be that person she could count on. I am going to find my sister, David."

He got that. He really got that. He put his hand to her face, running his thumb down her perfect, elegant cheek.

For a moment, she leaned in, a sweetness in her eyes. Then she took his hand away.

"Listen. I was thinking about what you said, about me being jealous—"

"I shouldn't have—"

"And I was jealous. *Am* jealous. And not because my sister thought she had found true love. But because she doesn't have a list of men who betrayed her in her life to tell her that…that there is no such thing as a man who will stay."

Please, God, I want to be that man. David ran his

hand down her arm, caught her hand in his. *Even more, I want her to see that You will stay.*

"But I want to believe that someday I will find that, David."

He nodded. "You will," he said, and it came out barely above a whisper, one that she probably didn't hear.

Because, just then, lights flashed from down the road, followed by an engine, and he grabbed Yanna and pulled her with him down into the brush.

As the car drove by, the phone in his pocket began to beep.

"I think that's for me," Yanna said, as she reached inside his jacket and pulled it out. She smiled up at him. "The tracker. The plan worked like a charm."

Oh, yeah, without a hitch.

Chapter Fifteen

Finally, *finally,* Vicktor had made it out of American customs and passport control, and thankfully they only asked him three times what medical conference he was attending. And his specialty as a physician. Vicktor knew this from before, when he'd been Vladimir Zaitsev on previous trips around the world. Thankfully, Yanna had done her homework. Despite her worry over her sister, she was a professional and, yes, there was a medical conference in Seattle. This weekend. Forty-eight hours—they stamped it loud and ominous on his visa.

He went out into the sunshine, or relative sunshine, because the afternoon shadows hung over the terminal. A taxi rolled by, but he ignored it, pulling out his cell phone and looking at the number of missed calls. Four. And one voice mail.

Gracie, of course, but she sounded strange in the

recording. Like she might have just been crying. And her words, "I really have to talk to you," didn't help.

Yeah, him, too. He pushed Save, then speed-dialed her number. The phone rang and rang and finally went over to voice mail.

For a second, the option of leaving a message stymied him. What was he supposed to say? He stood there, in the pickup lane of the airport, breathing in the exhaust, the cool air, the smell of desperate smokers, and knew he'd really gone overboard this time.

"You don't always have to fix everything. Sometimes I just want you to listen." How many times had he heard that from Gracie?

Yes, he did have to fix it. He just wasn't wired to watch his woman struggle without stepping in. And then Yanna being in trouble had stirred up the past, and how he'd nearly lost her to a serial killer, and his heart suddenly did the speaking for his brain.

He couldn't just turn around and get back on a plane.

Yet, all at once that seemed like a good idea. Because he envisioned the scenario when Gracie realized what he'd done.

"You're here?" Oh, she'd be glad to see him—or at least act like it, because that was Gracie. Sweet and polite and a terrible liar.

Maybe Vicktor should face the fact that he'd overreacted. He had a vague memory of Roman trying to talk him out of it. Very vague. He'd buy Roman a blow horn when he got home.

It was just a part of Vicktor's cellular makeup to

care—really care—about the people in his life. But perhaps this was a case of overcaring.

In fact, his being here had more to do with him, and the fact that he simply couldn't take a full breath without her. However, maybe she could. Maybe she didn't need him at all.

He'd have to live with that. "Uh, Gracie, it's Vicktor," he said, finally, into the phone. "I'm…in… America."

Then, because he didn't really know what else to say, but the obvious *I love you,* he hung up.

Vicktor stood there, wishing he was more like David, who did his job without freaking out about the woman he loved. David knew what to do, and how to do it right.

Gracie had always rocked Vicktor's world, kept him off balance.

Vicktor tapped his phone on his leg. He could probably call one of his old Russian cop friends he'd worked with in Seattle, like his pal Alex. But most of them had taken the oath, become American citizens, and agreed to certain allegiances. Like, turning in people in their country under false names.

Vicktor wouldn't be seeing any of his old cop cronies on this junket.

A smart guy would have probably thought further than the plane ticket.

Maybe…Mae…

Mae was different. She had shown up in Russia a few times under the radar. Wasn't she living with

Gracie? Maybe he could break the news to Mae, who could then sort of explain to Gracie that her fiancé was in town…to save her life? Oh, boy. And then she and Gracie could have a good laugh and he could be the easy brunt of the joke—Mr. Overkill—and come in with his hat in his hands, and wow, was he sorry, and Gracie might even find it cute. Attractive?

The hope clusters were about the last active brain cells working in his head, apparently.

He opened his phone and found Mae's number. He had to reenter it in American code, then pushed Enter.

She picked up on the second ring—there went his faint hope that all cell phones around the world were switching over to voice mail. "Hello?"

"Mae it's—" The words got stuck.

"Vicktor? I can't believe it! Gracie's been trying to get a hold of you for two days! You just disappeared off the planet. But she's in trouble—big trouble."

Big trouble. Vicktor wanted to put his fist into something—maybe the cement pole, however, that would only make matters worse—but yes, he knew it, *he knew it*.

He managed, *"Shto Slyochilas?"* Whoops, he hated when he switched to Russian, because it sort of highlighted his panic.

"It's a long story, but she got involved with what we think is a human-trafficking ring—"

"Sokolov, we know."

"We—who's we?"

"Roman and I, well, David and Yanna, too, but

that's another side of the story that you really don't want to know about right now. Gracie texted me, and Roman contacted a buddy in his office, and they've been watching this guy. Apparently he's a heavy hitter on their bad-guy list. So I don't know who she's mixed up with, but I'm not feeling good about this."

"Well, you were right because this Sokolov guy *is* bad news, and we got Gracie's friend away, but now Gracie's disappeared—"

He wanted to hit things again. "Disappeared?"

"Yeah, after we got Ina away, I thought they would round back to the hospital, only that was a long while ago and we haven't the foggiest idea where Gracie might be."

Calm down, take a breath. He moved to the side of the terminal wall, watching people as they flagged down rides or dialed their cell phones. "I'm not completely tracking with you—you got who away?"

"Just…this girl. What is of key importance here is that Gracie is gone. And we don't know where she is. Has she ever mentioned anything to you—a place she'd go if she wanted to drop off the planet, a place that is remote…I don't know…anywhere."

"Did you call her?"

"No, I thought I'd use my psychic powers, maybe get a newspaper and look up the horoscope—*of course,* I called her! Until I remembered that her phone was left in the hotel after the fire alarm went off."

Probably he needed to sit down. "Was she hurt? Please, tell me she wasn't hurt."

"What, no I don't think so, I mean, yeah, Sokolov pushed her, but I got there before he could—"

"In *the fire,* Mae!"

"What fire—oh, no, no fire. Just the alarm. That was Gracie's brilliant idea. I got away, but I think he followed her, or maybe had someone else follow her."

"So someone is after her?"

"Yeah, probably more after Ina, but now that Gracie was there—twice—he's probably figured out—"

"Sokolov?"

"Or maybe someone who works for him, but whatever the case, I'm getting worried."

Yeah, him, too. She hadn't flown halfway across the world on a hunch only to have that hunch confirmed. In epic scary-movie proportions.

Someone, and he was talking cosmically here, was on his side.

"Calm down, Mae, let me think. Which of Gracie's friends would she go to?"

"We're talking about *Gracie.* She's got plenty of friends she could turn to, but she wouldn't go there, not if she might put them in trouble."

He agreed with that. There was pretty much *nichevo* Gracie wouldn't do to protect her friends.

In that way, he supposed, they were a perfect fit.

"We were eventually supposed to meet back here—at the hospital—"

"Why are you at the hospital? Are you hurt?" Before Gracie came along, Mae had been his world, and he didn't just shrug that away. "Are you okay?"

"I'm fine. It's not me, it's Yakov and Luba, but they're going to be okay, too, if we can just find Ina and Gracie. The cops are here—including one of your old pals, Alex—and they're talking to the Feds about witness protection in exchange for their testimony, but first we have to find—"

So much for Vicktor's clandestine adventure in America.

Vicktor leaned against the cement pillar, his entire body feeling weak. "Okay, listen, we're going to find her, I promise."

The line went quiet. Then, "I'm sorry, are you…I mean…uh…I'm not trying to jump to any conclusions here but—"

"I'm in America. Standing here at the Seattle airport, but the last thing I need is to alert the wrong people so don't react. I don't need Alex to know."

"Oh."

Perfect. That's right, Mae, stop talking, glance at him. Way to be sneaky. "He's looking at you, right now, isn't he?"

"Uh, yeah." Her voice dropped, but only for a second because, now, in a voice that telegraphed, *no, I'm not trying to hide anything,* she said, "Well, do you know where I could find her?"

"I'm thinking." Vicktor blew out a breath, ran his hand through his grimy hair. He'd pulled out American cash from his ATM, had enough to rent a car. Walking back inside, he stopped at a map of Seattle. He'd lived here for a while, years ago, and collected vivid memories of hiking through Olympic National Park. Once he'd even headed west to Mount Rainier. He'd stared at it from a distance, thinking, yes, this must be paradise.

But he'd changed his mind, since he'd met Gracie. Anywhere—he didn't care where—was paradise, as long as she was with him.

Paradise. Oh…

"I might have an idea. I'll call you."

"Vicktor—"

"I promise, I'll call you."

"Be careful. Please."

Tell that to the woman he loved.

Big surprise, Kwan's limo led David and Yanna back to his yacht in Taichung. Yanna's entire body buzzed, and even wearing David's jacket, she felt numb clear through. Three hours on the back of David's scooter was like logging a thousand hours in the back of a Russian Kamaz with the top off.

Her insides might still be moving a year from now.

David had parked outside the harbor, hiding his scooter in the tall grass, and they'd hunkered down as the wind washed over them, watching, through her cheap opera glasses, the patrol of Kwan's body-guards. Oh, how she'd wanted to get onto that yacht, put that kitchen knife to Kwan's throat. Even suggested it.

"No, Yanna. We'll wait," David said, bringing down the glasses and giving her a don't-argue-with-me look.

Wait, wait for what? For Elena to be shipped off to Thailand or India or some other third-world country where she'd be caged and forced to…forced to…

"This waiting is killing me," she said, her knees pulled up to herself, David's jacket tight around her. "What if we never find her? What if, by the time we get to her, it's too late?" And it didn't help her discomfort that rocks and gravel were embedded in her backside, her legs. Or that her feet were ice blocks, even inside David's smelly socks.

David looked at her then, a strange expression on his face. "I know, Yanna. I know."

But that was all he said. He put his arm around her and pulled her to himself, keeping her warm.

In a way, David had always kept her warm, and right now, as he had his arm curled around her shoulders, pulling her to his amazing chest, smelling of cologne and perspiration and the soap he used in the shower this morning, his words found their way back to her.

I haven't dated anyone…

He'd been apologizing for kissing her, but she hadn't heard that. Not at all. Just…he didn't have anyone in his life, either. She hadn't expected that—well, maybe a little. He might have mentioned it during their online chats. But David was the kind of guy made for commitment, for marriage.

For a family.

He had *husband* written all over him, with his tenderness, the way he could look into a woman's soul and make her feel safe. And he would be an incredible father—wise and kind.

When he was home, that was. Because there was the other side of David, also. Driven. Dangerous. Focused. The kind of guy who would give his all for his country.

The kind of guy who would also drop everything—his patriotism, his duty, his career, his life—for her.

Which scared her, suddenly, more than she could put words to.

She didn't want this to end. Didn't want to say goodbye after they found Elena. In fact, if it were possible, she'd stay right here, clutched to his side, anywhere, anyhow, letting him take her on the ride of her life—in a boat, on a motorcycle, in his arms.

The thought made her tremble with how much she wanted it. He must have felt her move because he looked down at her. "What?"

Now she had tears in her eyes and that made her feel even more stupid, so she didn't look up at him, just buried her face in his chest. "I…" She took a breath. "What happens after we find Elena?" Her voice came out so softly she wondered if she'd actually spoken the words aloud.

He didn't get it. "I put you and Elena on a plane with Roman, and you go back to Siberia."

She ran her fingers over her eyes. No, she knew that part. And her silence must have confused him, because he pushed her away. The moonlight touched his beautiful face, filled his eyes, and the concern in them tightened her throat. Oh, she loved him. The magnitude of it washed over her. It wasn't a crush—had never been a crush. But until this moment, she hadn't realized how it would tear out her heart to leave him. Again.

Her breath caught and she felt like a fool when tears glazed her eyes. She looked away, wiping them, but he caught her hand. "What?"

"I just—" This shouldn't be so hard. He knew her better than anyone, probably. Except maybe this part, the part she should probably simply accept.

She wanted to spend her life with this man. She didn't care what she had to surrender. Where she had to live. Even, perhaps, what she had to believe.

Oh, brother, was she pitiful.

He touched her chin, brought her face back to look at him, ran a thumb down her cheek. "You are so beautiful, Yanna." And then, as if he might be thinking, feeling, exactly the same things, he leaned down and kissed her ever so sweetly, gently.

She was crying now, her tears salty in their mouths. She put her hands on his chest and pushed away, not looking at him. "I don't want you to leave."

"I'm not going anywhere," he said quietly.

She looked up at him. "No, I mean after this. I don't want to go back to online chatting, and wondering where you are. I want…" She searched his eyes, those devastating eyes, and it all caught in her throat—her longing, her fears.

"What…what do you want?"

You. "I want you to be safe." *I want you to be the man I come home to every night. Or vice versa. Or both.*

He sighed, wrapped his arm back around her, pulling her again close. "Ditto."

And there it was, glaring and painful, like a skewer to her heart, why they could never have more than this moment.

Because their world wouldn't let them. And probably, David saw the same thing. "Do you ever dream of getting out of the military? Of...getting.... married?" She could hardly believe she'd asked that, but let the words sift into the breeze, feeling him take them in on his breath.

"Yes."

Yes.

"Me too," she said, so quietly she surprised even herself. And then, she realized, that perhaps, she wasn't surprised at all.

David would probably never erase the image of Yanna wrapped in his coat, nestled close, falling asleep in his arms.

Nor would he forget the taste of her lips on his. He wasn't sure why he'd kissed her again. Or why she hadn't stopped him.

But seeing her tears, even if they had been all about worry for her sister, and probably even some fatigue, had only made him realize everything they couldn't have.

Wouldn't have.

Do you think about getting married? she'd asked. Oh, yes. In fact, to her. But he wasn't free to say that.

And when she'd replied, *Me, too,* jealousy's sharp fingers had driven into his heart.

Lately, over the past seventy-two hours, he'd begun to think about being her husband, more and more, until it consumed him. Waking up beside her, teaching his children to hunt and fish, to make pancakes—and he was a firm believer in equipping all children with life skills. But most of all, seeing Yanna become the amazing mother he knew she would be. Behind all those smarts and beauty, Yanna had a gentleness and commitment that would make her the top in yet another field.

But…and there it was, the big, looming, ugly *but* of his life. He was military to the core. It was all he had, all he did. He didn't know how to do anything else. And he'd take bets that Yanna didn't, either. Would their countries allow them to be on the same soil—even if they did resign? Cold War over or not, suspicions simmered under the surface of every political conversation, waiting to be stirred.

Of course, that very *but* was also the reason he loved her. Probably why he'd fallen in love with her, even in college. Because she understood him and the way he thought, and how it felt to be driven by some-thing bigger than himself. To want to make a differ-ence on the landscape of the world.

Which brought him to the big, flashing, neon-red reason…Yanna wasn't a Christian.

He'd kissed her, one last time, because, deep inside, he couldn't stop himself, and he knew that this was it.

After they found Elena, he would never see her again. It simply hurt too much. Tore huge chunks out of his heart every time he got near her. Every time they had an online conversation. After all these years, and especially the past few days, he was surprised he could still breathe, could still function.

Well, he couldn't really. Evidenced by the fact that here he was, sitting on a stakeout in a monkey suit with a beautiful woman in his arms rather than focusing on the party now spilling out into the night on the yacht. Kwan might have danced away, right under his nose, while David was caught by the expression in Yanna's beautiful eyes.

She was a distraction, and would always be one. And that could never be good for either of them. Which made him realize just how much he needed to stay away from her.

But he'd take the mental snapshot of her in his arms with him wherever he went. And he'd hope for happiness for her. *God, please help me let this woman go.*

Probably, he should be happy. He'd taken himself out of the picture. Hoo-yah, he was simply doing cartwheels.

"We'll be safe here."

Gracie turned the lock on the door to the cabin,

tucked into the woods, under the watchful embrace of Mount Rainier. The room smelled fresh, the balsam and pine scent reaped from the forest surrounding the cabins. The shaggy arms of night hovered over the cabin, and Gracie shivered as she turned on the lights, the heat.

It had taken her a few hours to get out of Seattle, hours she had spent cramming her heart back into her chest, of praying that Mae lost herself in the downtown traffic like she promised. Someone had to get to the police.

And someone had to hide Ina.

"I'm scared, Gracie," Ina had said. "Kosta won't let me go, he won't—"

Gracie took her hand off the wheel and touched Ina's arm. "Shh. You're going to be safe, I promise."

"You don't know him, you don't know what he does. The only reason I was still at the hotel was because Jorge wouldn't let him take me. He and Jorge had a terrible fight—I heard it. But Jorge told me that he wasn't going to let his brother take me. That he was going to find me and we would get marr—"

"Jorge is part of this trafficking operation, Ina." Gracie had tried to keep her voice from shaking, and really, she didn't want to snarl, but how could Ina be so stupid? Didn't she see that Jorge just wanted her for what she could give him? What he could get out of her? "Jorge was using you."

Ina folded her arms over her chest and stared out the window. "That's not true. Jorge loves me."

Oh yes, because every guy who loved his girl handed her over to his creepy Mafia cousin for what—two hundred bucks? She didn't even want to think where Ina might have ended up had Gracie not followed her gut instincts.

After winding their way around Seattle, making sure they hadn't been tailed, she really needed her gut to speak up, because she hadn't the faintest idea what to do next. The brilliant Master Plan B had been to separate and Mae would run back to the hospital to be with the Gromenkos while Gracie disappeared into the hills. They'd call—something that required the *cell* phone, which had been so conveniently left in the slimy hotel room back at the Ryss.

Which meant that Gracie hadn't the foggiest what might have happened to Mae. Perfect. "I'm hungry," Ina had said.

Hungry? Gracie wasn't sure she could ever eat again. "We'll get supper when we get where we're going."

"Which is where? I want to see my father."

"No. He's in the hospital, hopefully with my friend Mae, and I don't want to put them in any more danger."

"Jorge is innocent."

Did this girl have brain damage to go along with her other bruises? "Yeah, sure he is. Because it's normal for every boyfriend to sell off his girlfriend to the highest bidder."

Ina's face tightened.

"But assuming that Jorge was somehow forced into betraying you, his cousin—if they're even related—obviously isn't going to want you having a Q and A with the cops, let alone the media, so we need to get someplace safe and get a hold of Vicktor somehow."

"What's Vicktor going to do? Isn't he in Russia?"

That was the problem, wasn't it? Gracie released her death grip on the steering wheel, working the blood back into her hands. "He has friends here who will track down Jorge and Sokolov and nail them for what they did to you and hundreds of other girls like you."

If Vicktor was here, he'd also know what to do next. When she'd been on the lam from a serial killer in Russia, he'd been full of ideas.

Okay, so maybe not. Maybe he did this by the seat of his pants, too. He'd hid her at his father's house, and her friend's dacha—

That was it. As if she had a GPS talking to her, Gracie knew exactly where to take them both.

She finally felt her heartbeat begin to slow to a normal rhythm. No way Sokolov would find her here. Not a chance. Because *she'd* barely found it. Had it not been for the fact she'd ordered away for their brochure, and traced the route once or twice on the map, she would have sailed right past Paradise Cove without even tapping her brakes.

Ina, who had deemed Gracie unfit to be spoken to—Gracie had long ago given up trying to understand the mind of a teenager—flopped down on the sofa, putting her feet up on the wooden, made-from-logs table. Gracie closed the door behind her, locked it.

The cabin looked like something out of an old Western, log cabin walls, a rock fireplace, rusty horseshoes on a shelf above the worn leather sofa. On the log coffee table in front of the sofa, a candle sat in a basket surrounded by river rock. Gracie walked into the next room, a bedroom. She stood for a moment, wondering what it would be like to be here with Vicktor—as her husband. She'd even mentioned this place to him once or maybe twice, as someplace she'd like to go for their honeymoon. He probably hadn't been listening.

She sighed, exhaustion so deep she wanted to climb onto the huge queen-size bed, tuck herself under the red woven Navajo blanket and sleep for two weeks.

Right after she took a bath in that giant Jacuzzi in the corner.

She turned, and saw the other bedroom had twin beds, although no Jacuzzi.

Probably her tired mind had stopped thinking clearly because no one would be taking a Jacuzzi, because neither of them was on vacation.

They were, as the cop shows said, "on the lam." Not so much from justice, but from Sokolov and his band of thugs.

Gracie crossed her arms and leaned against the doorjamb, watching as Ina picked up the remote to the television and began to flip channels. She looked so…angry, as if her world had somehow upended.

Where was the "thanks for impersonating a house-keeper and saving my life, Gracie?"

Then again, Gracie had talked trash about Jorge, the Saint.

Apparently, Ina was utterly and completely under his spell. Well, she was a teenager.

"Ina, I'm sorry Jorge hurt you."

Ina's stoic face crumpled and she turned away. But Gracie saw her shoulders shake.

Gracie ached to reach out to her. "Listen, Ina, you're going to be okay. Someday you'll find a guy you can trust, and who will treat you…" *Like Vicktor treats me.* She closed her eyes.

She missed him. The past few days had stirred up the memories of that harrowing week when she'd been running for her life in Russia, and every single one of those memories included Vicktor. She'd been terrified, shaken by the death of her best friends, and Vicktor had been there. He'd questioned her, and even infuriated her, but he'd been gentle. And kind. And compassionate. And finally, he'd risked his life to save hers.

Ina turned to her. "I thought Jorge loved me." She wiped her eyes with the heels of her hands. "What's Vicktor like?"

Gracie sat on the wooden table, moving aside the stone centerpiece. "Vicktor is the most consid-erate man I've ever met. And a great cook. Tidy—everything has to be perfect, but he's not tame. In fact, he's always moving, always thinking. He has an energy about him that makes everything else in the room start to hum. And he has a protective gene that is more developed than most. But most of all, he loves me."

"Yeah, but how do you know he loves you?"

"Because…he shows it. He…" And suddenly Gracie drew a blank. "Well, he tells me, and he is faithful and honest and he worries about me."

"Do you love him?"

"Yes, of course."

But the answer came out so fast that Ina sat over there with a look of doubt on her face, and Gracie didn't blame her. Did she love Vicktor?

She loved his earnestness when he went after something. And she loved his desire to know God more. She loved the way he took care of his father, who'd been wounded by Vicktor's mistakes, and especially how he wanted to know every detail of her life. And not…maybe not because he was trying to drive her crazy and put some sort of tracking device on her. But because he genuinely wanted to know her.

Yes. Yes, she loved Vicktor. "I love him with everything inside me."

Ina was still staring at her. "So, if you love each other so much, why haven't you married him yet?"

That, at this moment, seemed to be the million-dollar question. Because she was an idiot? Because she hadn't been, and still wasn't entirely, sure that Vicktor wanted her, the real her? Because from her point of view, she seemed like a lot of trouble, personally. Maybe too much trouble. And take that all away and all she had left was her American citizenship.

She stared out the window at the darkness. "I don't know…maybe because I'm afraid that…that he loves me for what I can give him. Not for who I am."

Ina stared at her, a strange look in her eyes. "But isn't that what love is all about? Meeting each other's needs?"

Hmm. "What did Jorge tell you, Ina? That he needed you? And if you loved him…"

Ina looked away.

Oh no. Anger rushed into her chest. "That is a lie, Ina. A horrible lie. Love doesn't take…in fact…"

Vicktor didn't love her because she needed him, or even what she could give him, but because he just loved her. He'd loved her long before she had anything to offer. He loved her for what *he* could give *her*.

Her breath left her, as truth poured in, that truth she'd known for so long but never really let find her heart. Real love wasn't about receiving a response. Real love was about giving. And giving.

Even if it never received.

She looked up at Ina. "Real love says I love you, period. Not because of what you can give me. And not because I need you. Simply…because I am who I am. I learned that once, and sort of forgot it, I guess. But I know Vicktor loves me because…well, because I *haven't* married him yet and he keeps coming back. He still hangs around. Still hopes. And the next time I talk to him, we're going to figure that marriage part out."

Please, Vicktor, don't give up on us. On me.

Ina drew her legs up to her chest, looking about twelve years old and scared.

"Think about it, Ina. You didn't ask me for help, but I knew you needed me. So I came. And God is like that. He doesn't wait around until we call Him although, yes, He's not going to force you to need Him. Yet we do. The good news is that He's right there, loving us until we see Him, ready to rescue us. That's what Romans 5:8 is all about. When we didn't even know we needed Him, God loved us enough to save us."

Ina's expression changed. Tears welled in her eyes and she cupped her hands over her face. "Oh no. I did a terrible thing."

A thousand possible fill-in-the-blank answers rushed to Gracie's mind—things she didn't want to imagine, things that she'd name terrible—

"I called Jorge."

No, now *that,* she didn't have on her list. Gracie sat there, and it must have looked like maybe she didn't hear her because Ina looked up, tears reddening her pretty face, dripping off her chin. "Did you hear me—I called Jorge!"

"Okay, so you called him." Gracie lifted her hands. "No big deal, we're four hours from Seattle, and—"

Ina got to her feet, throwing the pillow across the room. It hit the window, skidded to the floor. "I *borrowed* the cell phone from a lady in McDonald's—and when you were checking us in…I called Jorge."

Gracie froze. She remembered that woman. She'd been on the phone, relaying a take-out order for her family. Gracie remembered thinking, *six* Happy Meals? She must have put the phone down, only to have Ina swipe it.

Which meant Gracie was an accessory to a cell phone robbery. Getaway driver/missionary. Perfect.

She tightened her jaw. "Well, he still can't find us. Because Paradise Cove isn't easy to find."

"No, you don't get it. I called him from McDonald's, from the bathroom. And then, again when we got here. I told him where we were."

Oh.

Oh.

"Okay, okay, uh…" Wait. "Do you still have that cell phone? Because maybe I can call Mae and—"

A noise, outside on the porch step, made her jump. She looked at the door, at the way the lock rattled and her only thought was…

So much for Paradise.

Chapter Sixteen

Yanna finally fell asleep against David, her head up against his chest, and didn't wake until the sun began to dent the horizon. David shook her awake and helped her onto the back of the bike. And drove her back to Trish and Cho's house.

She crawled into bed, shivering, and fell into a hard, dreamless sleep.

Unfortunately, while she'd been sleeping, David had briefed Roman, showered, and headed back out to Kwan's lair.

Without her.

She was going to strangle him. Yanna stood on the roof in a pair of Trish's yoga pants and a T-shirt, overlooking a thousand other roofs, the kitchen gardens overflowing with peppers and tomatoes in pots. She folded her arms over her chest, not sure where to put the anger that wanted to seep out.

Maybe she should scream.

Because she'd finally figured it out.

David had said he respected her. At the time, she'd found it sweet, a sort of peace offering after her abysmal decision to go after Kwan. But his kiss last night had been filled with pity, not passion.

Goodbye, even.

And now she realized it was just a lousy way to say, *I'll put you in a tower and throw away the key.* A man who respected her, who *believed* in her wouldn't leave her behind like a three-year-old while he tailed the man who had kidnapped her sister. And apparently, it was a fraternity, because Roman had gone right along with him.

Clearly, she'd have to strangle Roman, too.

Wrapped up in her fury, she didn't hear Trish approach from the open door to the terrace. "Yanna, how are you feeling?"

Yanna looked at the woman, so cute in her little pink maternity top, her short caramel-brown hair blowing in the slight wind.

She didn't want to answer that, so she shrugged.

"I know you're upset about not going along— David said you would be. But he was worried about you. He said you were tired." She touched Yanna, but she shifted away. "He has the cell phone."

"I'm not calling him on a stakeout."

Trish looked as if she'd been slapped. "Sorry. I agreed that you needed some time to rest. You looked worn pretty thin when you came in last night."

Oh, great, another person telling her how she felt,

what she needed. She tried to smile at Trish, something to soothe the fracture between them, but it didn't work. Trish didn't smile back, and in fact stepped forward, past Yanna, to stare down at the road, the scooter traffic. The wind chimes caught, tinkled their sound across Yanna's nerves.

"He's just trying to keep you safe, and help you find your sister."

"I know. It's just that…I didn't come to Taiwan looking for help," Yanna sniped, although, what would she have done if David hadn't been here? She hadn't spent enough time, probably, thinking about that. About what he'd given up for her—i.e., his mission, his goals, three months of disgusting undercover work stalking Kwan and his pals. She didn't even want to think about what he'd had to do to earn a trip to Kwan's yacht.

And now, after everything, they had even less than they had before. Before she had some sort of unfounded, ethereal hope.

Now, she just had reality.

"Sometimes we need help, even if we don't think so. Even when we don't want it," Trish said quietly.

Yanna glanced at Trish, who picked up a watering can and went over to the outside faucet to fill it. "Besides, I think David has some deep feelings for you."

Not enough, however. She folded her arms. "Here's the thing, Trish," Yanna said. "David might love me—might be crazy about me, but he can't act on it. For lots of reasons, mostly good ones, he constantly pulls away from me." She turned around, facing Trish, who was watering her tomatoes.

"I'm okay with that. I mean, yes, I…care about David. But I was living with reality, the fact that I will probably be alone for the rest of my life, or at least that David and I will never be anything, when he steps right back into my life. I don't want him, I don't need him. I just want to find my sister."

There, that felt good. Like pulling a knife from her bleeding heart.

Or not.

Trish moved on to the next plant. Examined the leaves.

"Maybe I'm *not* okay with it." She didn't have to close her eyes to remember David's arms around her, remember his breath on her neck, remember… "Maybe I am dying a little bit inside, but there is nothing I can do about it. David is a soldier—he always will be. And he doesn't have room in his life for a relationship. At least not for one with me."

Trish looked up, gave her a strange look. Sighed.

"What?"

"Are you sure that's why he pulls away from you? Could it be because you don't believe in the most important part of his life?"

Yanna frowned, but the words zeroed in and made her flinch. Trish was right. David wasn't just a soldier—he was a dreamer, the kind that made other people want to believe his dreams, too.

"David is all about fairy tales and God, but I've had an up-close-and-personal look at the world and I…I just don't believe God cares about people. Not like that. And that seems to be an issue for David."

"Do you know why that's an issue, Yanna?"

She stared at Trish, then sighed, turned away.

"Because David believes that this life matters beyond the now. That there is an eternity out there, and that the things he does here and now have impact on the future, his eternal future," Trish said.

See, a dreamer. Yanna stared out at the beautiful tropical island sky. It might be nice to believe that someone—someone big and powerful like God—cared. Was on her side. Watched her back, like David suggested. That the things she did mattered beyond now, that her life mattered.

For a second, she let those thoughts find a home. Wiggle inside.

Perhaps she…maybe she wanted to believe, just a little.

She wasn't sure why. Possibly because she'd always wondered what made David the man he was—a man of passion and strength. A man who hoped. Who didn't surrender.

A man she could count on even if it didn't go her way.

A man whose beliefs were so strong, so vividly written on every inch of him that it made her hurt that she didn't have that, too.

Sometimes, like now, when she felt the world was caving in, yes, she might want to believe.

But she wasn't going to say that, not yet, and not to Trish.

Behind her, she heard Trish put down her watering can. She came over to Yanna. "I envy you," Trish said.

Yanna shot her a look.

"I do," Trish said. "You are one of the smartest, most creative women I've ever met. The way you took apart those cell phones to make communication gadgets. And you were so incredibly brave at the teahouse. I just sat there drinking my tea, thinking I might wet my pants or something."

Yanna smiled. Yeah, well, Trish didn't have to know how close she'd come to that, too. More than once in the past few days.

"And I'd give just about anything for the way you fit into that dress."

Yeah, well, Trish had curves, cute ones, and Yanna opened her mouth to tell her so when—

"But I guess I'm lucky, too."

Huh?

"Because I don't have my brains and beauty to keep me from forsaking the grace that could be mine."

Yanna closed her mouth.

"It's not a weakness to believe in Someone. To depend on them. Especially if that person is out for your good. Your eternal good."

Yanna had the strangest, unsettling feeling that

perhaps Trish wasn't talking about…David. In fact, nope, because—

"The world spends an awful lot of time trying to come up with reasons why they don't need God. But you know, even if you don't think you need Him, it doesn't make His love for you any less. And I'll bet, when you turn around and take a look at what He is doing in your life, how much He loves you, you're going to rethink whether you need Him or not."

Maybe Trish might be talking about David, just a little, too.

Yanna opened her mouth, but nothing came out. Not words, at least.

Because at that moment, she wasn't a supersecret agent, but just a woman, a tired, overwhelmed woman, a woman who didn't know what else to do when three men rushed at her from behind Trish.

So, she screamed—and stepped in front of pregnant Trish to protect her as Kwan's men reached out to grab them.

"I see movement down there." Roman had his eyes glued to a pair of binoculars—real binoculars he'd purchased last night while David and Yanna were running around Taiwan, her in stocking feet and a silky dress.

While David had been saying goodbye. At least in his heart.

"Is it Kwan?"

Roman didn't answer for a moment, then, "No, one of his bodyguards. But he's definitely up to something. He's climbing into the limo, talking into a radio." He put the glasses down. "I think one of us should tail him."

David nodded. "I'm down with that. You go—I'll stay here and keep track of Kwan. Take the scooter."

David dug into his pocket for the key to his latest ride—Cho's scooter. Thankfully, his brain cells had been firing enough this morning to prophecy the scenario that he and Roman might have to separate to tail Kwan.

He'd given approximately zero-point-six seconds to the idea that he should wake Yanna. After finally flushing the panic from his system—probably around five this morning—he had made a final decision.

A decision he knew would seal their fate.

She wasn't getting near Kwan again. He didn't care if he had to duct tape her to Trish's kitchen chair, Yanna wasn't leaving the house until he brought Elena to her doorstep. And even then, only to get into the van, drive straight to Taipei, and get outta Dodge—or Taiwan, as it were.

And even after *that*, he had made Roman promise to keep an eye on her for a very long time, because neither of them was stupid enough to think Kwan wouldn't track her down, even in Russia.

Kwan probably had distant relatives on every corner of the planet, every one of them aching to be next in line for the so-called Serpent Throne. Taking out one FSB agent surely wouldn't give them a moment's pause. In fact, there might even be a bidding war. Which meant that after David got Yanna on a plane, and after he'd made Roman shadow her every move, he had to return to Kaohsiung and track down the real Kwan. And now, Serpent number two. They just kept breeding…

Again David had the overwhelming urge to simply throw Yanna over his shoulder and disappear. But that cavemanesque response wasn't what a girl like Yanna deserved.

Not at all.

He put his hand to his chest, right where it hurt as he watched Roman drive away.

Lord, please help us find Elena. And help Yanna see that You do care, You do love her.

He kept his eyes on Kwan's yacht.

His new cell phone rang. It was a cheapie he'd picked up at the market, with a disposable minutes card. He flipped it open, not able to read the identity. "Yeah."

"David—"

Just the tone, the way his name came out short, with pain, made every cell in his body tense.

"Trish?"

"David, they came, and they got her…."

Got…oh, no. Breathe. Just breathe. "Trish, are you okay?"

"Cho's hurt, and I…I…" Her intake of breath cut off her voice, and the sobbing that followed had David already putting the van into gear, already on autopilot.

"Hang on, Trish, I'll be right there. Just hang on. And lock your doors."

"Yeah…" she hiccuped. "Hurry, David…hurry."

Please, God. He roared out into traffic, nearly taking out a couple of scooters—*watch out, boys*—and sped through the next, yellowish light.

No, no. How had Kwan found—

Oh no. They'd been careful, and if Kwan knew where they were, he could have snatched them last night.

Unless he didn't want David, just Yanna.

Again, that didn't make sense, because David had seen him.

No, David had seen his *imposter.* He hadn't met the real Kwan, he knew it in his bones.

Then why kidnap Yanna? And how?

The bottom line was, this was David's fault for letting himself be distracted.

He dodged a car and honked his horn at a couple of pedestrians who thought they might be able to win in a metal-to-flesh game of chicken.

The alleyways of Taiwan had about a millimeter of clearance for the van, and he went through them like he might a computer game, fast, following his instincts. He did take out a planter—heard it fly up and splatter on the ground behind him—but didn't slow, and thanked God that he didn't also kill anyone.

Yet.

Please, don't let Kwan hurt her. *Please.* He wiped

an edge of wetness below his eye. Apparently, his fatigue and stress had overflowed his cup.

Oh, who was he trying to kid? If anything happened to Yanna he'd never make it. He'd curl in a ball somewhere, dark and horrible, screaming.

Why hadn't he pushed her—made her confront the idea that God cared about her?

No, why hadn't he told her he loved her? Really, finally, in good and bad, Kwan or no Kwan, over e-mail and up close, loved her?

Do you trust God, David?

He wiped away another tear as he pulled up to the Yungs' house.

I hope. *Please help me trust You, God.*

He braked, and the car screeched and he slammed it into Park, getting out before it had come to a complete halt. Then he was inside.

What he saw made him hold on for a second to the door frame. "Trish, how bad is it?"

Cho had been hurt—the bloody cut and Everest-size goose egg over his eye testified to something hard connecting with his skull. David winced just looking at it. In true horror-movie fashion, blood had run down his face and was pooled in the collar of his dress shirt. More blood stained his sleeve.

But it was Trish who had David's attention, the way she sat on the sofa, holding her stomach, breathing hard. Cho sat beside her, his hand on her stomach, and he looked up when David entered.

"What happened?"

A scratch down the side of Trish's face oozed rivulets of blood. Concrete meets face, and concrete had won. "They surprised us—Cho was downstairs—I didn't even see them coming. I just looked up, and they were inside."

Trish moaned, which cut off Cho's words and made him go white. "I have to get you to the doctor."

Trish couldn't take a breath, but then neither could David, or Cho probably, considering that his unborn child was probably fighting for life.

"Did they hit you?" David said, grabbing up the phone and tossing it to Cho. "Call nine-one-one again."

"No—I mean, yes, but Yanna took most of it. They came in with this long pole, probably the same one they used on Cho." Trish put her hand out, touching his cheek, her face crumpling as she mentally relived the attack. "And Yanna saw it coming and she stepped in front of me. It knocked us both down." She put her hand over her stomach, again, and made a face that prompted Cho to dial.

"Are you sure it was Kwan's men?"

"No, I don't know. I didn't ask. I just…just lay there as they hauled up Yanna. She was kicking and screaming, and landed at least one punch—"

Oh, swell. Give them another reason to hit you, Yanna. David sank down to a crouch because suddenly his stomach wasn't feeling so well.

"But they hit her and told her to shut up."

He put his hand up, wanting to stop her words but knowing he couldn't and instead covered his eyes with his hand. "Did they kill her?" Had he really asked that? Or worse, was he ready for the answer, because that thought knocked him off his feet and he had to sink all the way to the floor, one hand out to take the weight. He took some deep breaths. Nearly put his head between his knees.

Oh, Lord.

"No—they had a pretty tight grip on her when they left, but she wasn't howling anymore, in fact it almost looked like she was cooperating." This, from Cho, who cut off his testimony to talk to whoever had answered the phone.

Cooperating? David stared at Trish, who had ducked her head, breathing hard now through whatever pain gripped her. What would make Yanna not fight?

Elena.

They had Elena. And Yanna went with them because they told her so and she believed them.

He leaned back, breathing hard, sweating.

Get a grip, David.

Only, what, exactly, would getting a grip look like when the woman he loved had been hauled out to who knows where by a couple of human traffickers? *Unraveled. Unhinged*—now those words he could embrace.

Cho had hung up, and he turned to his wife. "The ambulance is on its way. Just try and stay calm."

Calm. It was possible David would never be calm again.

Cho looked up at him, gave him a grim look. "You're going to get her back, David."

He stared hard at Cho, at those dark eyes, a rabid suspicion that made him both ashamed and furious, rising from some haunted place inside him.

"He left that—" Cho pointed to a manila envelope on the table. Next to it sat Yanna's smashed laptop. "He said to tell you to wait for his call. Kwan will trade Yanna...for you."

Vicktor was prepared for Gracie to be surprised. To react, even to stare at him, maybe even yell. But he didn't think Gracie had that kind of aim. He barely managed to miss the flying—metal? Before it banged on the door, chipping out a piece of wood.

The second missile caught him in the forehead. Blinding pain made him hit the dirt, or at least the wood-planked floor. "Gracie, stop! It's me—Vicktor."

And then, silence. Pure silence during which he wondered if he'd passed out, because his head certainly spun, the pain centered right there in the middle, throbbing. He reached up and sure enough, not just a goose egg, but blood.

Oh, wasn't this a great way to make an entrance.

But he quickly put his hand back down because the floor had lurched up at him, and his cheek connected and he was down for a two-count.

And then Gracie was there. Right beside him, kneeling over him, a cool hand over his wound, pulling him up toward her, into her arms.

He leaned back, against Gracie, letting her hand stop the bleeding. Breathing hard, he looked up at her.

Her expression was shocked, but only for a second, because then her eyes started to shine with tears—or maybe fright—and she swallowed and managed a shaky smile.

He might just live.

Or slide happily into unconsciousness.

"Vicktor, I can't believe it. What are you doing here?" But she didn't wait for an answer, just bent down and kissed his cheek, holding him.

No, this wasn't going to work. He let her hold him a second longer, then leaned up, turned and, while she held his head, he put his hands around her waist, pulled her to him and kissed her.

And as if she were *ecstatic* to see him, she kissed him back. Arm around his shoulder, holding on, kissing him back like she hadn't seen him for months…or years. Like she wasn't remotely tired of him, or annoyed by him.

Like she still loved him.

He felt his panic begin to shake free—not the panic that had made him rent a car and drive as if he might be on the autobahn, straight to the place where she said she wanted their honeymoon—but the deeper panic.

The one that told him she no longer needed him. No longer loved him.

Gracie.

He might be trembling so he pulled back, breathing hard, and ran his eyes over her face.

She smiled up at him, her beautiful eyes bright. "I can't believe you're here."

"Surprise."

She shook her head, incredulity on her face. "How did you find me?"

He shrugged. "I know you."

That obviously touched her, because she nodded and wiped a finger under her eye. "You do."

"Yeah. Just a little." He cupped his hand under her chin. "And I was worried about you. You sounded weird on the phone, and when you sent me that text, well, Roman ran the name, and I did the math, and when I couldn't get a hold of you…I…"

"You hopped on a plane to America."

He swallowed. But she didn't stop grinning.

"You *hopped* on a plane to America."

"Yeah, okay, I did do that. But not because you're incapable or anything. It was just because…because I'm a panicker. I do stupid things, and it probably won't be the last time I do something really over the top, but in this case, I'm glad I came because—"

"Because we're in trouble."

This from the girl standing in the doorway to another room. A thin girl, about eighteen or so, with long brownish-blond hair and a face that looked definitely Russian. She wore American clothes, however—sweatpants and tennis shoes and a down vest—and, most important, held another horseshoe in her hand. "Were you the one who hit me?"

"No, that was me," Gracie said, taking her hand

away and looking at his wound. She made a face. "That won't be pretty. You might even have a scar."

"It'll be a memory." He found his feet, closed the door and locked it. "The time when Grandma nearly took Grandpa's head off."

Gracie made a little whimpering sound, and he reached down to pull her up. Then, one last time, because he had to, and because his heart was still pounding hard, he pulled her tight against him and held on.

She held him back. "I was hoping you'd come."

"Really?" he whispered. Please, let it be true, and not because she was in trouble and might be happy to see anyone on her side, but because she really meant it. Because she hoped *he* would be the one knocking at her door.

"Deep down inside, I think I'm always hoping that." Her smile faded. "Wait a second—how did you get into the country so quickly? You don't have a—"

He put his finger over her mouth. "A little bit illegal, here, *dorogaya.*"

Gracie's eyes widened, her smile now completely gone. "If you get caught."

"I won't get caught."

"But—"

A sound made Vicktor freeze. Footsteps, on gravel. Outside. And them with the lights on, televising their every move. He flicked off the lights.

"Get down."

But it was too late, because whoever was outside

had friends inside, too. Glass broke in the bedroom, then, before Vicktor could get them someplace safe—like, where, behind the sofa?—footsteps rushed through the house.

One came in behind Gracie's horseshoe-holding friend. He grabbed the girl around the neck and added a gun to her temple for oomph.

Vicktor stepped in front of Gracie.

"Jorge, put down the gun," Gracie said slowly.

But Vicktor's eyes were on the men coming in through the door. With an ax.

Welcome to America.

Chapter Seventeen

Vicktor was here. In America. *Here.*

And about to get killed. Because shortly after her Russian hero had jumped in front of her, the door with its flimsy lock had slammed open, and two men had rushed in, one holding the ax.

Which hit the floor right where she and Vicktor had been standing.

She ended up near the sofa—Vicktor must have thrown her—and as she blinked to clear her head, she saw Sokolov take Vicktor to the ground.

Meanwhile, Jorge had Ina by the hair. "No, Jorge!" Gracie called, as Ina clawed his arm.

She'd counted three attackers, Sokolov on Vicktor, Jorge grappling with Ina, and number three—sure enough, she threw her hands over her head as something came crashing down over her. She dodged, and it hit the sofa.

Her attacker lunged toward her, off balance.

Gracie brought up her knee, connected with his gut, and groped for one of those decorative rocks from the coffee table.

Her hand curled around it just as her attacker grabbed her throat.

She hit him with everything inside her, all her fury and frustration. An explosion of payback that probably saved her a couple thousand dollars in counseling. Blam! Right on his temple and the man went down.

On her.

She screamed, pushing him off her, kicking free and climbing out from under him.

Ina had vanished into the bedroom, but Gracie could hear screaming. She scrambled toward the sound.

Or—

Sokolov sat on top of Vicktor, and whatever had happened ended with Vicktor on the bottom. Sokolov held the sharp end of the ax an inch away from Vicktor's throat while he leaned into him. Blood coursed out of the wound on Vicktor's head.

Vicktor spoke some not very nice words in Russia, real low.

And Sokolov spit at him.

Then he elbowed Vicktor, hard in the face. Vicktor didn't even flinch, eyes on the ax.

Gracie looked at the rock in her hand, and fired it off.

She'd played high school softball for just this reason.

It hit Sokolov in the head, knocked him off just enough for Vicktor to push him away. And that was all Vicktor needed. Just like that he had Sokolov in a submission hold, his hand bent back, Vicktor's knee in Sokolov's spine, gripping his neck.

"Call the police, Gracie!"

The cell phone, the *cell phone.* Ina had been reaching for it—yes, there under the table. Gracie dove, picked it up.

A gunshot sounded from the bedroom.

Gracie dropped the phone. "Ina!"

"Nine-one-one, Gracie!"

But she couldn't think, couldn't breathe. Because she saw, in her mind's eye, Ina, lying on the floor, in a pool of blood, lots of blood, just like her friends in Russia, and she began to shake.

Sokolov swore, kicking at Vicktor.

Vicktor shoved his face into the floor. "Gracie! Call for help, right now. Pick up the phone."

But she just stared at him, unable to move.

He must have seen her fear, because his face softened, as did his voice. "It'll be okay."

And right then, she wondered what was so horrible about needing him? Because more often than she liked, her past rose up to haunt her, and she needed his voice in her ear, to break her free from the past. To remind her that she had, and would, live.

"You're okay, Gracie. I promise, it'll be okay. Pick up the phone."

She grabbed the phone. Punched in 9-1-1.

Froze. "If the cops come, you'll be arrested. They'll deport you—you'll never be able to come back."

"Call them." Vicktor looked up at her, eyes dark, fierce.

As he spoke, Ina came out of the bedroom, blood down the front of her, dazed, stumbling. "I shot him." She started to shake, dropped the gun on the floor. Then crumpled beside it. "I shot Jorge."

Gracie pushed Send.

Mission accomplished, she'd found her sister. Only, Yanna should probably work on her goal-setting techniques because although she'd found— or *hopefully* found—her sister, she'd neglected the second half of the plan, which was, *and escape alive.*

Oh, yeah. That part. Alive and without getting David killed in the process. Although, when she'd started out on this jaunt into her worst nightmares, she really hadn't realized how much company she might have.

Like Trish. Who had gone down hard onto her cement roof terrace, even though Yanna had taken the hit for her, and when Yanna had left, she'd been in a ball, writhing, protecting the life inside her.

If Yanna ever felt like believing big, and then, perhaps, *praying* big, it was now. Because she could use someone like God on her side. If He felt like listening or caring. And not only about Trish, for now Yanna had joined a group of women in various stages of hunger and pain and fear. They'd all been shoved into a basement warehouse room, under some thumping noisy club—Yanna guessed casino—and were probably bound for some far-off country to live the rest of their life in bondage.

And lucky her, she just might be among the statistics.

"Elena?" Yanna stood there staring at the four tiers of bunks lining the walls, women jammed shoulder to shoulder on them, like something she might see in a prison camp, complete with the smell of sweat and fear. Then the world turned dark as the door closed behind her, metal scraping on metal. It made every nerve in her body gasp. Her eyes struggled to adjust and make out the shapes through the pinpoints of light that broke through the grime of the shoe-box-size window.

"Elena?" She heard the fear in her voice. She had never been so afraid in her life and didn't know how to handle this kind of terror. Confirming that really, she'd never been cut out to be a secret agent.

"Yanna? Yanna!" Movement, somewhere at the end of the room, and then steps, running steps, broken sobs.

Then someone grabbed her, and she knew, despite the sharp bones and the smell of neglect…Elena.

"Oh, Elena." Yanna wrapped her arms around her skinny—now skinnier—sister and pulled her tight, shaking, not sure who might be sobbing harder. "I thought I'd lost you. I thought…"

"I thought I'd never see you again. I…they…" Elena held tighter, and Yanna didn't want to ask, didn't want to know what Elena had been through.

Maybe she'd ask later, when they were safe and back home. Her imagination was enough to cut off her breathing. She'd never let Elena out of her sight again.

"It's okay, Elena. You're going to be okay. We're all going to be okay."

Not that she actually believed that. Oh, she wanted to believe it, but she had heard what Kwan's men said as they'd left Cho's—trade her for David?

They meant, lure David in. And kill him.

She held Elena tighter, so tight that she knew it had to be for herself now.

"I was so scared. I'm such an idiot. Why did I believe that…that Bob, or whoever, wanted to marry me."

"You couldn't know," Yanna said, running a hand over her sister's greasy hair.

"I should have listened to you. Should have stayed in Russia, been like you—independent and strong. I'm so…" Her voice shook. "I'm so stupid."

"You're not stupid." Yanna backed away, holding her sister's face in her hands, tipping her forehead down to touch their faces together. "You believed in something. And that's not stupid. That's brave. The bad part is that you put your belief in the wrong thing."

It's not a weakness to believe in someone. To depend on them. Especially if that person is out for your eternal good.

Trish's words came back to her, and Yanna closed her eyes, pulled Elena to herself. *I want to believe.* She said the words to herself, to…whoever might be listening. *Help me believe.*

Help me believe.

"It's not so great to be like me, Elena. I wish…well, there is so much I wish for you. And for me. But right now, I gotta figure out a way to get us out of here."

Before, *please…God*—before David answered Kwan's page. Because without a doubt, Yanna knew he would want to.

And Kwan was banking on David's honor. On his loyalty. He'd seen the way David had gotten her off Kwan's boat, and even out of his house. Yeah, Kwan knew exactly how to get David's attention.

She closed her eyes. But why, exactly, would David trade his life for hers?

He wouldn't—no, couldn't. Because even though they cared about each other, they were just friends. Really good friends, yes, but in the end, David had a mission.

And that mission wasn't to save his Russian friend from human traffickers. He'd abandoned his agenda for the past few days trying to help her, but at heart David was a patriot. And if that meant sacrificing friends…

Breaking promises.

Yanna tightened her jaw. She had to do this alone and, despite Trish's words, depend on no one but herself.

She put Elena away from her. Then she reached up and pulled her earring from her lobe. "Anyone here still holding a watch? And maybe, some gum?"

* * *

"I want to marry you."

Vicktor turned at Gracie's voice and watched her as she came into the room, drying her hands on a towel after she'd done her best to wash the blood off Ina. Yes, Jorge was dead, thanks to a wild shot that had hit him dead center in the chest. How Ina had gotten the gun still wasn't clear, but Vicktor had an idea it had to do with the fact they'd found him dead not on the floor, but on the bed, the covers mussed.

Good for Ina.

If she hadn't done it, Vicktor might have, and wouldn't that be a nice addendum to his list of charges?

He had used duct tape from Gracie's car supply kit to tape Kosta Sokolov into submission. And while he'd done it, he'd paid particular note to his ring, the one with the snake and the red ruby eyes. Something about it was ringing bells, although he couldn't put a mark on it. Vicktor even taped Sokolov's mouth shut, because he couldn't take one more second of the man's Russian. Or his English, for that matter. Sokolov had too fluently grasped the less savory nuances of both languages.

Vicktor finished wrapping the tape around Sokolov's shoulders, securing him to the chair, and turned to face Gracie.

And her statement.

"I want to marry you." She threw the towel onto the table and looked up at him, her beautiful eyes no longer carrying a haunted, broken look, but now fierce, so fierce that it shook him.

"Yeah, me, too." He reached out to take her hand, because he wanted that almost more than anything. However at the top on his priority list was—hold Gracie. And second on the list—hold Gracie. Maybe number three was hold Gracie, too, but by that time, yes, maybe they had better be married.

But she moved away from him and folded her arms over her chest. "I want to marry you, now. Right now." She'd lost weight since he saw her last, and her jeans hung baggy on her. Her T-shirt had smudges of blood—his blood, probably.

He raised an eyebrow. "In that?"

"Funny. No. Or yes, I don't care. But I want to hop in the car and head west. We're only about a half day's drive from Vegas, and we'll get married. Today. Before they can find you and arrest you and…" Her chin quivered. "Take you away from me."

In the distance, sirens whined.

But in his heart, he heard only a sigh of relief. "No one is going to take me away from you, Gracie. I'm here, to stay. That's what you have to get here—I'm not going anywhere unless you boot me out of your life."

And for a second, he let his fears hang there in the open, because he had to know.

"I'm not going to boot you out of my life," she said softly.

Relief rushed through him, so much that for a second he thought he might be woozy again. He stepped toward her, but she backed away. The sirens grew louder.

"No, you don't understand. I really want to marry you. I don't want to wait. I hate this living on two sides of the globe, and I want to be your wife."

His *wife*. He hadn't realized how incredible that word might sound, and for a second, he was right there with her, in the car, breaking speed limits to get married. But as who? Vladimir Zaitsev? That thought brought him back to reality. Not only would America give him the heave-ho, but probably, since she would be an accessory to some sort of crime, i.e. marrying a fugitive, Russia would never let her in, either.

And then they'd live…where?

"Gracie, I want to marry you right. In a church, with our friends, and before God. I don't want Elvis singing at our wedding. I want you in a white dress because we both deserve that, and I want to know when I walk back down the aisle, I'm not going to be arrested and go through the next ten years waiting to see you."

Her eyes filled.

"Most of all, I'm not marrying you until you're ready. Really ready. And I know we haven't seen each other for a while, but tomorrow, when I'm back on a plane to Russia, and you're back in your apartment, you'll be able to think. Clearly. And that's when I want your answer. No—" he held up a hand "—I want it in a month."

Gracie bit her lip, but this time, when he stepped close, she let him, and he put his arms around her.

"Why do you love me?" she asked, lifting her face to his.

Oh, that was an easy question. The hard part was where to start. "Because you're beautiful. And smart. And you care about people. And you're brave. And most of all because you let me be the guy I am and don't get mad when I fly across the ocean just to check up on you."

She grinned, smoothed her hands down his chest. "I need a lot of checking up on."

"Yes, Gracie, you do." And then, because the police lights flashed across their window, and because he just might not have another chance for a long, long time, he kissed her.

Chapter Eighteen

"Can I just tell you that this is an abysmally bad idea, and although I really dropped the ball in letting Yanna run off without backup, I learned my lesson and you are not going to do this alone." Roman had said this as he sat in the van outside the harbor.

"You could say that, but I wouldn't listen," David had replied.

Only, maybe he should have listened, because right now, as Kwan's men frisked him, blindfolded him, then put him into cuffs that looked very much like the ones Yanna had worn—Kwan must order them by the carton—David could really use Roman on his right hand.

Or left. Or behind him. Just skulking around would be okay, too.

Anywhere that would put Roman in the vicinity of Yanna, and hopefully Elena, close enough to grab them while David obeyed Kwan's texted message to go down to Kwan's dock, and offer himself up as a living sacrifice.

Sadly, he hadn't seen hide nor hair of Yanna when he'd shown up, unarmed. But he went through with the exchange anyway because he'd be afraid. Really, bone-deep afraid that Kwan wouldn't wait around to negotiate, and would simply dump Yanna's body into the surf.

David didn't care what Kwan did to him, as long as Yanna was safe. He had promised to get her home, and with his last breath, he planned on keeping that promise.

He would have appreciated some providential help in keeping that promise, however—i.e., being shoved into the trunk of the limousine—the GPS-tagged limousine. But there was no such help, because by the way his knees hit his chin, Kwan's goons had crammed him into a much smaller space, probably one of those compacts he had a hard time riding in even when he was in the passenger area of the car.

Riding in the trunk had also skewed his bearings, which had probably been precisely what Kwan intended.

David had to wonder if maybe Kwan had planned this all along. He didn't really have to track David down—just take something that mattered, the *only* thing that mattered to David. And he'd come running, waving his hands above his head. Me, me, pick me.

Please, Yanna, be alive. David hadn't the vaguest backup plan, but then again, he'd been going full speed ahead, don't-look-back ever since he had found Yanna on the boat, and well, backup plans usually entailed a primary plan.

Which was…?

Stay alive sounded good. Except, he didn't expect that, not really. The thought filled him with literal pain, the kind that made him groan.

God, I so wanted to… He'd wanted to do a lot. Like tell Yanna he loved her—no, more than tell her. Marry her. Be a part of her life.

See her finally, fully healed from her past, from her betrayals.

However, at this point, he might settle for just seeing her alive. With Elena.

He'd name that Plan A.

David tried to listen for identifying noises, something other than street traffic. Like the tinny sound of Taiwanese music, maybe coming from a market, or shrine, maybe the sound of ships, although he knew they'd taken him far from the harbor. Or voices, someone speaking in the car, something that might tell him where they'd taken Yanna.

The car stopped and, in a moment, the trunk opened. Fresh air whooshed in, and hands yanked him out over the back.

He heard voices now, laughter, and felt the cool night air over him. Then, rock music, loud and raucous.

Rough hands pushed him forward and he nearly

fell down a flight of stairs. He got his footing near the bottom, but Seeing-Eye Dropout behind him shoved him through the door, into a basement, or perhaps a corridor. He heard feet scuffling against cement, smelled mold and dampness.

Breathe. At least he'd get another face-to-face with Kwan. At least he could go down kicking.

A knock at a door. It opened and a shove to his spine pushed him inside.

Someone grabbed his hair and kicked him in the back of his legs, and he didn't need another hint. He went down on his knees into something damp.

And then—and he had the slightest warning in the intake of breath, just enough to brace himself—something hit him across the face. Pain exploded in his head. He tasted blood, tinny and acrid in his mouth.

He righted himself, shaking his head, as if to break the grip of pain, but really to dislodge the blindfold.

It worked. He saw wan light, designer shoes, a puddle of something dark and brown beneath him. Please let it not be blood.

"I thought we had a deal."

Silence. He braced himself for another hit, but it didn't come.

And then, to his surprise, hands untied the blindfold.

David blinked into the shadows. Looked up. Kwan smiled at him. "Welcome back, Mr. Ripley. Somehow I knew you'd agree to my terms."

They were in a room, a basement room evident by the light feebly pushing the last of the day through the tiny window. There was no furniture in the room save a lumpy futon on the floor, soiled and smelling foul.

David gave his best I'm-going-to-kill-you-with-my-bare-hands look, and said, "Let her go."

Kwan looked up at the men beside him, and David half expected a kick, maybe to his midsection. In fact he tightened his stomach, waiting for it.

But Kwan knelt down before him. He reached out and touched David, his hand under his chin.

Every cell in David's body recoiled. But he swallowed, met Kwan's gaze. "I want Yanna."

"And I want answers."

David frowned. "Okay, the Red Sox finally won the World Series, the Democrats took over Congress, the price of oil has dropped this quarter, and you're a dead man."

Kwan shook his head, smiling. "I find you intriguing, Mr. Ripley."

"I think you're about as interesting as toe slime. So, why don't you get to the point, Kwan?"

Kwan backed away, nodded.

And now came the pain, another swift explosion, this time to his kidneys. David groaned, despite himself, and tried not to fall over. He fought to catch his breath, breathing now through gritted teeth. He looked up at Kwan, blinking back stars.

"You're a fool, David Curtiss."

David blinked at his use of his name.

"Major David Curtiss. Special Ops, I think?"

David stared at him, hating Bruce with everything inside him.

"Because what you don't know," he smiled, "is that I'm not Kwan."

David had known Kwan wasn't really Kwan. Just known it. How desperate did it make him that he wanted to pump his fist into the air and say, *I knew it!* "Oh?"

"And my boss, he's a nervous man. He wasn't real happy that you got away."

"What a shame. 'Cause I was thrilled."

"Yes, I told him that you were a flea, that it didn't matter, but he's a demanding man. And he doesn't trust anyone."

"Don't see why not. You're such a prize." David's words came out more like a grunt.

Kwan smiled, the scar from his jaw to ear stretching up his face. "He wanted me to kill you. But I knew you'd be helpful, although stupid. You did know I would be watching the teahouse, didn't you?"

David said nothing.

"I just wanted to confirm that you were working with Agent Andrevka. And then, when she joined my party…" Kwan actually pushed his tongue between his lips. "Yum. I can see why you want her to yourself."

David mentally had his hands around Kwan's throat, squeezing.

"Believe me, she'll forget about you sooner than you think." He stood. "Unless, of course, you tell me what I want to know."

David swept from his mind every image that Kwan had tried to conjure. "I'm not telling you anything."

Kwan drummed his fingers on his arms. "I disagree." He took a step back and David expected another nod, another kick to his kidneys. But Kwan only smiled.

A sharklike, nasty smile. David had the urge to head-butt him right in the teeth.

Kwan ran his hand over his chin, and David noticed again his ring, the one with the ruby stones set as snake's eyes. "You might have guessed that I'm not the only one my boss is grooming for the job when he retires. Unfortunately, Kwan likes to keep us guessing."

"What, you have a pension plan, a retirement community that Kwan fades off to while you helm the ship?" But behind his words, David's mind whirred. Kwan wanted to know who might come looking for him, should he take out his boss.

Suddenly this all made sense. Why Kwan hadn't just taken David out with a head shot, or hidden in a back alley. He wanted David face-to-face so he could get an inside glimpse at the bigger picture. Apparently, the good guys weren't the only ones who were struggling to pin down the identity of the Twin Serpents.

"You want to take out the competition."

Kwan smiled. Shrugged. "Who is the other man?"

"I have no idea." However, despite the tone and texture of his words—something that every good interrogator would know screamed truth—Kwan didn't believe him. He gave another lethal nod.

And this time, David found himself cheek first in the grime. Please, don't let that be old blood, because he'd now ground it into his skin, right next to his bleeding nose. HIV, TB, the list started to form in his head.

"I don't know who you're talking about," he said, fighting a groan. And he could say that because he actually *didn't* know. David knew that the Serpent's organization stretched from one side of the globe to the other, but he certainly didn't think they had conventions or a company newsletter. If David ran the Twin Serpents, he wouldn't tell one hand what the other might be doing, either.

Because it kept them all scared.

Obedient.

Only, bad news for Kwan-who-was-not, because even if David did know anything about the other Serpents, or Serpents-in-training under investigation, Kwan wouldn't have to waste his time trying to dig it out of him. If one terrorist took out another, the score was still down one, right?

And, if said terrorist then took out the current Big Kahuna, then wouldn't that make David's—perhaps, not David's because he didn't expect to live longer than the next hour, but someone in his line of duty— job a thousand times easier? At least they'd know who to watch.

So he looked up at Kwan, and gave a sort of wicked smile.

"Here's the thing. I *might* know what you're after. But you forget—just like you guessed, I'm a highly trained soldier, conditioned to withstand anything you do to me. I don't care what it is."

"Even killing your girlfriend?"

David didn't even flinch, expecting that. But inside, everything tightened into a fist. Somehow he kept his voice from quivering. "*Especially* if you kill her. I know that if I tell you now, I don't have a prayer of her getting out alive. But—" he wrestled himself back to a kneeling position "—if you let her go, right now, I *will* tell you. Everything you want to know."

He'd made an impact. Kwan stared at him, eyes sharp. "I won't let you go, you know. You're a dead man."

David didn't move a muscle, didn't blink. "I know."

Kwan looked up at the man behind David and nodded.

"They took away my passport as soon as I got to Taiwan. And then they brought me to the teahouse and put me in that room."

Elena had talked all through Yanna's experiment, maybe to cover her nervousness, maybe because she was so glad to see her that she couldn't stop. Or maybe because she feared losing her, and never telling her what had happened.

Yanna let her talk, relishing her sister's voice.

"What happened to Katya?" Yanna asked, wanting to know how Elena's friend had ended up in a Korean morgue, thankful that Elena hadn't joined her.

Elena curled her arms around her skinny waist. "She fought them. She didn't eat supper. I figured out later that some sort of drug was in my dinner, but Katya stayed back in the room, and I don't think they expected her to put up such a fight. When they came into our room, she freaked out, and one of them slammed her against the wall so hard it knocked her out. I never saw her after that."

Yanna looked up at Elena. Then she didn't know...

"Why?" Elena asked. "Did you find her?"

Yanna sighed, held up her contraption. "I hope this works." The battery to her nifty GPS had shorted out, but thankfully one of the girls still had her watch. She'd pried the diamond off her earring backing, and lifted out the destroyed battery. She blew on the inside gadgetry, just to make sure that it had dried out from its bath in the ocean. Then, she disconnected the battery from the watch.

She'd come up empty on the gum, but when she got creative with her requests, found a girl with a bobby pin. A little rubbing against the cement, and she removed the lacquer, the plastic, and broke the bobby pin in half, creating two pieces. She put the battery sideways between them, then touched it to the contacts inside her earring.

Then, she'd plucked two long strands of hair, winding them round and round the end with the battery, until it had been secured in place. She repeated with the other side.

"What are you doing—"

She looked up, and gave the voice in the darkness a look that said, in any language, *Zip it.*

While everyone watched, she climbed up on the wooden bunks and set the transmitter on the window. She pushed the backing into the works to activate the panic button, climbed back down and stared at it.

She had no way of knowing whether it might be working, well, except expertise, and hope.

Lots of hope.

Please. And this time, she knew exactly who she might be talking to.

Please, God. If You are listening, if You care... help.

That's as far as she got, because the door lock slammed back. Yanna turned and grabbed Elena, sitting them down on the bed. "Not a word," she whispered. "Not...one...word."

She didn't have to worry. Elena drew up her knees and scooted back on the bunk, way back.

Which was what Yanna should have done, because the man who entered flashed his mag light across the room, at the haggard, terrified faces of the girls, one by one, working his way down, searching.

Until he came to Yanna. He grabbed her by the arm, and yanked her to her feet.

"Yanna!"

Yanna turned and shot her sister a look that should have stopped her cold. But Elena apparently didn't care anymore, or maybe she knew something Yanna didn't, because she threw herself at Yanna, holding on with a grip that the man couldn't break. Even when he slapped her. Elena screamed but didn't release her death hold.

Yanna stepped in the second time, cutting off his slap with a self-defense block. *"Nyet."* She put her arms around Elena. "We go together."

The man stared for a moment, debate in his eyes. Yanna stared him back without flinching. She wasn't leaving her sister, not again.

He pulled her out of the room, and Yanna grabbed Elena's hand and dragged her along. Yanna didn't know if she should be leaping for joy or calling herself a fool. Especially as the door closed behind them, locking her nifty GPS unit, working or not, behind them.

Please…

She followed Kwan's man down the hall—hard not to since he still had her by the arm. As if she might make a break for it…okay, maybe.

He stopped before another metal door, opened it.

And there, kneeling on the floor, looking battered and beautiful and as if he'd done everything that she'd feared—David.

His eyes lit up when she walked in, just for a second, like maybe he knew something she didn't. And the smallest of smiles touched his lips.

It was the smile that hurt the most. Because she knew, oh, she *knew,* just what he'd done for her.

"Oh, no…David." She let Elena go and ran to

him, putting her arms around him, holding him, burying her face into his shoulder. "Oh, David, what did you do? What did you do?"

The door closed behind them.

"Listen to me," David's voice whispered into her ear, soft and urgent, and it just about broke her heart. "Kwan's going to let you go. And I'm going to buy you time. They want to know who the other Serpent is, and you know how that's going to turn out. But you gotta run, and I mean *run*. Don't wait for Roman. Just get to Taipei, and get out of the country and then I want you to disappear. I'm not kidding you, Yanna. I want you to bury yourself so deep in Siberia no one ever finds you."

What? He expected her to leave here without him? "I'm not leaving you here!"

"Don't be stupid." He pulled away from her. "You are leaving here with your sister."

He looked as if he'd been fighting his emotions, and his face twitched, even now, as if to hold them back. She touched his handsome face, ran her hand down it, over the bruises, the whiskers, and everything inside her broke. "What have you done?" she whispered.

Now, tears did glisten in his eyes, and one dripped down, onto his cheek. And she lost it. Really lost it. "I can't let you do this."

"You can and you will. Honestly, Yanna, if you care anything about me, you'll take this window of freedom and run. You'll get out of here. Because I can't watch them hurt you, and they will. I promise you, they will. And they'll do it slowly, in front of me, just to tear me apart. *Please,* go."

He looked away. "I'm so sorry, Yanna. I totally screwed up. Here I was thinking I was going to be some sort of big shot, save you and find your sister, and prove to you once and for all that men weren't the way you saw them. That you got a raw deal when you were a kid, and I hated that so much, but I couldn't go back in time and kill the jerks who did that to you, so I thought if I could just prove to you that…that men could be counted on, that maybe I could be counted on, then…" He swallowed and closed his eyes and another tear ran down his face, and he was shaking.

It made her shake. Only not from fear, or even cold, but at the desperation of his concern and care.

"Then…what? If you could prove it to me… then what?"

He opened his eyes and gave her the saddest, most pained look, as if the words hurt, even more than what Kwan had done to him. "Then maybe you'd believe, deep inside, that God could be counted on, too. That He cared. That He loved you. A thousand times more…"

She held her breath.

"Than me."

Than him? Everything inside her went still. But only for a second because then she was really crying. Loudly.

Because, she *did* see. Everything. All the truth David had been trying to tell her for years.

She looked at David, his incredible eyes, the way he put everything he was into what he did. She felt the truth burrow deep, right down to the middle of her soul.

Maybe God *did* love her.

Because He'd given her David Curtiss. A man who would believe in her. Run after her.

Love her.

"David, don't give up on me. I do want to believe. And not because you're a superhero and willing to do this, but because…because I want to believe in a God who would give me a man like you. You make me believe that God loves me."

He stared up at her, closed his mouth, swallowed. Then gritted his teeth because his eyes filled. "I wanted this to be different."

Yeah, her, too. She looked up, wiping her face. "I'm sorry. I just…"

"I know you needed it to be different. That you wanted a happy ending, for all of us, but—" He closed his mouth, stared at her. "You gotta go. Please. Before Kwan changes his mind and decides to hurt you. Because I couldn't live with that."

His words hung there between them, ugly and raw, and she shook her head, because, no, he wasn't going to live, not at all.

Oh, David. And then, because she had to, because she *was* going to leave him, but when she did everything inside her would shatter, and then there'd be nothing left, she took his face in her hands and kissed him.

Really kissed him. With everything inside her, just like she had ten years ago, but differently, because this wasn't about youth and passion.

This was about her telling him that she wasn't going to let him die without knowing that she loved him right back. She leaned away, putting everything, all her emotions, all her love right there, in her eyes for him to see. "Thank you, David."

He stared up at her, a broken look on his face. "Yanna—"

She didn't let him finish, just kissed him again. And although his arms were behind him, he leaned into the kiss and gave it all he had. And he didn't pull away, either, not once, just kept kissing her, over and over until hands grabbed her arms, pulled her away.

"No!"

Kwan shoved her away, toward the door, where Elena caught her. "No!"

David was breathing hard, his eyes on her as they pulled her out of the room and shut the door behind her.

Chapter Nineteen

If Kwan wasn't going to keep his promise, David wouldn't, either. He crouched on the floor, breathing hard, his heart beating its way out of his chest, and tried to steel himself for what might lie ahead.

He'd heard what Kwan said when he closed the door, heard it in Mandarin, loud and clear, like a blade separating his ribs and taking out his heart. "Take them to the yacht. We'll kill them when we get out to sea."

David closed his eyes, tried to focus on his breathing. This wasn't over. Not until Yanna was free. He just had to hold out until he knew Yanna was safe.

Only, exactly, how would he know that, because he guessed that might get technically challenging with him locked in the basement, bleeding from his ears.

Oh, Lord.

Everything, *everything,* he'd done had failed. Finding the real Kwan, rescuing Elena, getting Yanna to safety. Even trying to show Yanna that she could trust in God to deliver them. Yeah, that had been a resounding success.

Help me, Lord. Help me hold on to my faith. Because kneeling in the puddle of grime, his head pounding, knowing that as soon as Kwan returned things would get ugly, he felt himself slipping. Fast.

Help me, Lord.

Who do you have in heaven? Roman's words rushed back at him and David grabbed them for all he had, gulping them in. *There is nothing I desire on this earth but the Lord. He will guide me and then bring me to glory.* The words from the psalm riveted into his head.

Do you trust God, David?

David leaned forward, head bowed. He'd grown up, his faith embedded in him, believing that God loved him, had a purpose for him. It had become the fabric of his life, the very substance that formed him.

He heard the dripping of some far-off water pipe onto the concrete. Feet scuffling outside. Doors slamming. Heard a woman's cry.

He clenched his jaw.

God, I want to trust You. I do. I...trust... You.

And just like that, he felt it, a breath or wind or maybe a touch so powerful it swept through him, through his breathing, into his heart, his bones, his cells. He drank it in, gulping whole this feeling of strength. Of wholeness.

He lifted his head. Breathed out long and hard. Stared at the door.

He could do this. He could, and would stay the

course. And when he died, he'd know that he'd accomplished his mission.

Because, while he might do just about anything for his country, he would *die* for Yanna. And she, without a doubt, had been the mission. Kwan and his ilk would always prosper or seem to, and people like David, believers in truth, would always fight them. But they didn't fight only an earthly battle against evil. They waged a cosmic one, for lost souls. And if David could pour out his life helping one woman—*the* woman—to see that God loved her, by being the face of grace to her, then…yes, this was why he'd come to Taiwan.

Why he'd lived the life he had. Made the choices he'd made.

The choice to love Yanna, from a distance. To pray for her. To be truth and commitment and support in her life.

He heard her words again, now letting them inside to touch him. *You make me believe that God loves me.*

To believe that God loved her. *Thank You. Thank You for letting me see You touch her life.* David breathed in. Out. *Thank You.*

He lifted his chin as the door opened. Bring it on, Kwan.

"You look like you've been hit by a semi and dragged down the street."

Huh? David blinked against the light pushing into the room from the hallway, his eyes wide as he connected the body to the voice. The body crouched next to him, grabbed his arm. "You okay, pal?"

Roman? David opened his mouth, but nothing came from him.

"Can you stand?" Roman tucked his hand under David's arm. "How bad are you hurt?"

Aside from his legs wanting to give out and his brain in knots… "I'm okay. I'm—where's Yanna?" Okay, now he was fully functioning, at least zeroing in on his priorities. He turned his hands toward Roman. "Get me out of these."

Roman nodded, turned toward the hallway. "Bruce! We need a handcuff key here!"

Bruce? "Oh, no, Roma, Bruce is—"

"Really glad to see you." Bruce came in holding his 9 mm pistol, and slapped a key into Roman's hand. "We thought you'd be fish bait by now." He stepped back from David, which was a good thing because it gave David about five extra seconds to debate what he was about to do as Roman unlocked his handcuffs.

He did it anyway.

"David, let him go!"

But David wasn't listening, just squeezing. He had Bruce up against the wall, one hand around his neck, the other pinning Bruce's weapon hand to the wall where he could see it. Bruce had his hand around David's wrist, was trying some kung-fu bone-twisting, hold-breaking move on him, but David had gone into pit-bull mode.

He wasn't moving until Bruce coughed out every one of his sins.

So what if it might be hard to talk with his oxygen cut off—he could nod, right?

"Were you the one telling Kwan where to find us? Only you knew I was having a meet with him, only you knew about the safe house in Taichung. Why, Bruce, why?"

Oops, that wasn't a yes or no answer. But Bruce was shaking his head anyway, kicking him, punching him in the face. David didn't budge. Not when, in the back of the chaos, he saw Yanna on the boat, white with fear when Kwan told David he was going to kill her. Not when he remembered their contact at the safe house, and Trish Yung's crying in pain, and—

"David! Stop!" Roman had him now around the neck. "Bruce didn't do it!"

"He's the mole, Roman, he's the mole." David's voice had pitched to a deathly low level, all his energy on keeping his hold.

Bruce had started to turn white, was blinking his eyes.

"He nearly killed Yanna, nearly killed me. He hurt Cho and Trish and her baby." His voice cracked. "And Chet— what about Chet?"

"Chet's alive. And you're killing Bruce. You don't want to do this. If he's the mole then we'll find out, but—"

"David."

The voice, calm and sweet beside him, cut through his haze of anger.

"David, let him go."

He looked over at Yanna. Her eyes were wide, and she was shaking her head. "Please."

David closed his eyes. *You make me believe that God loves me.*

He blew out a long breath, and impaled Bruce with a glare.

Then he let go.

Bruce slumped down against the wall, gasping in breath. David stood over him, breathing hard. "So help me, if I find out you're the mole…that you're behind hurting my friends…"

"He's not. He saved your life, David." The voice came from behind Yanna, and David looked up to see his old partner standing there in the doorway, handgun at his side. Chet.

A very alive, sturdy-looking Chet in a pair of jeans and a button-down shirt. He must have swiped them from someone, because he didn't have it buttoned all the way due to the fact that he couldn't get the shirt around the bandage that crisscrossed his chest. David hurt a little in the same place, seeing him. "What are you doing here? You're supposed to be in the hospital."

"I got wind of this story about my partner running around Taiwan, busting up bad guys. You have all the fun."

David locked eyes with Yanna. A very alive Yanna. Then, right there in front of everyone, he reached out and pulled her to himself. And she hung on, as if she had always belonged there.

Which, she had.

"How'd you find us?"

"Yanna's wizardry," Roman said. "When I lost you at the harbor, I went back and called Chet, who called Bruce. He fired up their GPS system and began to search—not that I thought we'd find anything, but I thought maybe, hopefully, you know, Yanna's pretty smart." Roman flashed her a smile.

"Yeah. Too smart for our own good, sometimes." But David pressed a kiss to her forehead.

"Anyway, Chet and Bruce knew you were here in Taichung, so they hightailed it down here, and we were down at the wharf, eyes on Kwan's yacht when his people called and said they'd picked up Yanna's panic code. From here."

David shot a glance at Bruce as Roman reached down and pulled Bruce to his feet. David stepped away from him, eyeing Bruce, who looked shaken, still rubbing his throat.

"Did you get Kwan?"

"Yeah, he's in custody, and my people are searching the building." Bruce's voice came out hoarse, and David guessed he probably had some swelling. "We'll take him back to headquarters, and then the fun starts. You…you can be there if you want."

David looked him over, sorted through those words. *Translation—if I was the mole, would I risk letting Kwan rat me out, right in front of you?*

"You need to see a doctor, probably," David said.

For the moment, that was the closest to an apology he could get.

Bruce gave a nod. Apology sort of accepted.

"Elena—"

"We found two rooms of women—you're going to be sick when you see their ages. And at the loading dock, two empty containers, with bunk beds built in the sides," Chet said.

"He was going to ship them in containers?" This from Yanna, who had stepped away from him, just a little, but not too far. Please, not too far.

"People—kids, men, women—they're trafficked from all over the world, shipped to foreign countries where they're trapped and helpless. Americans in Malaysia, Koreans in America. It's a giant operation, and Kwan is just one of many. When he's out of the picture, another slimeball will ooze into his place." Bruce's voice emerged hoarse, at best.

"You should know that there's another one out there—another Kwan Jr. that Kwan's grooming."

Bruce nodded. "We know. But we have to take down one Serpent at a time."

"I want to talk to Kwan," David said.

"First, you're going to the hospital," Yanna said, moving to put her arm around him.

He looked down at her, those beautiful eyes trusting him. He had to keep his promise—the one he had made to himself. And to her. "No," he said quietly. "First, I'm going to the airport. So you and Roman and Elena can go home."

* * *

And she was expected to live without David, how? Especially after he'd nearly given up his life for her, something she felt sure she'd never have been able to live with.

Yanna closed her eyes, feeling the pressure crack her ears as the plane descended into Russian airspace, toward the landing strip in Khabarovsk. Elena sat beside her, a whitened grip on her hand that she hadn't loosened since they'd stumbled out of Kwan's basement dungeon and into the light.

She'd even hung on as David pulled Yanna into his arms one last time.

And right there, in front of Roman, who had most definitely been watching, based on his openmouthed grin as he'd escorted them through passport control, David had given her a kiss that told her he had heard, *really heard* her words to him.

You make me believe that God loves me. She put her other hand over Elena's, feeling her sister's grip tremble slightly.

God had done this. He'd helped her find Elena. And saved David.

God, please help me to believe in You. To trust You. As she thought the words, the knot that wound through her chest, the one she'd learned to live with, suddenly began to loosen. She felt it, even as she took a deep, tremulous breath.

Maybe this was what hope felt like.

She opened her eyes. Glanced at Roman, who sat

across the aisle from her. Though he had his eyes closed, she didn't for a second believe he was sleeping, but he did look at peace.

The same expression David had worn as he'd pressed his hand to the window that separated them from passport control. If it was the last thing she'd remember, it was the look of love in his incredible blue eyes, the way they shone, the way he stared at her, as if imprinting himself on her heart.

God, please, watch over him.

As she prayed, she looked out the window to the cirrus clouds scraping sky, and decided that was how she was expected to live without David.

With hope.

They touched down, a bumpy landing in Khabarovsk. A flight from America had come in just prior to theirs, and as she and Elena followed Roman through the military line of passport control, she couldn't help but think of David. And wondered where he was, if he was mopping up the mess in Taiwan, and with the information he'd pry out of Kwan if he'd have to go back undercover to sleuth out the "other" Serpent, which meant she didn't have a hope of seeing him in the near or even distant future.

The precious hope that had filled her chest took a spiral down to her knees.

Especially when she saw Vicktor.

"Oh, my—what happened to you?"

Vicktor was sitting in a vinyl chair in front of one

of the passport desks, boasting a black eye and a vicious welt on his jaw. She'd heard the border guards were cracking down in America, but seriously…

"What happened to you?"

Roman sat down beside him. "Tell me that Gracie was glad to see you?"

But Vicktor's gaze was on Elena, who still had a hold of Yanna. "You found her." And the smile in his eyes warmed Yanna clear through. He sprang to his feet and pulled Yanna to him. He smelled a little ripe, as if he'd been in the same clothes for three days. Which, by the looks of him, he had.

He put her away from him, searching her for injury, as if he wasn't a walking *Fight Club* billboard. "What happened?"

Yanna opened her mouth, not sure where to start, but Roman filled him in with the high points. Elena crept even closer to Yanna.

"And David's still there?" Vicktor asked, when Roman got to the part about them getting on the plane.

"Trying to track down this other Serpent Kwan wanted to know about. What happened to you?"

Vicktor looked at Roman. "Gracie was in trouble. She got in the middle of a human-trafficking ring—"

"Big surprise there," Roman said.

"She was just trying to help a friend, and it got ugly. Sokolov tried to kill her—"

"Which meant that you got into the middle of it." Yanna reached out and touched the welt on his jaw. "That looks like it hurt."

Vicktor rubbed the welt, wincing. "Sokolov had a ring…" Vicktor wore a strange look.

Yanna's hand went to her cheek, as memory made her wince. "Gold snake, with red rubies?" she asked.

She saw the answer in his eyes even before he answered.

"The other Serpent in training…Roman—"

"I'm already there," he said, dialing his cell phone. He looked at Yanna, his eyes light when he got a voice at the other end. "Hey, Preach," he said, turning from them.

Yanna looked back at Vicktor, who was frowning. "So…Gracie was happy to see you, Dr. Zaitsev?"

He wore the sweetest blush.

"And just how long before you're allowed back in the country?"

His smile fell.

Oh, perfect.

"But the good news is, I think Gracie is ready to marry me."

At least someone would get their happily ever after. But as she watched Roman talk, she had to hope that maybe, just maybe, hers wasn't far behind.

Chapter Twenty

"Ready, when you are."

Yanna heard the voice over the radio and peered at the computer screen, which revealed the ancient hotel room—not unlike the room she was in next door—with the black molded plastic double bed, the gold polyester spread, the black velour drapes. An unopened vodka bottle and two glasses were set on the table, and next to that, sat slim and beautiful Zina Bruskho, aka "Madame," the field operator for this mission.

"You're on, Madame," Yanna said, speaking into her lapel mic.

Yanna watched, her breath tight, surrounded by her techies as Madame answered the door, and in walked their target. Qyin-Wo. Chinese Minister of Justice.

It felt amazingly empowering to be on the catch end instead of the run-away side of the mission. Sometimes in her new position as Assistant Director of Surveillance and R & D, Yanna still saw herself handcuffed to a chair, watching Kwan flick out her small knife.

She'd come a long way, baby. In fact, as Qyin-Wo walked into the room, all two hundred and fifty robust pounds of him, and Zina let him pour her drink, Yanna knew she'd been working toward this view all her life.

Watching killers like Qyin-Wo go down.

This view might not be as beautiful as a fourth-story window overlooking lush gardens, but it also came courtesy of a fourth-floor office in the FSB Headquarters off Lubyanaka Square, which overlooked a four-lane road, one of the busiest in all of Moscow. Soon, come spring, when she opened her office window, she'd hear the coughing cars, the pigeons cooing from the metal sill of her ancient window, smell the cooking oil from *chebureki* vendors infiltrating her office. Of course, the paint was peeling from the frame, and the glass rattled when the wind swept by on its way east. Some said that once upon a time, the KGB could see all the way to Siberia from the offices in Lubyanka, but Yanna knew it was only legend, because she couldn't even see Red Square.

Still, her new office had a window. And red brocade drapes, and a parquet floor, and lime-green walls and pretty soon, pictures. She'd bring some from her new flat—ones of Roman and Sarai, taken at their Christmas engagement party, and Vicktor, and Mae and Gracie in Seattle, and David.

Of course, David. Although she didn't know where he might be at the moment. Maybe still in Taiwan, although Trish and Cho—who'd had a healthy baby boy two months ago—hadn't heard from him, even though he'd sent them a huge bouquet of blue flowers and a teddy bear the size of Russia. Even Roman didn't know where to track down his friend. He hadn't talked to him since the airport in Taipei, when David had neatly booted her out of his life.

Yeah, that hurt.

A lot.

And even being offered her dream job, which came with an entire department of R & D geeks for her to harass, travel perks and a three-room flat, it only slightly dulled the pain of a broken heart.

Still it was better than being a basement tech grub, stuck in Siberia with a broken heart.

"Are you getting his words?" she asked one of her techs, who was fluent not only in Mandarin but in manning the digital recordings.

"*Da*, Director Andrevka," he said. Yanna folded her arms over her pressed blouse. Director.

Hmm. David should see her now. Maybe he'd answer her online pages, the ones left in their chat rooms.

It had been five months. After two, she'd stopped trying. Now, if she could only stop hoping she'd find his e-mail waiting for her.

It was very possible he had decided that being with her, knowing her, had made his life so much more complicated than he'd ever imagined, and he couldn't repeat that ever again.

Her brain, the part not connected to her heart, could admit that loving a woman with high-security clearance, when he had his own high-security clearance, well, there were certainly international issues there.

She couldn't really blame him for his silence. Not really.

But, *ow.*

In fact, his absence had left a great, big, weepy, raw hole right in the center of her chest. Which had made it difficult to breathe, but she'd learned, finally, to bandage that wound with her job, and Elena, who had re-enrolled in Moscow University to finish her law degree. Yanna was also trying out for the Moscow Volleyball team. And wouldn't David be curious to know she was going to church. Moscow Bible Church, which had a progressive group of new Christians. Roman had given her a Bible, and with a little coaching, she'd begun to read.

She wouldn't call herself a scholar, by any means. But every day she felt a little more whole. A little more healed.

And maybe, someday, she'd be okay.

Definitely okay. And not because she'd forget David—that might resemble trying to forget about her heart beating in her chest—but she might someday believe in her heart what her brain told her. That God did love her. And that He had a good plan for her life. With or without David.

And that good plan had turned out to be making her not only director of what she loved to do, but also, because of her new exuberance to wipe out human slavery, she'd been the point woman for tapping the offices of Zhenshini & Lubov. Which, as it turned out, was indeed a front for trafficking.

She stepped back from the techs—how she used to hate when her bosses hovered over her—and watched the drama in the next room. Madame had sat next to Qyin-Wo on the bed, letting him refill her drink. She smiled up at the man and it made Yanna press her hand to her stomach.

Zhenshini & Lubov had proved to be only one of dozens of fronts. And after months of surveillance and taps and intercepted messages and chat-room peeking, Yanna had discovered that everything routed through one man, the leader of the network of low-life scums.

The Chinese Minister of Justice. Only, taking him out would be überfun because while he was in Russia, he had diplomatic immunity.

She'd often wondered if Wo might be a distant relation to Kwan. He was definitely someone in the Serpent nest—she could see the ring from here.

And, well, since he was actually the one in charge of justice in China—and wasn't that some sort of joke—she hadn't a prayer of handing over that information to Chinese government officials in hopes of retribution.

Furthermore, assassination was out of the question. Really.

So, instead she'd planned a little sting operation. Only problem was…she had to resort to working with the Americans. Their role in the world allowed them access to international laws, and they just seemed to get the ball rolling. Maybe because the rest of the world still thought Russia shot first and asked questions later.

But as usual, the Americans were late, which left her to run the op in the next room. At least the surveillance part.

Back in the hotel room, Zina had now perched herself on the desk, out of view of the camera. But Yanna's technology clearly framed Qyin-Wo in the picture. And then, in line with their intel, came another knock. This was the contact with whom Madame had agreed to meet to start channeling her trafficked women through.

Because Zina really was a madame. A repentant, wired, she-would-do-serious-time kind of madame. The kind who knew exactly how to work with these two players.

The kind who had family back in Khabarovsk. And Yanna, well, she might be learning how to be a Christian, but she still knew how to play by Russian rules.

The camera caught Zina as she opened the door to player numero two.

Qyin-Li.

Only, maybe Yanna should adjust her screen, because Qyin-Li wasn't Chinese. Or even Asian.

The man had the distinct features of an American.

In fact, she'd seen him yesterday at the Chinese-American-Russian summit on international trade.

And bing, it all made sense. Qyin-Wo, one of the Twin Serpents, had come to Moscow to meet his counterpart.

The other Serpent. Aka Lee Quinn.

The Director of the American Institute in Taiwan. The American attaché to Taiwan. Father to the man who'd taken Yanna hostage.

Zina closed the door.

The two men embraced as if they'd known each other for a lifetime. Mafiosa bosom buddies. Yanna shook her head.

A knock came at her door.

"Tell the maid to go away," Yanna said, her eyes on the screens. The less the hotel management knew about the FSB's little party, the better.

She heard the door open, whispers, but her focus was on the screen, on Wo and Li, and every word she was getting on her digital hard drive.

"I should have guessed you'd be here."

Yanna froze. Really, everything inside her simply stilled, and she just stood there, looking at the screens.

And then his hand pressed her shoulder, and her breath came out in an incredulous huff. She turned, and for a second, everything vanished—the room, the five techs who weren't sure what to do when their director gasped and turned from the operation visible on her flat screen.

Because there he was, David, dressed in a pair of pressed black dress pants, a gray dress shirt, a black tie, clean shaven, his hair blond, his face nicely healed and smiling—at her. He looked like he was going to a wedding.

Or a funeral. Which was perfect because she was going to kill him.

"Hi," he said.

Oh, she had the greatest urge to slap him. "Hi," she said softly, her voice completely betraying her.

"Sorry I'm late. I got hung up in traffic."

Traffic? Where…in Chechnya? Maybe the Middle East? He must have also picked up the ability to read her mind because he had the good sense to appear sheepish.

"You almost missed it," she said again, softly. Yeah, really missed it—in fact, she wasn't sure they'd ever get back what he'd missed.

He looked at the screen. "How are we doing?"

"We? I'm sorry, are you part of this operation?"

He gave a laugh that wasn't really a laugh. "Yeah. Who do you think gave the A-OK on the American side? Vicktor's fun and games in America—although a political snafu for him—worked out in our favor. Your tip on Kosta Sokolov turned out to be rich in information. We were able to work on Kwan in Taiwan and Sokolov in America and guess what— both of them were working for the Serpents. We've been after Lee Quinn for a couple months now, but we wanted to confirm he was working with Wo, who is his half brother. In fact, the Qyins—or Kwans as they were called in America—have quite an interesting family tree. Apparently propagating heirs across the globe is a nifty way of not only creating international blood ties, but producing operatives that blend into society. And they're not afraid to steal from each other—which was what the Kwan we met was doing to his half brother, Kosta Sokolov. Sokolov had a tidy trafficking operation importing Russian girls into the States until Kwan got wind and began to intercept them. Which is why you and Elena, ended up in Taiwan." He looked past her, at the screen. "So, how are we doing?"

Huh. Yanna had been privy to some of Vicktor's fallout after his shackle-and-chain return to Russia. But all he'd gotten for his AWOL activities was three months of desk duty.

She'd heard through Roman, however, that Vicktor had recently been entertaining ideas of leaving the FSB and settling down in some neutral country with Gracie.

"Are we ready to go in?" David asked.

We? There was no *we* here. Yanna turned, directed the question at the two techs with headphones glued to the exchange. Yanna watched on the screen as Qyin-Li stood up. Shook Wo's hand.

"Go."

The FSB pounced. Shouting and chaos and

finally Yanna watched as her agents took down the Twin Serpents and their human-trafficking ring. Gotcha.

"Surely their way is slippery," David said softly. Yanna shot him a look. He shrugged. "Something Roman said."

He watched the rest in silence, saying nothing, even when the two men looked right at the camera and threatened to do unspeakable things to her, her men, and their families for ten generations.

Yeah, right back at ya. "Send that to my office, and make a billion hard copies," she said to the two techies still in the room.

"Good job," David said.

Well, she'd been highly motivated. David put a hand on her arm. "Can I talk to you?"

Talk to her.

He wanted to *talk*. She wanted to scream. Maybe they could find a happy medium.

But he still had magical powers in his touch, even well-groomed and speaking softly—maybe more so. She followed him down the hall, where two overstuffed chairs sat in an alcove, overlooking Red Square.

Yanna leaned against the wall, the cold, wallpapered cement seeping into her blouse. She wore her hair up today, but a strand had leaked out, falling long beside her face. She reached up and pulled the pins out.

David stood there, watching, and she saw him swallow and take a deep breath. "Okay, here's the deal. I know you wrote to me, over and over, and that

I'm a total jerk. But after you left Taiwan, I had to stay and interrogate Kwan, and even after that we were still working out who the real Kwan was, and I just…I just couldn't contact you. Not without jeopardizing everything."

"One e-mail. Just one. *Dear Yanna, I'm still alive. And we're still friends.* And maybe, *Hey, I thought of you.*"

David took another long breath. She looked away, unable to face the sudden hurt in his eyes. What did *he* have to be hurt about?

"I thought of you every minute. You were never…" He swallowed. "Of *course* I thought of you."

"What were you afraid of jeopardizing? I hardly think that one e-mail to me would have destroyed your investigation of—"

"Us."

She blinked at him, and suddenly, he looked so…well, exactly the way he'd looked as she had said goodbye to him in Taipei. As if he'd taken his heart and pinned it to his chest.

"I don't understand."

"I didn't want to jeopardize us."

She didn't move. "Define *us*. And by the way, not writing is probably the one thing you could do to destroy what we…what we had."

He ran a hand through his short hair. "I had to take that chance. Because *us* means you and me. Together. Figuring out how to be loyal to our countries, and still be loyal to each other. Getting married. Living here in Moscow. Having kids, learning how to make pancakes. Together."

"Pancakes?"

"Yeah, you look incredible in an apron, and, well, I really…" He looked away then, and his expression held everything she'd hoped to see. For month after silent month.

"I miss you, Yanna. And I can't stand one more day living on the other side of the world. And if I had to spend another night chatting with you instead of…being with you, I thought I'd scream. Yes, I want to get married. But to you. *Only* you."

She thought she had finished crying over him. Infuriatingly sweet David Curtiss. She ran a finger under her eye, but he reached out and stopped her.

"I couldn't contact you because I asked to be transferred to Moscow, to work in security at the embassy, and if they knew that the woman I loved lived here, then I'd never be cleared."

"You…you're moving here?"

"I'm currently bunking on the sofa in my new office, since I arrived only yesterday. But yes, starting tomorrow, I'll be looking for a flat. Somewhere in the vicinity of Moscow University."

Near her flat. "You've been doing your homework."

He nodded and took a step closer to her. Wow, he was a beautiful man, with incredible eyes and wide shoulders. The way he looked at her had her forgiving him over and over.

"Yanna, I love you. And I can't live another day

without you. I've loved you for years, but I didn't want to get in the way of God's love for you, which I know now was…maybe stupid. But I believed that if I let you down, you'd think God let you down, which I know really sounds arrogant, but most of all, I thought it was more important for you to know that God loved you. And I was willing to wait for it. But what you said at Kwan's place really hit me. Something about me helping you believe that God loves you. And that's what I want to do. Show you how much God loves you by loving you the best I can, every day for the rest of my life. It's not as good or perfect, and I am going to let you down, but I want to try. Really try. Please, forgive me?"

Forgive him for breaking her heart, and then putting it back together? For seeing more for her than she saw for herself? For loving her enough to die for her?

Well, maybe.

She smiled up at him. "I love you, David." She'd been waiting to say those words, honestly and without fear, for most of her life. "I really love you. And yes, I want to figure it out. I have waited my entire life to be with you, and we'll make it work. Even if I have to go undercover."

"Oh, please. No." But he smiled as he cupped her face with his hand. He wove his fingers into her hair, then ran his hand around the back of her neck. "I love your hair," he said in a voice she could barely hear.

"I love your smile."

He rubbed his nose against hers. "I promise not to leave you, ever again."

She lifted her face to his, and he kissed her. And this time, he didn't pull away. In fact he put his arms around her and held her tight. And kissed her some more.

And she knew, way down deep, where he'd taught her to believe, that David Curtiss would keep his promise.

QUESTIONS FOR DISCUSSION

1. Yanna's little sister, Elena, goes off to America to marry a man she's only met on the Internet. Today, with people meeting on various Internet sites and groups, what do you think about Internet dating? Would you date or marry a man you met on the Internet?

2. Yanna takes drastic measures to go after her missing sister. Not all of us have sisters, but is there anyone you would do (or have done) something drastic for, or have gone out of your way to help? How and why?

3. David has gone undercover, and has been forced to make choices he finds horrifying for the sake of the larger picture. Have you ever been faced with a moral dilemma that blurs the line between black and white? Is that line *ever* blurred for you?

4. David chooses to save Yanna, sacrificing his mission. Why does he do this, and how does it differ from the situation with Chet?

5. Have you ever traveled overseas and visited an open market? Describe your experience, and the strangest thing you saw or ate.

6. Gracie gets herself in trouble when she starts getting involved in her teenage friend's life and finds herself embroiled in a human-trafficking ring. Were you aware of the human-trafficking problem in America? What do you think can be done about it?

7. When David and Yanna meet up with Tricia and her husband, Tricia decides to help Yanna at the teahouse. Why does she do this? Have you ever done something "edgy" like this? When and why?

8. Yanna and David have an elegant evening at the opera house. Have you ever attended an opera or other black-tie event? Tell about it.

9. David believes that having a relationship with Yanna will keep her away from God. Do you agree with him? Why or why not?

10. Do you think Vicktor is overprotective? Why do you think he behaves this way?

11. Yanna uses her talents as a techie to save the day. Do you have any skills that you think would make you a great agent?

12. What is your favorite scene in the book, and why?